East Coast Blues
A 1960s Odyssey

JOHN EVES

This book is a work of fiction and any resemblance to actual persons is purely coincidental. Some real people from the era are mentioned but are not principal characters in the story.

Published by John Eves
Publishing partner: Paragon Publishing, Rothersthorpe
First published 2018
© John Eves 2018

ISBN 978-1-78222-634-5

Book design, layout and production management by Into Print
www.intoprint.net
+44 (0)1604 832149

Chapter 1

Many writers and lyricists have written about the pain people feel over the loss of buildings and places that hold memories for them and when I saw what had happened around the Manor Ballroom where so many of the memories of my youth had been created I knew exactly where they were coming from.

I felt an almost physical pain, a shortness of breath and a strange hollow feeling in the pit of my stomach. This was the place where I had come on Monday evenings to see some of the biggest names on the rhythm and blues circuit in the mid-1960s. The place where I met a couple of my girlfriends, drank with my mates and got into bother. Standing there I could almost smell the cellar bar, the stale beer, the thick smoke-filled atmosphere and feel the stickiness of the beer-soaked dance floor.

The hall was still there but now just down the road was a block of old people's flats. That's a bit ironic, here we are fifty odd years later and they have changed the place where we grew up into a place for us to come to die! It made me sad to think of the kids I knew back then and how we were now all getting old, how could those trendy young people suddenly become OAPs? And what about those no longer with us, Maureen who died young from breast cancer, James from a heart attack and, of course, Col. Let alone the parents and relatives who had fought us, guided us and who managed to love us despite all of that.

It was nearly fifty years since I had been back and I wouldn't be here now if it wasn't for the death of my aunt. Not that it was that long since I had seen her, we had remained close throughout her life and I had always found time to visit her in Lavenham where she and my uncle had retired. But to come back to the town; that had been too big a step, too much pain, too many memories. My cousins had however decided that she should be buried in her home town and I couldn't refuse the invitation that they sent.

Having decided to come back, I felt that it might be the right time, cathartic even, to visit the sites of my time living in the town, what I had thought of as my exile, maybe I could bury the sadness and guilt once and for all. To see if all the prayers I had said in the intervening years had had any effect! There seemed to be some hope in that I found myself thinking that it wasn't all sadness and loss that was affecting me. Maybe it was because I also had good memories of the place, remembering the American Blues legends I had seen there; the British performers who had gone onto rock superstardom, Clapton, Steve Winwood, Rod Stewart and the rest. We had been fortunate that, because of the proximity of the local American airbases, such talent had been drawn to a small provincial town and that had enhanced our lives. Anyway, what had I expected, did I really think it would be the same as 50 years ago, really expect all my old haunts to be the same? Of course not. The Cock and Pie pub, so lovingly known as The Prick and Pudding was still there but the Vaults Bar on the Cornhill, where I had spent so many hours drinking with friends was derelict, with a forlorn For Sale sign hanging from its wall. As for the Gondoliers coffee bar; well I couldn't even remember where it had been! Even my place of work had disappeared.

As I walked around revisiting those places, the memories had flooded back and deciding that a drink might be in order, I returned to the Cock and Pie. In so many ways it had not changed; the basic seating arrangements were still there, I could identify 'our table' and the table where I had had to use a bit of muscle to sort out a couple of lads who hadn't shown me the right respect was still exactly the same as I remembered it. The bar was in the same place and it was still reassuringly low-key, although it didn't serve food back then. I stood at the bar with a pint of Adnams bitter; 'If you let your imagination run you can smell the sea air in it', I said as I chatted to the young barman explaining why I was in the town and how I had used to be a regular.

He laughed and said, 'Must have been a popular drinking hole back then, you'd be surprised how many old people we get in here reminiscing'. I'm not sure if that was meant to make me feel better but it didn't, although I did wonder if I would know any of the other old people who came in to reminisce. Leaning against the bar with a second pint I realised that I couldn't just leave it there. I had to go down to Felixstowe; the visit would have no meaning if I didn't close that circle. The thought of it made me go cold but I had to return to the place where it had happened.

When I left the pub the sun was shining and the sky was a clear blue, it boded well for a trip to the coast. The drive down to Felixstowe along the A14, with all the container traffic, was so different to the old single carriageway route which we used to take on a Sunday afternoon; that wound through the villages and outlying built up areas of the town. The seafront and promenade were however still in the right place and parking the car at the southern end I got out to look around. How sad our seaside towns have become I thought, looking across at where Manning's amusement park, dominated by the scenic railway, used to stand. Now all that remained were a couple of shabby buildings full of games machines, a hot dog stall and vendors selling ice cream and doughnuts, the oil giving off a sour smell wafted across the road to be swallowed up by the brisk east wind.

I walked along the promenade towards the pier; I could see that that was still there. I recalled so vividly how, in the mid-1960s, on a warm summer Sunday afternoon, the curb alongside the prom would be lined with scooters, all types of Vespas and Lambrettas, every one of them polished to perfection to be shown off to the other guys. The Mods, also dressed to impress, wearing new clothes that they had bought the afternoon before, would parade along pausing to chat to the small knots of girls that had also congregated there. Often a new shirt would be purchased on Saturday, worn that evening then washed and ironed ready to be shown off again Sunday afternoon.

The June afternoon was clear and bright but with a slight chill in the air from the east wind. The combination of breeze and sunlight played on the surface of the sea to make it sparkle and the gulls cried out as they swooped and soared in the thermals. Today there were a few mothers with their pre-school children in pushchairs, one or two hardier mums sitting on the shingle playing with their kids and large numbers of elderly people out taking the air. I tried to cut them out of my images but they wouldn't go, this was the reality, no longer a place for aspiring youth but a waiting room for God. But then what right had I to judge, at 72 years old I probably should see myself in that category. Please; God Forbid.

Eventually I arrived at the pier, at least the old pier pavilion had gone, replaced by a 1980's corporation designed sports centre, that at least was one memory I wouldn't have to face. No more Saturday night dances with big name bands and rows of scooters standing outside. No more fights and blue flashing lights of police cars and ambulances. No more deaths in the car park. The pier was still there though, families still came to walk its length and take in the bracing east coast air before letting the kids have half an hour on the slot machines. Some things never change. Some memories never die. The car park was in the same position as it had been back then, although now with a smart brick surface. I walked over to the middle and instinctively knew that I was in the place where that early summer evening, fifty years before, it had happened. I almost expected to see the blood stain. In my mind, I always imagined that moment of death. I felt sick and my mind reeled, no, this was not going to bury the memories or salve my conscience.

That death had stayed with me throughout my life and more than that it had shaped what I had become during my life. It was no use trying to hide behind a denial of the events leading up to it; I knew exactly the circumstances that had led to it. My own culpability, the way others had been drawn into the web of violence that had such a tragic outcome and the individuals that had been involved in the story.

A story, I supposed that this would have been one way to describe it and after fifty years it seemed that way. The characters had been real enough but from a distance they now seemed surreal. A story of how the Mod culture of the 1960's had gone sour through the mindless violence of a few. Oh yes, the press liked to project all Mods as being violent, but it wasn't like that nor was the violence just directed at Rockers, so much more was between individuals and groups within the Mod community and it was that violence which tended to be the most extreme. It was that way because, as in any youth culture, there were jealousies, power struggles and disputes, mainly over girls.

Chapter 2

I wasn't a Face, but I was well up the ranks of the soldiers and a lot of them, and certainly all the seven and sixes were envious of and looked up to me. I had my own little coterie of supporters and this made me feel special, invulnerable.

'Why do you say these kids are all at sixes and sevens?' Mum asked me.

I laughed, 'No Mum, seven and sixes, kids who can't afford the proper gear and go and buy T-shirts at Woolworths; they cost seven shillings and sixpence and we take the piss out of them.'

'That's a bit mean dear, they are only trying to fit in.' She was a sweetie my mum.

Even though I say it myself I was quite a good-looking bloke, I had blond hair cut in the latest fashion, pulled forward at the front and cut to stand high at the crown, no bleeding spots to worry about and skin that the girls all commented on, probably because I nicked Mum's moisturiser.

I had grown up in Romford in a middle-class family, although some of my teenage acquaintances, who were mainly from working class families referred to me as posh. This was because unlike their fathers, most of whom worked on the docks, on the market or in the Ford factory in Dagenham, my old man was a builder and a successful one at that. I didn't go to the local state school but was educated at a highly regarded private school.

'You're a posh bastard, you went to a snob school,' the guys would say to me, although the fact that I had been to St. Anthony's seemed to go down quite well with the girls.

It also helped that my parents were generous. Dad bought me a customised Vespa GS 160. Metallic red with chromed side panels, lights, mirrors and straight-through exhaust to give it that distinctive crackling exhaust note; it was the dog's bollocks and was the subject of much envy. My parents were however disappointed in that I had refused to go to University; I had got good 'A' levels that would have allowed me to go on, but it wasn't for me. I was too involved in the local youth culture, the North London Mod scene, and I wanted to live, not go away to bloody study.

That didn't mean that I wasn't prepared to work. Dad was a prominent Mason and had managed to get me a trainee accountant's job with the local council. As a trainee accountant, I was given blocks of time at off to attend East Ham College and by getting my head down and studying hard during those weeks at college I had already become partly qualified, a couple more exams and I would be there. This meant that I was earning good money without having to do hard labour or overtime in the factory. Yes, I was in a privileged position. I had money to go to the clubs and to go to the boutiques in Carnaby Street and the Kings Road. I was always dressed in the latest gear and had the best-cut suits which we got from the local tailors. I remember going to this little terrace house in an East End back street with Ritchie, a mate of mine. We knocked on the door and it was opened by a short Jewish guy with a dark complexion, his black hair topped with a traditional skull cap. He was wearing a black jacket which, despite being worn over a tatty old woollen waistcoat, was obviously beautifully cut from a top-quality cloth.

'Come in, come in boys. What can I do for you?' He asked. We showed him a picture of the latest style of Italian suits being sold in exclusive West End shops.

'We want a couple of these Manny, dark blue Mohair.'

'That's not Mohair.' He replied. 'What you want is fine Italian wool suiting.' And he produced a bolt of material from behind the sofa. It was soft and fine. 'This is the finest you'll get your hands on and, if you want it, I'll make you suits to be proud of. You know I was trained by the best in the Row and I still work there now so you'll have to keep quiet about where you got them from.'

We knew this was all a bit of schmutter, everyone knew that many of the Saville Row tailors who lived in the East End did a bit on the side. Manny, like the rest, was proud of his reputation. Indeed, most of the local coppers would be out on a Saturday wearing a bespoke suit that was got for a fraction of the price it would have cost up West.

'Now let's get you measured up lads, got to get it right you know.' Manny seemed to take forever measuring me up and then asked he asked me, 'which side do you dress?' I looked at him blankly. 'Which leg does it hang down?' Manny pointed at my groin.

'You mean me what's-it, does it matter?' I said.

'My son, of course it matters, if I don't adjust for it the suit will never hang right.' I was gobsmacked, this wasn't something I had ever considered before so I had a little feel and replied,

'The left I think Manny.' By then we had collapsed in fits of laughter and Ritchie was fumbling extravagantly in his trousers.

'Boys, boys you have got to take this seriously you're not at the Thirty Bob Tailors now, these suits will be a work of art. On my life, they'll be fit for Royalty, trust me.' And they were; I felt a million dollars when I was out for the evening wearing it.

Richie was my closest mate, he was very different to me in that he had left the local secondary school at 15 to work on his dad's stall on the market. That didn't mean that he was stupid, in fact he was so sharp that he was in danger of cutting his self. Richie could sell anything to anyone and usually did. If you listened to him shouting the odds at the market on a Saturday you could tell he had been born to it. Richie was also a sharp dresser, even if at times he went for the more extreme styles, bright colours and patterns tended to be his thing. And his Vespa scooter; no-one else would have got away with florescent pink side-panels but get away with it Richie did. Richie had brought his scooter on the hire purchase, £24 down and the rest on weekly instalments. His first act on a Saturday after helping his old man set up the market stall was to go to Grimsteads and make his payment, it didn't do to be late paying as you never knew who might come knocking on your front door. As well as Richie there was Dave who did his best to ape me and what I wore one-week Dave would wear the next. This used to irritate me somewhat and a couple of time I had to have serious words with him about it. To look at, the guys could have been brothers, both had hair that stood up on end no matter what they did to it and both had that East End pinched look about them as if they needed at good meal and, although they were always well groomed, both looked as if they could do with a good scrub.

At this time there was another guy who hung about with me. Bruce was an American, his father was a visiting professor at one of the London Universities. Wanting his children to fully experience the society in which were spending three years he sent them to English schools. However, even though he was a sociology professor from California's Berkley University, he drew the line at sending them to the state schools. Bruce was a big guy, affable, gentle and very bright. I was given the job of mentoring him when he first arrived at school. From the time that we first met, we got on well together and during the time he was in London Bruce spent a lot time with me and my mates. Although even then I used people, his main use to me was that he was black; he was a bit of an exotic to be shown off. Most Mods lived in parts of London or the Home Counties which had few black faces; the more so in the New Towns and estates of the south east of England and even in Romford not many black lads would be seen on the streets. However, Bruce fitted right in, he could handle himself well and had a great street vocabulary. During one scuffle someone called him a nigger, Bruce ran the guy headfirst into a wall and to our great satisfaction screamed at him, *'you white motherfucker if I was at home I'd and go get a gun and fucking burn you, call me a nigger again and I'll fix you for good'.* No one challenged Bruce after that, even the local Faces would keep their distance, and I made sure I always kept him close. After he returned to California with his family I kept in touch though being a pen pal to his sister and it was from her that I kept up with what was happening musically and culturally over there.

The most prominent of the local Faces was Max and I had known him since I was at junior school. Max had a customised Lamberetta GT200 in white with metallic electric blue side panels, also from Eddy Grinstead and, as much as I loved my Vespa, I coveted Max's Lamberetta. When my dad had taken me to select a scooter, that was the one that I had aspired to but I was soon brought down to reality when Dad said that it was out of his price range and that I would have to be satisfied with the Vespa. I hadn't argued and it was a great machine, but oh that Lamberetta! Max spent a fortune on his clothes and appearance, never a hair out of place, he was a good-looking guy with high cheek bones and dark hair which he had styled at one of the top salons in the West End. He worked on the docks, the male members of his family all did. My old man said they were more like the Masons than the Masons and they really looked after their own. Dad regularly warned me about getting involved with them, but at that age you never listen, do you? Max did more than work on the docks, he also made money from other, less legitimate, activities. If you wanted anything Max could lay his hands on it, this included Italian flick knives and, more profitably, he was also the sole local source of amphetamines; Purple Hearts, Black Bombers and the like. It was said that his family also had close ties to the East End gangs and that you didn't want to cross them.

Max was not only a local Face he was, what we referred to as, one of the hard Mods, a really tough guy, no that didn't really do him justice; Max was vicious and enjoyed it, so you made sure that you were on his side. I wouldn't say I was a friend of his; we went around in the same circles but very few got close to him and anyway I liked to think I was more independent than that. Needless to say, he always pulled the best-looking birds, behind his back the guys would tell you he paid for them. Not as you would a tart, but he would pay for them to go to the best stylists and buy them clothes. He liked his girls to look good on the back of his scooter, as though they were the final accessory that he needed. Besides that, he didn't treat them very well and rarely would you see the same girl on his scooter for long. But they were his until he said so, they didn't dump him. I first met Max, when I was a kid, at the local boxing club. My old man had decided that I needed to learn how to fight after some local lads had ambushed me on the way home from my private junior school.

'Next time that happens I want you to be able to give those little toe rags a good hiding,' he said. And I loved it. Not only did I enjoy the discipline of the sport but also the actual fighting. Soon none of the other local lads would try and pick a fight with me and I also did fairly well in my bouts in the ring. That is until Max showed up. He was bigger and nastier even then and the first time I got into the ring with him he gave me a real pasting. I gave up boxing when I was thirteen, my new school didn't approve of either the boxing or their pupils mixing with common boys like that.

1963 was the year that launched the Beatles and while artists like Cliff Richard still topped the charts these acts would soon be toppled by the whole raft of bands from up north. It was the time that young people really started to break free. The Teddy Boys of the 1950s started it, but they were constrained by conscription and post war austerity. However, by 1963 the kids had full employment, cash in their pockets and an ever-widening range of fashions. It was in the late summer of 1963 and Max and his crew were at Clacton as were my mates and me. Clacton-on-Sea; we had started going there that spring, fifty or so miles up the Essex coast made a nice run out on the scooters on a Sunday afternoon. Dressed up, with leather coats and fishtail parkas, the girlfriend on the back of the scooter, it was a great way of burning off the Saturday night hangover. People would ask, 'why don't you go to Southend, its closer?' But the parents went there and you wouldn't want to run into them when you're having fun would you? The only problem with Clacton was the local 'swedes' and there had always been friction between the two groups. It didn't help that the local lads, some of them in cars, would try to chat-up our girls, they thought London girls were easy. Well after fifty miles on the back of a scooter, even on a warm day most of the birds would be pretty damn cold and if some swede offered them a lift back home in a nice warm car, they were often tempted. The fact that there might be a price to pay on the way didn't deter some of them neither.

'Oi, you!' I turned round and saw Max across the promenade with a group of his mates, he was dressed the part, striped blazer, cream trousers and desert boots. 'Come over here, I wanna talk to you.' I went over to him, hoping I hadn't crossed him in some way. 'You and your mates come here regular, don't you?' he stated rather than asked. I nodded. 'Well we're pissed off with these local twats comin' on to our girls and we think something needs to be done about it.' I couldn't have agreed more; the girl I had brought out that afternoon had only just told me she had got a lift home and I had had great hopes for a bit of 'hows-yer-father' to warm her up when we got back.

'What are you thinking?' I asked him.

'I think we need to come up here mob handed and sort these little turds out, teach them to keep away from the girls. Cut a few, warn the rest off.'

I never liked the idea of blades, they had spilled over from the razors and flick knives carried by the Teds in the fifties, but some of the hard mods still liked to carry a blade and I had already turned down an offer from Max to get me, "a nice little Italian blade off one of the ships coming into the port".

Despite this, the idea of a good scrap appealed and when he asked if I could get my mates on board I said, 'sure thing', and anyway I wouldn't have said no, I didn't want to look as if I carried no authority amongst my mates. He turned away,

'I know where to find you, I'll let you know what's happening.'

Before anything could be organised the summer came to an end and it all went away with the Autumn. Trips to the coast were replaced by trips up West to the clubs Fridays and Saturdays. The scene was really starting to take off. The Flamingo Club had Georgie Fame and The Blue Flames as its resident band and, together with the Marque and the 100 Club, most of the new R and B bands like Long John Baldry and His Hoochie Coochie Men and Zoot Money's Big Roll Band could be seen performing there. It was at the Flamingo we first saw the Stones; that is until they got fired for being too poppie. At the other end of the scale was John Mayall and his band, the Blues Breakers, but many of the mods considered him too much of a Blues purist portraying himself as a middle class intellectual in the old jazz club mould and who failed to understand the mods liking for more upbeat horn driven tunes. Even so the scene then was still more about jazz and blues, albeit as interpreted by the London-based groups and a lot of black dudes hung out in the clubs as well as the up-and-coming mods. Unlike some of my crew I loved the blues, not the raw Country Blues, that was a step too far, but the Chicago blues of people like John Lee Hooker and Muddy Waters. Never mind the Blues being the music of alienation, I liked it because It helped me be seen as different to the crowd and stand out. I would trawl the Soho specialist record stores to seek out obscure American imports to rave about. It was on one of the imports that I found a track to which I really related. It was a song that would turn out to be prescient and which would stay with me over the years. East Coast Blues, about a guy struggling to find his way in a strange city, it had a simple guitar riff, basic lyrics and a repetitive chorus but it was sung with such bitterness, in a voice that expressed the rejection the singer felt was being metered out to him. I bored my mates senseless with it.

Down and out in New York City
ain't got nothing more to lose,
down and out in New York City
just me and the East Coast Blues.

The Flamingo Club in Wardor Street was our venue of choice, it had started as a jazz club and then become a favoured haunt of the West Indian lads. It was edgy, but after a while the Mods took it over. Despite this, many of the black guys stayed around giving it a real cosmopolitan feel. After a few beers we would wander up to the club and down the stairs, pay our ten-bob entrance fee and go in. The atmosphere was like walking into the Amazon rain forest with condensation running down the walls. This was over-laid by the smell of cheap perfume, body odour, smoke and sweat from the dancing bodies and was accompanied by a throbbing Rhythm and Blues soundtrack. The stage was at the far end with a few stained and worn seats in front of it, to the left on a raised platform, was a coffee bar area from where you could oversee the stage and the rest of the club, a foot or so below and from there check out the girls. You had to be desperate to buy anything there though as a Coke would cost you half a dollar, almost twice the price of a pint outside. But none of this mattered as it was the place we wanted to be, especially when they had their Friday all-nighters. If we planned to go up west to the clubs on a Saturday evening however, we would often go shopping in Carnaby Street or the Kings Road in the afternoon, sometimes the clothes that you started out in were dumped as new gear was bought and worn that evening. Yes, we were the original dedicated followers of fashion. The lads in many ways worse than the girls!

There were many Mod crews around London at the time, each with their own manor, including those associated with Highbury, the Archway, Somers Town, Elephant and Castle and Mile End. These gangs consisted of anything from between fifty to a couple of hundred in strength at any one time. Turfs were strictly patrolled and borders laid down. Mods intruding onto other's turf risked a beating if caught. However, this tended to be put aside when we came together in the Soho clubs and there was never too much trouble in those venues, so long as you knew your place. Faces like Max ruled the roost and you made sure you didn't get in their way unless invited. The guys like myself, who were there with their mates, tried to make a space for themselves, while the hangers on just sort of hovered around the edges. If someone didn't pay for some pills, then they got smacked and you never tried to chat up the girls that were with the Faces or with crews from other areas; that was asking for trouble.

And that is just what happened when one of the local Romford lads tried to chat up a girl who was with some lads from Croydon. A fight broke out and the guys were bounced out onto the street. It had to stop there as there were a couple of coppers over the road. But the Croydon lads weren't satisfied, 'It's about time someone sorted you Romford ponces out! You better watch your backs next time.'

A few weeks later we heard through the grapevine that the Croydon lads were planning to come up to the Hill mob-handed and that we could expect to get a good beating. Max was in his element, sending out calls-to-arms like a medieval monarch calling on his Barons for support. This was a matter of honour.

'But Max, the Croydon crew are really hard bastards', someone said.

'Bollocks,' Max growled, 'They invade our patch they'll get lesson they won't forget'.

Most of us weren't as sure. The Croydon lads hadn't got their reputation for nothing, but no one else wanted to challenge Max and be accused of being scared, especially as the girls were there watching us. No one wanted to lose face in front of them, that would have done your pulling power no good at all. Anyway, the girls were worse than many of the guys, 'Go on, a good fight will be great, really exciting, we'll cheer you on, show those South London cows a thing or two'.

In many ways that summed it all up, North verses South. The North was still ruled by the Krays while the South came under the jurisdiction of the Richardsons, these two sets of gangsters had their fingers in most activities and many local businesses paid their weekly insurance to the gangs for their protection. Their patches centred on the Old Kent Road in the South and the Eastern Avenue in the North. Mod rivalries would change somewhat the next year but then geographical rivalries were still dead serious. I confided in Richie, 'The thing that worries me is that the Croydon crew have a lot more numbers to call on and if they all turn up we'll be in deep shit and they are likely to be tooled-up, only Max's guys carry weapons regular, it won't be just about fists and boots'.

'Don't worry Ace I'll get you one of these.' With that Richie produced a tube wrapped in multi-coloured plastic beads.

'What you going to dazzle them with your magic wand? You might as well wave your dick at 'em and hope they die laughing,' I said.

Ritchie frowned, 'It's a length of hose, stuffed with copper wire and if you hit someone in the face with it, those beads will rip their face off more effective than any blade. I'm telling you mate it's a good piece of gear to have in your pocket. Plus, if the coppers pick you up you can always claim it's a toy for your little cousin coz it looks so pretty.' He then went all serious and added, 'and there's no chance you stick someone with it by mistake and face a murder charge.' So, I ordered one, just in case.

The Croydon crew turned up one Friday at a gig by a local band at one of our pubs. As we feared they came mob-handed, there was bloody dozens of them, all looking for trouble. We heard they were coming and were waiting for them. They rode around the car park, the scooters reflecting the street lights in their chrome side panels and their straight through exhausts crackling like early machine-guns, making as much noise as they could in a show of strength. They had obviously come ready for a fight, I was fingering the cosh I had obtained in my pocket, wondering whether I would have the nerve to use it. I had hit plenty of guys but never with anything other than my fists or boots, somehow this all seemed more serious. We stood with our backs to the pub entrance and I clearly heard the doors being locked behind us as the landlord made sure his pub was secure. I saw a couple of guys try the gate to the back of the pub but that was well secured, the only way out was to the front, through the Croydon lads.

'No place to run'. I said to Richie who was standing next to me. He just laughed.

By now the girls who had come outside with us had realised it was going to get nasty and some were holding on to each other and others had started crying, their bravado evaporating under the harsh neon of the pub lights.

The Croydon lads did a last circuit of the car park and then stopped, their scooters facing us. I looked over at Max, even he looked worried and I thought, it's not all bad then if there is someone out there who can scare the shit out of that hard bastard. But he was surrounded by his close coterie of heavies, some I saw had coshes and knuckle dusters, Max pulled out a flick knife and held it by his side. That's when I got really scared. The Croydon lads pulled their scooters up on their stands and just sat looking at us. Three guys got off pillions and stood facing us, their Faces were taken everywhere by pillion, no driving for them. They stood there tapping what looked like rounders bats against the palms of their hands challenging us to make a first move and a group of local lads were daft enough to have a go, three of them were clubbed to the ground in an instant with their mates quickly backing away. The Croydon guys were really hyped up and started to give the lads on the ground a good kicking. Then before anything else could kick off all hell let loose. With a roar about thirty motor cycles came into the car park, most with a pillion passenger. The riders and passengers were dressed in leathers, many with 59 club patches sewn on the arm. They pulled their bikes up in a line between the Croydon lads and us and dismounted. I could see some of them carried bicycle chains, another throw-back to weapons of choice of the 1950s Teddy Boys. Their leader strode up to Max and with a loud sniff said, 'we've come to give you an 'and.'

A nod was all he received in response but an alliance, albeit temporary, had been made. The message was clear to everyone present. With that the odds changed and, with them being a long way from home, the Croydon lads' response was to kick their scooters into life and disappear like scolded cats. Some of the rockers chased after them for a while and kicked a few of them off their scooters before coming back to the pub.

Much beer was consumed that evening;

'How'd you hear about it?' I asked a rocker with greased down hair and a deaths head painted on the back of his leather jacket.

'There was word on the track at Dagenham, so we talked about it down the 59 club, you know our place on the North Circular, and thought we'd give you a look. 'Specially when we heard it was some wankers from Croydon invading the patch. Can't 'ave that, can we? We also heard you ponces were gonna get a good beating from the South London boys and that offended our sense of pride so over we come. Looks like a good job we did, although it's a shame they buggered off before we could lay into them proper.'

So, it turned out that geographical loyalties outweighed sub-cultural rivalries, at least that time. Although it didn't stop us giving some of the rockers a smacking when they came into one of our dances a few weeks later. But that was different, weren't it? They were taking liberties!

Chapter 3

The rest of the winter went along as normal. I had a succession of girlfriends but none lasted more than a few weeks and certainly there were none that I would have taken home. Most of them were what we used to call 'slags' anyway, easy on the eye and ready to go all the way if you could just find somewhere to do it. And we usually did. A mate's party, a front room when the parents were out, a bus shelter for a knee trembler and even the back porch after you'd taken her home. Well you needed some recompense for going out of your way, wouldn't you?

It was early in 1964 and we were at Tottenham Royal, probably the top music venue in North London at the time. It was a strange place in that the stage was decked out like an old-time dance hall with swags of gold curtains and gilt decorations. They had, what we thought then, a bloody awful house band called The Dave Clark Five, who had just broken into the pop scene in a big way with Glad All Over, and who we thought looked like a right bunch of nancies. They dressed in matching dark blue blazers, white trousers and white high necked collarless shirts, the sort of outfits you could imagine a bunch of young Conservatives wearing and thinking that they looked cool. Not at all what we would have described as fashionable, but for some unfathomable reason, the girls loved them, which meant that the Royal was a great place to go to try and pull. However, the Royal also put on some of the more credible groups like the Pretty Things, The Downliners Sect and other mainstream Rhythm and Blues bands; that night they had booked the Animals and, although they were a bit Northern, they played much more the type of music we were into. We went to the Royal quite a bit because despite all its faults, it was the place to be seen in our neck of the woods.

One of Max's soldiers pushed his way over to where I was standing, 'Max wants to see you.' Again, my first thoughts were what the fuck had I done wrong, how had I upset him? But then he went on 'he's planning a little trip to Clacton and wants to make sure you'll keep your side of it and bring your mates along. He'll be down the boozer tomorrow night; you better not keep him hangin' abart. He hates that.'

'If it's that important why don't we talk tonight?' I replied sounding bolder than I felt, indicating to where Max was talking to two older guys in suits.

'Max's busy. And a word to the wise my son, those guys he's talking to are the Kray twins so make sure you don't cause no trouble 'cause they don't like trouble when they're out enjoying themselves.'

Max was on speaking terms with the Krays, the most notorious gangsters in East London, bloody hell maybe my old man was right to warn me away. But it was exciting after all.

Next day, Max arrived at the pub where we were waiting for him as instructed. He walked in, he was the Face, he didn't have to ask, am I? He just was. Wearing desert boots he came into the bar, his feet seemingly not touching the floor, silently, surrounded by his soldiers. Whenever he walked in somewhere others made room, the epitome of a hard mod, he was the Face. I felt a pang of envy, that's who I wanted to be, but Max and the others like him seemed to have something more, something that I could only aspire to and I would have done anything to obtain that. Max spent the first few minutes evidencing his position, getting everyone drinks, flirting with the girls and generally making sure we all knew that he was the main man.

'Oi,' he shouted, getting everyone's attention. 'Easter's coming up and I want you all out on the Monday coz we're going to Clacton to sort the fuckin' swedes out before the summer comes. Make sure they know their fucking place. You get me. Any problems with that?'

Surprise surprise, no one had. We all agreed we'd tag along to Clacton on Easter Monday and support Max in his crusade against the locals who he had decided had shown him disrespect.

'Come tooled up.' was his last instruction then staring at me he said, 'Ace I wanna word.' I hung around and after the rest had moved away Max came and sat down next to me. 'I need a favour Ace.' I nodded. I hated to think what I might be getting into but whatever it was it would only add to my credibility. 'I gotta go to a meet with some guys who don't like some of my boys and I just need someone at my shoulder who I know won't offend them.' I shrugged I couldn't imagine that Max would go anywhere that would actually put him danger. 'I gotta meet Reggie, a little business to sort, just need you to cover me back on the way, there won't be no problem. Thursday at eight, meet me at Gants Hill station we'll go on from there. Right?'

'Do you mean Reggie Kray?' I asked with some incredulity because these guys already had the reputation that would follow them to the grave.

'Yeah, is that a problem?'

'No', I lied, 'It'll be interesting.'

'Jus' keep your fucking mouth shut an' you'll be OK' I just need some company.' I was confused but I was committed so I just went along with it.

Thursday as agreed I met Max at Gants Hill tube station and we rode the line to Bethnal Green, the real old East End. From there we walked down to Cheshire Street to the Carpenters Arms.

'Why didn't we come on the scooters it'd been quicker?' I asked.

'Ronnie says they make too much noise; an' you don't wanna upset him.' The pub stood on a corner and when we opened the door a haze of smoke and beer fumes spewed through the doorway. I looked around and saw the twins sitting in the corner. Reggie, looking for all the world like a successful business man, dressed in a bespoke Prince of Wales check suit, white shirt and paisley tie, talking with a thin, mean, wizened-looking guy. Ronnie sat at the next table drinking with a good looking young mod with longer than fashionable strawberry blond hair and wearing a blue and white striped calico jacket.

'Go get me a pint.' Max said and I went up to the bar under the close scrutiny of the clientele. I brought the beer back to Max and he stood nervously gulping at it. Although they were only in their early thirties, the Krays had an awesome physical presence oozing unspoken threats which warned you not to take liberties.

'Get me another, go.' Max had all but finished this second pint when Reggie waved him over. I followed just behind him.

'What you doing here son?' Reggie asked.

'Me old man told me to come an' give you this', Max replied reaching into his inside pocket and pulling out a thick envelope.

'I do hope George hasn't been silly and left me short son.'

'No Mr Kray the old man's broke his arm and can't get out, he says to tell you it's all there.' Before anything else could be said the street door opened and two non-descript short blokes with dark complexions and slicked back black hair walked in.

'Why if it ain't the Maltese pimps,' Ronnie said loudly, 'they got some nerve.' Reggie held up his hand as if to say stay calm. The two sullen Maltese came over to the brothers. Before they could speak Ronnie says,

'You've been running girls in one of our clubs, that's outta order, right outta order, Joe.'

'Ronnie it's all a big mistake. Your boy, Phil from the club, he says it's all right to run the girls outta there.'

'Well it aint! You got that? Phil's been a real silly boy. You keep your girls well away or there'll be trouble and we don't want that do we Joe? We all gotta know our place, aint we? Just be a good boy and sort it out. Now I'd buy you a drink but I'm busy, so see yourselves out.' With that dismissal the two slunk out of the pub as Reggie spoke to his brother.

'Ronnie, Phil's been silly once too often, bet he's takin' a back hander from them two, get someone to 'ave a word, make sure he don't do it again.'

'I'll do it meself Reggie, it'll be a pleasure,' Ronnie said.

'Don't hurt him too bad, just teach him a lesson Ronnie, you got a keep 'em dahn aintcha!' This last phrase was addressed to us. 'Now you aint introduced your mate to us. Whatcha think Ron, nice looking boy, could be your nephew?'

'Too old for my taste and I don't do glasses.' Ronnie replied and I saw a look of relief cross the blond mod's face.

'This is Ace Mr Kray, he's a mate from Romford.' Max said.

'Good for him. Glad to see he's not one of those leery kids you usually knock around with. Get yerselves a drink and wish your old man well from us,' and with that he turned away.

Max took a moment to realise that we had been dismissed and so we went to the bar as instructed and ordered a couple more pints. I would have been much happier to have just left, but as Max said later, 'I don't want them thinking I'm too scared to drink in their pub,' he added 'you know those two never swear, my old man says that the worst they'll ever call you is silly. If they say you've done something silly, then you can expect at least a good smacking and maybe worse.' I was just glad to be getting home and hoped that they would forget they had been introduced to Ace from Romford, I didn't fancy being asked by the Krays to do them any favours and I certainly didn't want to know what that envelope was all about. But at least supporting Max would add to my reputation and I'd been introduced to the Krays, I'd make sure the lads heard about that and Max would know now that he could rely on me and he would owe me one now. I should have known better.

Easter came and with it particularly dismal weather, they reckoned that it was the worst Easter Bank holiday weather on record, but this wasn't allowed to put us off our trip to Clacton. Bank holidays were seen as a real bonus with the extra day off from work and we were determined to make the most of it. Sunday had been spent cleaning and polishing the scooters and nagging mothers to make sure shirts and suits were properly washed and pressed. In this we weren't much different to our old men who would spend Sunday mornings cleaning the car before putting on a shirt, tie and jacket and heading out for a Sunday afternoon drive.

As arranged, we all met up at a transport café on the A12 before heading off to the coast. Scooters decked out with mirrors, extra lights and many with whip aerials sporting foxtails or some pennant. The riders dressed to impressed, their good clothes covered by ex-US air force parkas, desert boots on their feet and college-style scarves around the neck, most of the scarves nicked from students who had been foolish enough to wear them to dances and in the clubs. A few wore helmets but not many, they weren't seen as cool. Under the parkas those who could afford it also wore three quarter leather coats but given that these could cost a couple of weeks' wages you needed a good income to stretch to one. If you were lucky the whole look was finished off with a good-looking bird on the back; the ultimate accessory. They would of course be dumped when we arrived and left to find their own amusement while we went off to the boozer to get up some courage before the action started. As it happened I was between girls and anyway I didn't fancy having to worry about some bird if we were going to see some action so I went solo.

When we arrived, Clacton was cold and wet, the sea a sullen dark grey merging seamlessly with the slate grey sky. It was as welcoming as only a wet seaside resort can be. We were also cold and wet and the birds were doing nothing but complain. All we wanted, even more than a beer, was a hot drink. We were greeted by a bunch of lads from Stratford who told us that the cafes were refusing to serve London mods. That really pissed us off, what was wrong with our money? We wandered along the prom trying to find some local mods to smack but they seemed to be staying out of sight and out of the rain. We were cold, bored and looking somewhat bedraggled, not the image we had hoped to present.

'Look over there!' someone shouted. Over the road, overflowing out of a café, were a bunch of motorcyclists. 'How come they get served and we don't?' The guys outside the café stood pointing and laughing at us and in that moment the idea of looking for local mods disappeared. Max led the charge but we had to dodge between the steamed-up family cars driving along the sea front, this slowed us up and the greasers legged it.

'Come on let's get the greasy bastards.' Max shouted and we went after them. Soon a running battle had broken out all along the sea front, fights between groups of guys, the girls standing by shouting encouragement. I punched a guy in the mouth and then my mates and I gave him a good kicking as he laid curled up in a foetal position his arms covering his head. Cars were brought to a halt as people spilled into the road, some fighting, some just families trying to escape the violence, dads shouting, kids screaming and the mods trying to nail any greaser we could find.

I heard someone shout, 'Watch out the rozzers are here!' And soon I could hear the police whistles. It was then I saw Max and his soldiers wading into another rocker laying on the ground and giving him a real kicking. They were enjoying themselves so much they didn't see the police come around the corner. It was all over quickly, Max's boys legging it and Max being held by two big coppers while their mates chased after the others.

I turned to Richie and Dave and said, 'Come on let's scarper, I don't want to get nicked'. They seemed to like that idea so we and the other guys rounded up the girls and went back to the scooters. While we were doing that, I saw Max's latest standing by his scooter. 'You know he's been nicked Julie, don't you? I said.

'How the bloody hell am I gonna get home then?'

'Can't you go back with one of his mates?'

'They most came in pairs and anyhow how do I know they've not been nicked as well?'

I thought, this could be another way to really get into Max's good books so said, 'I'll give you a ride back, Julie if you want. See you home safe. Just leave a note on his handlebars to let him know you're OK.' This she did in lipstick on his fly screen, I thought, that'll piss him off, she's braver than me.

We made our way back to Romford wet and cold and feeling that the whole thing had been a bit of an anti-climax. Except of course Max had been nicked, that had been worth seeing and I'd rescued his girl. That had to have a value didn't it?

The big surprise came the next morning at breakfast.

'I hope you weren't involved in any of this? The old man said, flashing his Daily Express at me. The headlines screamed "Youngsters Beat Up Town - 97 Leather Jacket Arrests".

'You know I wouldn't be seen dead in a leather jacket, it must have been some rocker group' and I left for work with a smile on my face. When I read the same story in the Daily Mirror they made it sound a whole lot worse, Mods and Rockers fighting on the sea front terrifying women and children. Ruining the weekend. It seemed that everyone on the bus was talking about "the riot at the seaside". I felt really chuffed to have been there. When I arrived at work the Chief Accountant was giving vent to his opinion.

'It's about time they brought back the birch or at least National Service to instil some discipline into these yobs. The Telegraph says it was Scooter Boys who were terrorising innocent families. I hope they lock up those who were arrested, that will teach them a lesson they won't forget.

'I'm sure it's all exaggerated Mr Jones,' I chipped in.

'It's in the Telegraph so it must be right. I can tell you if any of my staff were arrested for such a thing they would be out on their ear.' As he turned away I pulled a face and winked, half the office had to stifle their laughter while the older members of the team tutted about disrespect and knowing our place. But I had been there, once that became known, I was the man of the moment amongst the younger members of staff. I just thanked my lucky stars that we had scarpered when we did.

The following Friday Max was back in circulation and down the pub telling everyone how he had been fined £50 and that his old man had thought it so funny that he had paid it for him.

'Over 'ere Ace,' he called, 'you fucked off quick Monday, scared were you?'

'No Max, we stayed until the Police broke things up. How come you didn't get done for carrying?'

Laughing he replied, 'when the rozzers pounced, I managed to slip my blade into Micky's pocket, 'lucky he weren't picked up weren't it? But anyway, I 'spose I got to thank you for taking Julie back home. Hope you didn't take no liberties?'

'Course I didn't Max, she's your girl, but I thought she needed to be got home.' He gave me a hard stare,

'Gertcha, I know you didn't do nothing, you got more sense than that aintcha? You done good seeing after Julie. I gotta buy you another drink my son, this is getting to be a habit.' I was in his good books, it didn't get much better than that.

For the rest of that summer the newspapers were full of stories about mods and rockers. Following our lead at Clacton everyone seemed to want to find some action and there were riots, as the papers put it, at Margate, Brighton and other resorts on the South coast. Mods were being portrayed as a menace to society and, in general, a threat to civilisation. We loved it. However, few of the Romford guys got involved in the later battles. It really was too much effort to trek across London and then another 50 miles or so to spend a cold weekend sleeping on the beach just to chase a few rockers. Some did go on the train when they heard about the planned seaside invasion of Brighton, but for many, that turned out to be a wasted journey as the police put them straight back on the train home or, if they protested, gave them a swift slap and arrested them for threatening behaviour. A lot of us felt that it wasn't worth the trouble and the police were cracking down hard on, what they saw as, trouble makers. I certainly wasn't interested in getting a criminal record, that might well have led to me losing my job and I felt that I had it made, good job, good money, a great social life and a nice home to crash out in. As for Clacton, we still went there most weekends but, beside the occasional scuffle with the locals, there was no more real trouble and we just enjoyed the summer.

Chapter 4

I really fucked up, how was I to know that Max still considered Julie to be his girl? When I saw her in the pub late that summer we got talking,

'Thanks for helping me out back at Clacton Ace, you were a real gent.'

'That's OK Julie, it was a pleasure, I'm just glad Max wasn't offended.' Julie didn't comment. So, I brought her a drink and we carried on chatting.

'Y'know Max didn't like that you took me home, he's never let me forget it. Gave me a real hard time, kept on about it. In fact, he's dumped me coz of it, kept saying I should have waited till I knew for certain he weren't coming back. Said I should have looked after his scooter and that he couldn't trust me.'

'That's not fair. I think you got that wrong; Max thanked me for taking you home, he was real grateful.'

'I wouldn't bank on it, he's just an insecure jealous arsehole' Julie snapped. 'Found himself a new model now, blond tart from Ilford, I hope she gives him a dose.' I'm a bloke I didn't know what to say so I bought her another drink. She carried on, 'You know you're a much nicer bloke than Max, I've always fancied you, not as flash as Max, just really fashionable.'

'Thanks, you look pretty good yourself, I can't think why Max has given you the elbow.' She leant forward and put her hand on mine.

'I'm pretty good at a lot of things and I've never really thanked you properly,' she said and I began to think this could be a good evening here. By now Julie and I had had a few drinks and she was getting quite sloshed, so when asked if she fancied coming outside for a bit of fresh air she replied, 'Why not I could do with a bit of fun,' and I knew she wouldn't need much persuading. After a bit of a snog she became as hands on as me, whipping me flies open and pulling on me old man as if she was bell ringing. By that time, I had her dress up over her waist and her knickers round her ankles; the next stage was inevitable. Inevitable but not easy. Leaning against a stack of cases of empty London Pride bottles which not only rattled the whole time we were at it but also threatened to fall on top of us. The whole experience would have been particularly memorable if it wasn't for the consequences. Afterwards we stood holding each other for a while and I suggested maybe we could see more of each other,

'We'll see,' she replied' I'm not sure what I'm doing yet.' We went back into the bar and found a table in the corner. Julie sat down looking somewhat sullen,

'You all right girl?' I said.

'Yes, of course why? Just don't tell anyone what we done and get me another drink.'

The pub was a regular haunt of the local mods so there was nothing unusual about the number of guys from different crews in the bar and I really hadn't taken any notice, especially once I had other things on my mind. If I had I might not have taken Julie outside in the first place. I had just ordered a couple of drinks at the bar when I felt this shove and the next thing I knew I was up against a pillar and one of Max's soldiers was right there in my face,

'Max aint gonna like this,' he said, 'Micky and I saw you take Julie outside, she's his bird an' she should have fuckin' known better than to let you get her pissed. She would never have gone outside with a little twat like you if you hadn't got her pissed, you're both in deep shit. And you my son; forcing Julie could be the last time you shag anyone after Max has finished with you'.

'You're wrong' I managed to stutter, 'she came on to me!'

He hit me in the stomach and said, 'you lying little turd, Julie wouldn't even look at a tosser like you if she weren't pissed'

He hit me again and as I collapsed gasping for breath and saw him walk over to Julie, pull her from her seat and say something to her. What it was I don't know, but she screamed and ran from the pub.

No wonder she was edgy, if she'd lied about Max being finished with her, even if he had got a new girl, then we would both be in trouble. Max wasn't renowned for having a forgiving streak and if he was already doubting my motives for giving Julie a ride back from Clacton it would be difficult convincing him that tonight hadn't been planned all along. I could picture him looking at me and telling me I had been silly!

I decided to keep a low profile the days following this but by the end of the week no one had been in touch and I was desperate to get out see my mates and find out what was happening. Mum and Dad were driving me crazy, they couldn't understand why I wasn't going out. They worry when you go out, then when you have a couple of days in they worry the arse off you wanting to know why. I just hoped that by now it had blown over and the heat gone out of any anger that Max had felt. After all, Julie had said she was no longer his girl, so maybe it would have been of no consequence. He might even be grateful that I had taken her off his hands. Maybe his guys hadn't told him, but I wasn't holding my breath. Even so I consciously kept away from the more popular venues where I might bump into Max or any of his soldiers.

Down at my local, where I usually met up with the guys if we hadn't decided where to go on to, I ordered a beer and sat in the corner waiting for the guys to come in. However, they didn't show and I was on my second before Richie came in. He nervously glanced round the bar; I thought Christ he looks a bit shifty tonight.

'Hi Richie, what are you drinking?' I called over to him.

'Shit I didn't think you'd be here, but I'm glad you are, I didn't want to come round your house.' He sounded strange, panicky even. I went and got him a cider.

'Ace,' he said, 'You're in big trouble.' Max has put it out that he's going to cut you so badly that no girl will ever look at you again.' I couldn't take in for a moment what he was saying.

'Don't be a twat Richie it wasn't that serious, Julie and I just had a bit of fun, she told me Max and her were over.'

'That's not the way he sees it Ace. He's really pissed off. You should 'ave heard him down the club. You should be really scared. He has already put the tart in hospital.'

'What Julie? He wouldn't.' I was beginning to feel panicked.

'He bleedin' has, hurt her bad, gave her a real beating and cut her face. That's why the guys aren't here' they don't want to get involved. You're on your own mate. The guys are scared and so should you be, they've left you high and dry.'

'What about you?' I asked

'They all think I'm a twat for coming tonight but I thought I owed it to you to let you know the score. But I can't stay. Max reckons he will sort out anyone who is seen with you as well. Sorry mate. I hope it works out but you really are on your own. You should have kept it in your trousers and let her be'.

'Shit Richie what am I supposed to do?'

'I really don't know Ace, we can't take on Max,' then added as an afterthought 'If it were me I'd get away somewhere. I've gotta go. Bye Ace, take care and good luck mate. Sorry.' He even left his pint untouched.

I had to think. It was easy for Richie to say I should get away but I had a good job to hold down, my family and friends were all here. I didn't have anywhere to go. Sitting in the pub I started to feel really exposed, the brown nicotine-stained walls and matching furniture seemed to be closing in around me I had been involved in scraps before but had always had my mates beside me; always been on the winning side. Where was Bruce when I needed him? Probably in a paddy field in Vietnam by now. I was completely on my own. Everyone I looked at appeared to be hostile. Even the juke box seemed to mock me as someone put on The Stones, It's All Over Now. I considered going to Max and explain what had happened, but quickly eliminated that. I knew Max well enough to appreciate that he wasn't the forgiving type. If he had decided that I had damaged his standing he wouldn't stop until he had proved he was the top dog. I would be made an example of to warn everyone else to show respect, he'd have learnt at least that much from the Krays. The only option for now was to go home, maybe I could sort something out but just what I hadn't a clue.

Parents are strange creatures. Most of the time they ignore you, just as much as you ignore them, then you arrive home early one night and your Mum takes one look at you and asks.

'What's happened? What's wrong with you, you look as white as a sheet, in fact you've been acting funny all week are you going down with something?' Then despite the veneer of the tough guy I broke down. I told her the whole story, well I didn't actually say that I had shagged Julie, but she got the message. And do you know she didn't bat an eyelid, no tearing of hair, shouting or whatever, just a cutting,

'You stupid little fool, hasn't your Dad warned you? I'll talk to him.' Even when you're twenty they think that they can protect you and make it right. I wasn't so sure.

When dad got home from the Lodge she told him what had happened, I suppose I should have done it but I guess it shows that I am a coward at heart, and he came bursting into my room.

'After all I've bloody done for you; you stupid little sod. You've good prospects and now you've fucked it all away.' Strangely it was his use of the F word that shocked me most; I had never heard him swear like that before. 'I told you to keep away from those fucking thugs, I warned you, but no, you couldn't listen, could you?' I just stood there and took it. After he calmed down a bit he told me to follow him downstairs, I hung my head and did as I was told, I had no fight left in me, by admitting what had happened I had acknowledged my fear and the hopelessness I felt about the situation.

I have to admit, the old man was a doer, no sitting around crying in his beer for him. The only answer he said was for me to disappear. Christ that sounded dramatic, made me sound like some criminal on the run,

'I don't want to leave Romford dad, surely that's not necessary?' But he soon put me in my place.

'You know Max's family are filth, they have links with the very worst rubbish. If they say that they are going to sort you out it's no idle threat, it's a promise. If we don't get you away, you'll end up in a hospital; or worse.' He then added, 'and I've my business and reputation to think about,' then as an afterthought, 'and your mother's peace of mind, so you'll do as you're bloody well told.'

The next few days were all go, at least on my parent's part. Mum got in touch with her sister Jean, in Ipswich, and persuaded her to let me take up lodgings with her. I was given no say in the matter. The old man called in all his favours at the Council, a senior councillor and my boss Mr Jones, both Lodge members of course, were spoken to and asked to make enquiries about any jobs in the Ipswich area and were also asked to find ways to let me go without notice. They were told I was needed to support my aunt through some difficult times, nervous breakdowns were hinted at and they at least pretended to believe that. It's a reflection of the job market of the time that within forty-eight hours Mr Jones had come back and told Dad, not me, that there was job that I should be able to get at a small rural council based in Ipswich. The Deputy Clerk was a fellow Mason so it shouldn't be a problem. With that my future was sealed, I was to be packed off to some hick town with some crappy job in a tin-pot organisation, no mates and no social life. Although my dad put it more succinctly, 'at least you'll keep your balls!'

Chapter 5

With my parents following with my belongings, I had ridden my scooter north up the A12 through a damp September Saturday afternoon and felt some relief, elation even, at being able to escape Max's retribution, but now as I took in the faded wallpaper of the spare bedroom, with its roses wilting down the walls, the cheap pale pink foam-backed carpet, curling at the edges and matching Candlewick bedspread. I was in pieces. My welcome had been less than warm, I introduced myself to my aunt and uncle as Ace and was immediately told that they disapproved of the diminution of my given name and that they expected me to use and be called Alan, particularly in front of the children. I looked around the room again and self-pity threatened to well-up and drown me. I remembered my own stylish and spacious bedroom at home. Home, did I have such a place anymore? Mum had furnished that room for me with the latest fashions, matching light oak furniture, a desk for my record player, shelves for the record collection and dark blue bedding and curtains. Now the records lay piled in the corner. They and my Dansette record player had been greeted with hostility by my Uncle,

'We don't have a gramophone in this house; and pointing to the box of records, I don't know why you brought them along, I'll not have them played loud!'

I had never lived in an old house before; it seemed dark and dingy after home, there, that word again. The orange light from the street lamp on Norwich Road played strange tricks with the colours in the room and I drew the thin pink curtains in a vain attempt to shut it out. Sitting on the narrow single bed, with its thin mattress and creaking springs, all that seemed to go through my mind were those recurring lyrics:

Down and out in New York City
ain't got nothing more to lose,
down and out in New York City
just me and the East Coast Blues

Alone in a strange town, I wondered what my mates were up to, it was Saturday night after all, probably gone up West to one of the clubs, they would feel safe doing that again now I was no longer around. Strange town no mates, looking at a new job and only my cousins for company. A 13-year-old girl and 11-year-old boy, only bloody kids.

'They'll show you round next week,' my aunt had said. What'll they know, I thought, I'm on my own now. I really was on my own, both Mum and Dad had drummed that into me constantly in the days since it had been agreed that I would come to Ipswich,

'Under no circumstances do you get in touch with any of your old mates and you'll have to stay away from Romford for the fore-seeable. If I were you I wouldn't even go down to Colchester and for God's sake stay away from Clacton.' It all seemed a bit extreme but I had started to wonder just what the old man had heard on the grapevine. After all the guys on his building sites were well up with all the local gossip and rumours.

I would have liked to go out for a drink but where to? There was a pub opposite but I had no idea what it was like. I suspect-ed that if I asked my uncle it would go down like a sack of shit. Bugger, I'd only been here an hour on my own and already I was bored out of my mind.

'Come down when you've settled in' my aunt had said. 'Make yourself at home', but it wasn't, was it? I was an exile and now could not see beyond the darkness of my self-pity and, what I had decided were, my *East Coast Blues*.

'Next week you've got that interview to look forward to!' my fa-ther had said as they were leaving, 'remember to mention George Jones's name, he called in a lot of favours to get you that interview, but they'll need reminding'. Then poking me in the chest, 'You'll be all right.'

I wondered how much it had cost the old man to sort it all out.

'And I have told your aunt that you will pay your way once you get settled, don't let me down! I have given her a couple of months' rent but then it's down to you. Make sure you bloody do pay her, you're not living free at home now, it'll do you good to stand on your own two feet. And for God's sake keep out of trouble'.

'Some chance' I thought, 'in this shit hole!'

Later that evening I went out for a look around. Opposite, as well as the Emperor public house, there was a parade of shops and a Renault garage. A bus stop was just up the road and from the destination on the front of the bus that pulled up I could see in which direction the town centre lay. I wandered up the road towards the town and found another pub on the corner opposite a motor cycle dealership, The Inkerman, I wondered if all the pubs in the town were Empire based, it was as if I had gone back in time! But I thought I would give it a go, it wasn't directly opposite so shouldn't upset anyone. Inside it had the same nicotine stained walls that I was used to with red velvet benches along the walls. Faded grandeur came to mind, like the big Victorian houses that stood across the road. There was one old boy sitting at a table nursing half a pint of weak-looking dark beer. I could see that there was no fun to be had here, nevertheless I ordered a pint of bitter, I didn't like to order anything fancy they would have probably thrown me out as a degenerate. The beer was a Tolly Cobbold brew. It was bloody disgusting compared to the London beers I was used to, I don't think it had any alcohol in it, certainly didn't taste like it. After I had finished my pint I was tempted to go up into the town and see what was going down but as I didn't know how far it was and I didn't want to push my luck with my aunt and uncle so I decided to give it a miss.

Although I couldn't see it at the time, my aunt had come up trumps in agreeing to take me in. I don't know how much of the story she had been told, I suspected not a lot. The kids certainly didn't know and that first weekend they questioned me relentlessly about why I had left, what they thought of as the Nirvana of

London. My mother and her sister Jean had been born and raised in Ipswich and while Mum had moved away Jean had stayed and married Michael a well-respected local doctor. His surgery was at the side of the house and their decision to let me stay certainly wasn't because they needed the money. Both kids, Rachael and Peter, went to the local grammar school and my uncle ruled their lives with a rod of iron.

'You can come and go as you please,' he told me, 'but Peter is only allowed out to see his friends at weekends and the same goes for Rachael except she is allowed to go to the church youth club on Thursdays, but only if she is up to date with her homework. I don't expect you to give them any ideas contrary to that. Is that understood?' It was clear from this that he wasn't as happy to have me in his home as my aunt was, but I readily agreed not to lead them astray. At least I wasn't expected to have them hang around with me cramping my style, although at that time I had no idea whether there would be any style to cramp. The Dansette however was a great hit and although my collection of Rhythm and Blues records was outside my cousins' zones of appreciation they loved the Motown stuff that I had and after they returned from church spent most of that Sunday morning in my room listening to records.

'Oh, I do wish Daddy would let us have a record player,' Rachael said more than once. He doesn't even like me listening to the radio, says it will distract me from my school work. I told him all the other girls have record players, it's just not fair.' I said nothing I wasn't going to go there and create more problems for myself.

'Would you like to come to church with us?' my aunt had asked, 'There are a lot of young people who come along, you might get along quite well with them, make some nice new friends'.

'It's not really my thing,' I replied, 'I think I'll try to settle in a bit first if that's OK.' She didn't seem too put out by that and I was left in peace for a couple of hours. After Sunday lunch, and at least that was bloody good although I did miss the pre-lunch pint or two with my mates, I got on the scooter and went for a ride round. The place was dead but at least I sussed out where places were, the town centre, which of course was all closed up on a Sunday, a few possible pubs and where I had to go for the job interview. After that it was back to the house for another boring evening but at least it gave me the opportunity to catch up with some of the studying that I had got behind with.

That at least impressed my uncle who pointed out, 'Just take note Rachael. Alan goes off to study not because he has to but because he wants to better himself.'

'And move out of here', I muttered under my breath.

My interview wasn't until the Thursday so I had time to kill and decided that if I was going to live here I ought to get to know the place try and find out where any action was. So, on the Monday morning I decided to walk into the town centre, it was a couple of miles but that would kill some time and allow me to take in what was about. On the way in I passed a big motorcycle and scooter showroom and stopped to check it out, it wasn't a patch on the places around Romford but I would at least be able to get my scooter seen to if necessary. Further down the road was Coes, a traditional menswear shop, brown paintwork surrounding the windows and models in the sort of suits and sports jackets that even my dad wouldn't have been seen dead in. Then nothing more of interest until I got to the Town Hall in the centre.

There was another old-fashioned menswear shop, two department stores, that looked as if they had come out of the 1920s, together with a couple of hotels. My God was this all I had got to look forward to? I strolled the High Street from the Town Hall to a big Co-op store at the other end. Nothing. No style at all. On the way back I took a left by a Burtons the Tailor, God forbid that I would be reduced to shopping there, and finally found a half-decent men's shop. At least the stock was only half a season out of fashion. I spent half an hour browsing and left with a new tab collar shirt that would do for the interview but saw nothing that matched the style of the gear that I would have bought in Carnaby Street or the Kings Road.

None of this lifted my spirits and depressive thoughts swirled round my mind. What would happen if the Stour Council didn't want me? Where would I earn a living? What if my aunt and uncle got fed up with me? What if I didn't meet anyone to be friends with and ended up on my own? Life seemed unbelievably bleak. Just down the street I came to a coffee bar, The Gondoliers. Even that rubbed in the difference I was faced with when you considered it against the buzzing coffee bars we frequented in Romford and especially those in Soho. I went down the stairs anyway to get a coffee. A juke box stood in the corner churning out the latest pop song by Cilla Black, while down one wall was a counter with a Formica top and a Gaggia espresso machine at one end. The opposite wall lined with booths and chairs with half a dozen or so school girls huddled round one in the middle, all seeming to ape the look of the singer they had obviously selected on the Juke box. The girl serving at the counter looked like a mod from her hair style, although what she was wearing was hidden underneath a pale blue nylon overall. I ordered a coffee which came in a flat glass cup with a tired film of froth on the top. I thought I would try chatting to the waitress as she was nearer my age than anyone else I had met so far,

'I'm new in town, is it always this quiet?'

She shrugged, 'depends.'

I continued, 'Is it livelier in the evening?'

'Sometimes.' She replied without looking up. Don't you hate it when people won't even look at you when you speak to them?

'Is there somewhere that mods hang out in the evenings?

'Depends what's on I 'spose.' At that point I gave up, not sure that even if she had told me any venues I would have bothered with them given her lack of enthusiasm. I took my coffee and sat down under the scrutiny of the schoolgirls, I was certainly not going to speak to them. That was far beneath me. They giggled amongst themselves making it obvious that they were talking about me. The juke box had stopped so I went over and read through the playlist, it was all predictable with the top ten and other pop songs prominent.

'Put on Herman's Hermits', one of the girls called over. I selected some Stones and the single Chuck Berry that was listed.

'Boring!' Chorused the girls. I ignored them and drank my coffee.

Walking back from the town along the Norwich Road I passed a couple more cafes, Quick Snax and the Two Ages. Both of which looked somewhat seedy but as it was lunch time and the Two Ages had a couple of guys in leathers standing at the counter, I decided to risk something to eat in Quick Snax. I sat down with a ham roll only to be joined by a pasty-faced woman.

'ello love looking for a bit of lunchtime fun?' It took me a few moments to fathom out what was being proposed. I checked out the other customers and realised that they were mainly female and all seemed to have the same sallow complexion. Christ, I had stumbled into a place where you picked up a local prostitute. I would later find out that Quick Snax was notorious and that the Two Ages was where the rockers met of an evening. Apparently, the rockers kept a friendly eye on the girls and sorted any problems for them.

'Sorry love, I only came in for a sandwich.'

'Oh, I thought you were too good to be true. But sometimes you never can tell.'

When I got back to the house my aunt asked, 'How did you get on. It must be strange, not as lively as Romford is it, do you want something to eat? I couldn't help but smile she was so keen to see if I was getting used to the changes,

'It's different', I replied 'but I am sure I'll get used to it all and I had a ham roll in Quick Snax on the way back from town.'

'Really, I'm surprised that the only roll you got in there was ham, you could've got more than you bargained for. I should have got your uncle to warn you about that place,' she said with a sly smile on her face.

'Well I was approached by a rather strange woman and she didn't ask if I wanted more tea,' I replied, hoping that I wasn't overstepping the mark.

'That would have finished your education for sure, although I don't think my sister would have been too happy.' I realised that she was teasing and that she had a sense of humour very much like my mum. Maybe we would get on alright if I was a bit careful. 'While we're getting on OK, do you mind if I say something to you?' she continued. Now I felt concerned, she went on without waiting for my reply. 'I wouldn't go around here talking like a Cockney if I were you, a lot of people here aren't much impressed with Londoners. It would be such a shame if you got off to a bad start, especially at your interview, because of something so simple. I know you can speak well because you do when you speak to your Uncle.' I looked at her and smiled back, she had sussed me out right away. I knew I put on a bit of a London accent, back in Romford I did it to fit in, despite the school that I went to doing all it could to knock It out of me.

'Thanks, I'll remember that Aunt,' I said, 'I need all the help I can get up here,' and I meant it.

Chapter 6

When I arrived at the offices of the Stour District Council for my interview I had had quite a shock. After the large, modern office block in London this was a complete surprise, the building had once been an Edwardian gentleman's house but now housed the staff of the Stour council and it came with manicured gardens and a circular turret. My old boss had got me the interview, despite the less than good relationship that we had in the office, and it turned out he had given me a glowing reference. Before I left Romford, he had even phoned to warn me that I would have some adjustments to make when I moved to Suffolk.

'It will be different working in a department of six after being in one of over a hundred you'll have to conform more than you do here if you want to fit in.' I didn't even get the chance to go in and say good-bye to people at Romford, they probably thought I had been sacked because of my attitude. When I arrived at Stour, I was shown up to see the Deputy Clerk, Mr Jenkins. He spent some time asking me completely inane questions, none of which related to the job, I think he was trying to find out why I had moved up to Ipswich.

After about fifteen minutes of this he picked up the phone, 'Bernard, I got this new young man for you in my office, you better come and give him the once over before I offer him the job as your assistant.' I thought, you can see where the power sits here. Then Mr Jenkins looked at me and said, 'I'm not absolutely sure about you young man, but I promised the Lodge that I would do my best to get you in so now it's up to you. You might even like to think about joining the Lodge given how much you owe us. I'm sure if I proposed you I could get you in. Rob in the office here would second you if I asked him.' Before I had to answer there was a tap on the door. Bernard walked in, he was a tall slim man in his mid-thirties, with a friendly open face and thinning hair.

'Bernard let me introduce you to Alan, he will be filling that vacancy you've got.' Jenkins said. We shook hands. 'I'll leave you to get to know each other. Bernard will sort out your salary and starting date etc. I've got to be somewhere.' With that he left. Bernard sat down behind Jenkin's desk and smiled. He then proceeded to quiz me about my qualifications and experience and seemed genuinely impressed, he also seemed to swallow the story that I was here because of some family crisis.

'Well,' he said 'I thought I was going to get lumbered with some deadbeat but it looks as if you're exactly what I need and more experienced than I would have expected. We don't get many well qualified people wanting to come and work here. I better think again about what I was going to offer you salary-wise.' I had been expecting to have to take quite a cut in salary given I was moving into the sticks and would lose my London salary supplement on top of that. But Bernard came up trumps and with a dig at Mr Jenkins said, 'if Bill makes me engage someone better than I ever expected to find he can damn well find the money for me to pay you properly. What do you say Alan?' I even found myself starting to look forward to starting. While acknowledging that I could have stared immediately he suggested I wait until the following Monday, 'it'll look better that way. We don't want people getting the wrong idea. Oh, and best not mention your Masonic friends.' Bloody hell I thought talk about wheels within wheels, but I also noticed that he had said your friends, not our friends!

However, even that visit and the warning from my old boss didn't prepare me for the working environment I found. It was at 8:45am that I got off my scooter and walked into the building on that 1964 Autumn Monday, I was wearing my second-best suit, dark blue Italian-cut with narrow lapels worn over the new pale blue tab-collared shirt and maroon knitted tie. I took my parka off before entering the cashier's office and rang the bell on the oak topped counter.

Bloody-hell I thought, not even a screen. If we were that lax in Romford the punters would be over the top and have had it away with the cash in an instant! The door at the back of the office opened and a tall gaunt guy in an old badly-cut tweed jacket and shapeless grey trousers walked in. Not only did his shirt have a frayed collar but his tie looked as if it preserved a record of every meal he had eaten during the last month.

'Hello, I'm Ken' he said, 'You must be Alan, Bernard's expecting you, come on through' and he opened the hatch to allow me behind the counter.

When I had met Bernard the previous week I must admit I had taken an instant liking to him. He was in his mid-thirties, quite young to be holding a top finance job, even at a small council like Stour. This morning Bernard was at his desk and got up to welcome me.

'Good to see you, and in good time too, I can see you're going to set a good example to the other youngsters here!' At least he's wearing a suit, I thought, although he could do with some advice on style.

The previous week I hadn't seen the actual office in which I would be working and now I thought that that was probably a deliberate ploy because it came as quite a shock. No modern working environment here. Bernard's office was a space, in what had probably been the drawing room of the original house, delineated by a row of grey metal filling cabinets, while his desk, which had certainly seen better days, looked as though it belonged to a different century. The rest of the room was taken up with four equally run-down desks set facing each other with no space between them. There was a musty smell about the room as if it hadn't been properly cleaned for years; it probably hadn't because every space seemed to be in use, both on and off the desks. Files, piles of papers, filing trays and handle-less mugs stuffed with pens and pencils.

'We're quite cosy in here' Bernard said, probably seeing the shocked look on my face, adding 'but it does us alright'.

At a desk by the window sat a mean-featured man, with round tortoise-shell glasses; also in his 30s but looking older, wearing a blue blazer with what looked like an old-school tie which had also seen better days.

'You've met Ken, he's our cashier, and that's Tony over there he's my assistant. Tony this is Alan, I told you about him. Tony will show you the ropes Alan. You will be sitting opposite him and will be taking some of the load off him.'

Tony looked back without saying anything and gave what might have been meant as a smile but looked suspiciously like a sneer. What's his problem, I wondered? Bernard continued, 'You will be taking over some of Tony's duties, especially on the accounting side. Life's getting more and more complicated and we need a qualified person's view.' Was that it? I wondered if Tony hadn't quite got what it took for the professional side of the job? I was sure to find out in time. 'The two youngsters will be in soon enough, doesn't matter what I say to them they never seem to be on time' Bernard said.

'You are too bloody soft on them Bernard,' Tony said. 'I hope this one doesn't follow in their steps'.

I'm going to have trouble with this one, I thought and said, 'My time-keeping's good enough, you don't need to worry yourself about that!'

'Now, now Tony,' Bernard said, 'let's try to make Alan welcome'. Tony gave me his friendly sneer again.

At that moment the door from the entrance hall opened and in burst two young men, one wearing a parka similar to mine and the other a tatty leather jacket both of which they hung on the back of the door. Under this outer wear both were wearing shirts and ties but no jackets. The slighter built one had long blond hair combed back behind his ears and one of the friendliest smiles I had ever seen, while his parka-wearing counterpart, who sported a poorly-executed version of my own more stylish haircut, was also grinning from ear-to-ear.

'Morning Bernard, morning Tony, good weekend? They chorused. 'We had a great one; party at the Nurse's home; bet you wish you were young again, hey Tony? He never was young, born old weren't you Tony?' The words all coming so fast and confused that I couldn't tell who was saying what.

Tony went red and said, 'Shut up you silly young fools we're not interested in your sordid private lives, you young people sicken me, all you ever talk about is music and sex!'

'Cool it man!' the blond lad said with a smile,' this is 1964 after all, you wait 'till your daughter becomes a teenager Tony!'

'Settle down lads' interjected Bernard 'and stop being rude to Tony, show him some respect and don't give Alan here a bad impression, we want to keep him for a while'. The guys stopped and looked at me; they both smiled and immediately made me feel comfortable.

'Welcome to the mad house,' said the blond guy, 'I'm Peter, you better watch out for that suit; Tom here would kill for one like that! Think of the birds you could pull wearin' that boy.' Tom stepped forward,

'Hi it's good to meet you, is that your Vespa outside? It's got a terrific paint job. Is it a real Eddy Grimstead?' 'It makes my poor old thing look really rough.'

Bernard explained that Peter Collins was the Income Assistant and that Tom Richards was the office junior, it turned out that they were eighteen and seventeen respectively. At 20, I felt like an older brother rather than a more senior employee and realised that if I were to make a mark around here these were the guys who I would have to cultivate as my disciples.

Most of that first day was taken up meeting the rest of the office staff. Yes, I had to be introduced to them all. All twenty-seven of them. My last place had more typists than that. And talking of the typists, all four were really good looking, even Mavis the secretarial supervisor who was at least forty must have been quite a looker in her time. The youngest typist, Yvonne, had the shortest skirt I had ever seen, even in London, and when she reached up to get a file off the shelf above her desk provided an eyeful to everyone else in the office. As she was introduced to me she gave me one of the cheekiest smiles I had ever seen. I would learn later, from the guys, that she had a reputation for being boy mad but she was too young for me and not at all my type. The other three girls were older, in their early twenties, Debbie was dark haired and very stylishly dressed, a real stunner but she was also married to a copper so was absolutely off limits. It turned out that she had an identical twin and this led to much fantasising amongst most of the men in the office, old and young alike. Janice was more sedate with brown hair that hung down onto her shoulders and clothes that were quite staid in their style. I would later discover that she lived in a hostel for girls as she didn't hit it off with her folks. Finally, there was Tracy who was quite petite, no more than five-foot-tall with blond hair tied in a ponytail and the most incredible piercing blue eyes. She was dressed in an old-fashioned fifties style flared skirt; I instantly fell in love. I soon found out that many of the other men in the office were similarly smitten. My desire was quickly dampened by Tom and Peter when I raised the subject at lunch time while I was eating the corned beef and pickle sandwiches that my aunt had made me,

'I should keep away if I were you,' Peter advised.

'Yeah, she's engaged to a tough rocker, you wouldn't want to cross him,' added Tom. 'That's why she dresses like that, we think she wears suspenders as well.'

'Just you keep on dreamin' Tom,' Peter continued 'but seriously Alan a little flirting yes, we're thought too young to be a threat, but you; as I said, I would keep away boy.' My recent experiences were still too raw and I decided that for once I might just take that advice. I had had quite enough of tough boyfriends and the fact she was engaged just reinforced her unavailability to me. But oh, she was lovely!

While being introduced around I met the Clerk of the Council, the top man, Mr Blenkinsop. Now in his sixties he looked like a throwback to the 1920s. Long white hair above steel rimmed glasses, an ash stained pin-striped jacket and black trousers. A real eccentric, he sat behind his old desk puffing on a malodorous pipe,

'Welcome to Stour young man, Bill Jenkins has told me all about you. I'm sure you'll get on like a house on fire once you settle in.' The way that his pipe was sparking I thought that he was the one more likely to create a blaze. I would soon learn that one of his eccentricities was his insistence on opening every bit of post that arrived at the offices and then calling up someone from each department in turn to collect it from him. However, in case there was any cash in the mail, one of the finance staff had to be there with him to log any payments into a ledger and which at the end of every session Blenkinsop would sign. During post-opening his pipe was at its most lethal, not only spraying sparks and ash onto every surface but also regularly being dropped on to the piles of post. Many a cheque was brought down to Ken with singes on them and on one memorable morning a small fire had to be beaten out as post ignited under the onslaught of this mini Vesuvius.

By the end of the day my head was spinning with names and titles, it was clear that Stour didn't often have new staff come in from outside, with most of the staff having been there all their careers. Tony was a good example of that, he had joined when he left the grammar school and had worked his way up, never taking a formal qualification and had now gone as far as he would ever go in his career. No wonder he was bitter. Bernard had qualified under the previous Chief Financial Officer and when he had retired Bernard had simply been handed the job. Bernard actually said to me during that first day, 'Stay here until I retire and this job will be yours, Chief Financial Officer by the time you're fifty!'

I am sure that I shuddered visibly as I replied, 'That sounds like a plan.'

Tony was up and gone by five o'clock and Bernard shortly after, that was also a change from Romford. There was usually a backlog of work to be cleared and Mr Jones didn't expect you to leave until he did, sometimes an hour or more after close of business. A lot of us thought he stayed on deliberately to wind us up. It was one of the things we had fallen out over.

'Come on Alan we'll take you for a beer, tell you the truth about the place.' Peter said. This was more like it. I gave my aunt a call and she sounded pleased that I had already started to find my feet.

'That's OK, Alan you can eat with your uncle and I when he's finished surgery. You'll enjoy that more than eating with the children.' Until then I had been given my tea at 5pm alongside the children who, when their father came in from the surgery, were packed off to do their homework while I was left to watch the TV.

The nearest pub was The Rose and Crown, just up on the Norwich Road, and we walked there as the guys said it wasn't a good idea to leave scooters outside. I soon understood why as it was right opposite the Two Ages coffee bar where the rockers congregated, although 5pm was a bit early for there to be many in there. As we walked up the London Road I was treated to a constant running-commentary about the neighbourhood which wasn't the most salubrious in the town.

'That block of tenements is where most of the local prostitutes live and you wouldn't want to be round here late at night,' Tom related,

'a lot of them travel between here, Birmingham and London doing a couple of months in each place so that the police don't get to recognise them so easy.' Peter added,

'That house on the corner, they say you can pick up your hard drugs there and at the top of the street is a girl's hostel for those who have been thrown out by their parents.' Bloody hell I thought this really is a classy area.

'Is that where Janice lives?' I asked.

'Yes, there was some trouble at home, we've tried to find out what but have drawn a blank. But she's a real nice girl,' Peter said.

In the pub, I bought the first round and Peter told me that he preferred to be called Col, even though it wound Tony up something rotten. I then told them that my mates in Romford all called me Ace and that that would probably upset him even more, so it was decided that that's what they would also call me. Tom wanted to know all about my scooter and he went on to tell me how much he envied me. I could understand why, his Vespa had a home-sprayed paint job with a white flash on the side panels made from self-adhesive plastic, they didn't even match. In Romford I would have dismissed him as a seven and sixer, not worth bothering with given his cheap clothes and tatty scooter, but this was Ipswich and I needed friends.

During that first session, Col and Tom decided to treat it as part of my induction as to who was who in the office, warts and all. Col started, 'Wally in Pubic Health,' he paused to laugh at his own joke, 'he's a dirty old sod always trying to touch the girls, if he can get past Mavis. He's also got a filthy mouth on him. Always taking the piss out of anyone younger than him.'

'I got that impression,' I said, 'he seemed to think I would enjoy his rendition of Crying in the Chapel when I was introduced to him.'

'Silly old twat,' was the joint reply, 'just ignore him.'

'And as for Mavis, it's generally thought she's having it off with Doug, the Chief Planning Officer. I wouldn't mind getting inside her knickers myself.' Col said.

'Behave yourself, she's old enough to be your mother.' I said.

'Doesn't mean she wouldn't be a good screw,' Col replied, 'wouldn't make me a bad person. She might even teach me a thing or too.' After a couple of weeks away from my mates it was great to get back into this sort of banter and the guys were really starting to make me feel better about the whole situation, especially when they told me that at the weekend they would introduce me to the social scene in the town.

'Anyway, we've got to go, it's Bluesville tonight, you can come with us if you like.

Chapter 7

That had been the first time I had heard of Bluesville and as we walked back the guys explained that it was the best music venue in the area, with top U.K. acts and American Blues singers appearing each week. Monday nights it was the place to go and the place to be seen. Now I started to see some focus to my new life and hopefully with the help of the guys it might just be the start of a real social life, maybe even some opportunities to establish for myself some influence in the town, after all I was surely a bloody sight smarter than most of the locals in both style and intellect. But I would have to wait until the next week, because after already rearranging my meal I couldn't simply rush into my Aunts and say I was missing my meal with them to go straight out.

The rest of the week was all about settling in as everyone seemed to advise me.

'Take your time to settle in young man,' the Clerk had said.

'When you've settled in you'll learn to ignore Wally.' was an oft repeated comment. And from Wally, 'Once you've settled in you can focus on getting into the typist's knickers, I wish I was young again I'd show 'em a thing or two.'

While the young typist Yvonne, who was coincidentally, hanging round when I left one evening promised me that, 'When you've settled in you can give me a ride on your scooter and take me out for a drink.' To which my thoughts were, sixteen and making such obvious passes at guys, she needs to be kept at arms-length. I could do without those sorts of problems at work.

'While you're settling in you need to learn all about which parishes are where and who their councillors are, then you can really start understanding what we do and you will also need to understand how to balance the daily journals and cash books,' was Tony's pedantic advice, on which Bernard soon corrected him.

'Alan's here to support me Tony. You know that very well. He doesn't need to know all the minutia, that is your role.' This put-down seemed so unlike Bernard that it left me wondering what was behind it. It also led to Tony storming out of the office for an hour to get a haircut. When I asked Col and Tom if that was usual they told me,

'Bernard says as your hair grows in office time you might as well get it cut in office time!' I found such attitudes strange after the strict regime at Romford where the Chief Accountant sat at the head of the office on a raised dais and demanded to know where you were going every time you left the office. The juniors even had to ask him permission to go to the toilet. One day he publicly reprimanded one of the girls and demanded to know why felt that she needed to go so often.

When she snapped back, 'I'm having a heavy period. Are you happy now?' he tried to have her disciplined for being coarse and rude to him. The whole office had then got behind her when she complained to the Union which hadn't impressed the boss at all.

Bernard's contribution to the settling-in advice was,

'Have a browse through the books Alan, while you settle in.' This was probably the greatest shock of all. The accounts were literally a book, bound in embossed pale cream calves' leather it was about eighteen inches tall and twelve inches wide, all hand written and manually balanced. No mechanisation at all and certainly no computer like we had at Romford. Bernard later told me that he was the only one allowed to make entries in The Ledger for which he had a special Parker fountain pen. 'Your job will include keeping the journals and passing the totals over to me to make the entries. When you've settled in I will probably let you do the Capital Accounts as well. We are putting sewers into a lot of the villages so there is quite a lot of capital expenditure to be kept track of.' This was yet another eye-opener. Villages that didn't have sewers? I didn't know such deprivation still existed.

The nice thing about the office however was that everyone knew everyone else and, outside a little clique around Bill Jenkins, which I would later discover was centred on Masonic membership with a touch of sycophancy thrown in, there were few departmental or personal rivalries. Most people seemed to get on together and wanted to work for the general good. Even the councillors seemed to all get on, which was again different from my last place where party politics ruled every aspect of the council's work.

The first week slipped by quite uneventfully until the Friday. During that week taxpayers who had ignored all the final notices for unpaid taxes had been sent summonses to appear in court for non-payment. In the middle of the morning loud voices were heard coming from the cashier's office and shortly after Ken came through into the office looking flustered. 'McWilliams from the Coach and Horses is in there,' he nodded towards his counter. 'He's got a shotgun with him and says if we take him to court he's going to shoot me.'

'Oh, he said that last year,' responded Bernard. 'I'll go and have a chat with him.' I was ready to hide under the desk and call the police but no one else seemed concerned. After about half an hour Bernard returned waving a cheque. 'I expect it'll bounce but he seems happier now, says if we fancy a drink just to call in anytime.'

'He's a real character,' Tony said.

'But what about the bloody shotgun?' I said.

'He don't mean nothing serious,' Ken replied. 'Probably wasn't loaded.'

This was my introduction to the genteel life of administering rural Suffolk in the 1960s. The Ipswich Borough Council were naturally more up to date in their working practices and the Suffolk County Council yet a step further up the ladder of good practices, or at least as they saw it. But Stour? They didn't care less. The working practices had served Mr Blenkinsop well since he had started as the youngest Clerk of a Council in the country, thirty-five years previously in the 1920s, and he could see no reason to change them now.

Chapter 8

My first weekend of social interaction was filled by more introductions, both to people and to the local brews. Tom and Col were determined to make me welcome and get me into the local scene. On the Friday we went to the Vaults Bar in the centre of town, then on the Saturday to a dance where a local band were playing.

Col who had taken on the role of educating me explained, 'Nick and the Nomads are the best local band we have. They've been playing in Hamburg, like the Beatles did and have just come home so everyone's going to the dance to see them. It'll be a great introduction for you. All the girls will be there.' He gave me a leer and added, 'Bein' a new boy and with your style you'll be a great bird magnet so I'll be stickin' close to you boy'.

I must admit it was a good night. The venue was at the local college and the band were in truth excellent. The girls were mostly good looking and, as Col had said, they paid me a fair bit of attention and I liked to think it wasn't just because I was a new boy in town and had brought a few rounds of drinks. Over those two nights I was to meet most of the people who would become my circle of friends in Ipswich and who, I was determined, would see me as the top dog. I knew it would take a bit of time, the lads had already told me no-one was seen as a Face in the area so there wasn't the hierarchy I was used to, but I could still see myself as the top guy amongst my peers with all the credibility that would accrue from that. It helped that everyone I met wanted to know about the London scene and that I was able to tell the guys about the clubs and bands and talk about the shops and fashion to the girls, and what I didn't know I made up. It gave me a real kick just to see how they lapped it up and I felt that they were beginning to see me as some sort of icon. For me this was a very promising start to my aspirations.

Two of the girls immediately stood out Cathy; who was small blond and very cute and Maureen who was her complete opposite in that she was a brunette, tall and who, while you would never have said she was beautiful, had so much self-confidence that she exuded a magnetism that few of the guys, including myself, could resist. I soon found out that you didn't go out of your way to cross Maureen though, although she was only seventeen she could bring you down with just a few choice phrases and a look from her almost green eyes that would flash warning signals if she had been annoyed. You were better to back off at that point rather than incur her wrath. Strangely for me, neither would ever become a girlfriend although both became close friends, which was a type of relationship that I had never experienced before with girls. Down in Romford girls were for two things, to try and have sex with and to look good on the back of your scooter. Certainly, down there none of us had ever gone steady. That would have really cramped our style.

When I asked Tom if he had ever been involved with any of the girls he said, 'It doesn't seem to work that way Ace. We all hang out as a group and sometimes one or other of us will bring a girl or boyfriend into the circle but when that's over they disappear again and all remains the same. I'm not saying that we don't occasionally have a snog at a party but, so far, it's never led to anything. I think that's because we have all known each other since our early teens and we value each other's friendships too much.'

Most of the girls in the group either went to the grammar school or one of two private schools whilst most of the guys I initially met were also grammar school educated. I soon found out that this led them to see themselves as somewhat of an elite and I was happy to align myself with that image. This demographic did, however, mean that the group were starting to face the fact that within the next year or so many would be leaving for university and they all seemed determined to make the most of each other's company while they could. Tom was one exception to this in that he had gone from secondary school to the local college and then straight into work. Col was also different in that although he had gone to the grammar school he had decided to get a job after his 'A' levels the year before.

Three other guys hung around on the fringe of the group and were more my age group; Geoff who worked as a storeman in a local factory and did bar work on the side, which meant that he wasn't always with the group at weekends. Then there was Alf. Alf was a bit of an enigma. Col told me, 'Alf's parents are landlords of one of the less savoury pubs in the town, we never go in there it's too rough, and we aren't sure what he really does for a living. He never gives you a straight answer about any of his background, but the girls love him. He's the only one of us who's got into Maureen's knickers although she blew him out pretty quickly after that'. As I said I was being given a detailed education by Col. Part of the attraction of both Geoff and Alf appeared to be that they owned cars and so could take the group out and about and I wondered if that accounted for why they were included by the others. The third guy, like myself, was an outsider in that he had moved into the town rather than having grown up in Ipswich. He was my age and was also a trainee accountant. Len had been found a place with a firm of local accountants by his father who was in the Royal Navy. Len was also unique at that time in that he had his own flat and was therefore completely independent.

In style, however, all three were very different. Alf, short and swarthy with hair that was always slicked-back as if he was trying to mimic a 1950s American pop star. His clothes always good quality but dated in style, he looked a bit like some of the East End spivs that I had known. Geoff on the other hand was slightly portly and he tended to come out in his working clothes or plain open-necked shirts and grey slacks. In other words, Geoff had no style at all. He was, however, one of the kindest people you could ever meet, would do anything for anyone and the girls all liked him for those reasons although, I doubted whether they would consider going out with him. Finally came Len who seemed to wander in and out of the group at irregular times. Len had no particular loyalties, some weeks he would go out with one group of people the next with another and then we would find him with us again for a few weeks. Len was always smart. Not in any one fashion, but his clothes were expensive and classic and that also marked him out. He wasn't much liked by the others and the guys were more than a little jealous of his flat which he wouldn't let anyone else use for entertaining their girlfriends. It gave him a definite advantage. I was lucky though, I fitted straight in. My style and London clothes stood out and as all the girls were mods this went down well with them. My Vespa was the only genuine Eddy Grimstead model in the town and the guys were impressed with me for that. I was the smart new kid in town.

I discovered that their social life mainly revolved around Fridays, Saturdays and Mondays, although I would discover that, come the spring, Sunday afternoons also came into play with nearly everyone going to the seaside at Felixstowe. Monday night was when Bluesville happened and that made Mondays, in many ways, more of an occasion than the weekends. The Monday following my introduction to their friends, Tom and Col took me along to the Manor Ball Room, which was then the venue for the Bluesville Club. The kerb was lined with scooters and the pavement outside thronged with young people all dressed in their best gear. That night Georgie Fame was appearing; a personal favourite of mine, who I had seen many times during his residency at the Flamingo Club. I had spoken to him a few times in those days and half hoped to further increase my reputation by being able to have words again at some time during the evening. We all met in the Mulberry Tree, around the corner from the venue, for a beer before we went in and Tom pointed out some of the other guys from the area, 'Over there in the corner, the guy in the maroon jacket, that's Alex. He a bit of a hard case, I would avoid him if I were you, he might want to look big by giving you a hard time. Over by the bar the blond lad in the leather coat is Rick, he's a nasty little shit.' I smiled and thought that's two I will need to take down a peg or two. None of this lot have a clue.

After couple of beers we walked round to the ballroom and through its front door and my heart stopped, I mean I literally found myself having difficulty in breathing. I had come all this way to get away from London and the first time I go to a real gig London comes up to find me. If I had read the posters for the evening I might have noticed that it was being promoted by Nanda and Ron Lesley. I knew them from London's 100 Club on Oxford street where they promoted a lot of the top Rhythm and Blues acts as well as visiting American Blues singers, and there they were standing in the entrance hall. They were well known at the 100 Club for mixing with the customers and for being approachable if anyone had a problem. Often Nanda would be seen comforting some girl who had been dumped by her boyfriend or who had had too much to drink and who needed to be sobered up a bit before being sent home. I had often spent time chatting to them about the acts and the scene generally and I was well known to them both. Nanda looked enquiringly at me, 'Bloody hell Ace, what are you doing here, we hadn't seen you for so long we thought you'd died or something?'

'No,' I replied, 'I just moved up here with my job'. But I knew that wasn't a satisfactory answer. What if they went back and mentioned to one of my old mates that they had seen me in Ipswich? That would soon get back to Max and I didn't want him and his soldiers coming up looking for me.

'Nanda', I said, 'can I have a quick word with you and Ron?' We went off to one side and I said, 'I had a bit of trouble with one of the guys in Romford and have had to come away for a bit, it was all getting a bit heavy'.

'Anything to do with that girl who got hurt?' Ron asked.

'Christ you're well informed', I replied.

'There's not a lot happens with the kids we don't hear about and she was one of our regulars. It was a bad do; she didn't deserve that. That thug Max weren't it?'

I was staggered just how in touch they were. I gave them an abridged version of what happened and then said, 'Look is there any chance you could keep this quiet? I have only just started to settle in here and I don't really want to have to move on, I don't know where I would go from here if I'm honest.'

Nanda put her arm around my shoulders,

'Don't worry son, Ron and I will keep it quiet. You know we don't like violence at our venues and I can't be doing with any sort of violence against women. Your secret's safe with us ain't it Ron?' He smiled and nodded. I was so relieved, no wonder they were so well respected by all the kids who went to their clubs and I felt confident that they would be as good as their words.

'But one thing in return Ace,' Ron said, 'We don't get any trouble at all up here, the Ipswich kids are as good as gold. If they scrap they must do it off the premises, we don't see any of it. They come here for the music and a couple of drinks. Do you get my meaning? I would hate to see any of the London attitudes brought up here.' I agreed with him but couldn't help wonder whether within that request didn't lay a threat of "or else". Ron went on, 'Another thing Ace, you're well out of it if you've had issues with that Max. I heard he beat a guy up so bad that they say he has brain damage and might not get out of hospital. They also say that he did that for the Krays. Something about selling pills on their patch.' I just nodded in confirmation. After that it all got a lot chattier and they told me that they didn't come up to Ipswich often but that tonight, during the interval, they would be promoting a special season for the autumn. Nanda handed me a handful of flyers.

'This looks terrific,' I said.

'It will be,' Nanda said, 'we're promoting these acts across all our venues, we don't think there has been such concentration of Blues artists appearing across the country before, possibly not even in London. You can give your mates the heads up if you like.' She slipped me half a dozen tickets for the John Lee Hooker gig and added, 'these should put you in a good light with your new friends.'

When I went back to join the others you could see that they were impressed that I knew Nanda and Ron so, to add to my reputation, I hammed it up a bit and made it seem I knew them well and that I just wanted to catch up on some mutual friends. I also told them about the Blues Festival and handed out the flyers which impressed them even more. I kept the tickets back until

AMERICAN NEGRO BLUES FESTIVAL 1964

Nanda and Ron Lesley proudly present at

"IPSWICH BLUESVILLE"

Manor House Ballroom, Ipswich

Monday 5th October

JOHN LEE HOOKER

The worlds greatest Blues Singer/Guitarist with

John Lee and the Ground Hogs

Admission 6/6

Monday 12th October

LITTLE WALTER

Composer of "My Babe" "You'a better watch yourself"
A prominent member of Muddy Waters Band
with the

Art Woods R & B

Admission 6/6

Monday 9th November
The one and only Big Boss man

JIMMY REED

*Harmonica/Singer/Guitarist
Composer of "Shame, Shame, Shame"
and numerous great Rhythm and Blues hits.
here and in the U.S.A.
Backing Group to be announced*

Brampton Press Ltd., (T.U.) Brampton Park Road, London, N.22

I knew on whom they would have the most impact. Overall it was a real result. The rest of the evening was as good as it could have been, great music and new friends, who were also able to show off a bit in front of some of the other punters by showing them the flyers in advance of the formal announcement. By the end of the evening I was already feeling comfortable and I knew that this would certainly be the routine for future Mondays. It would also be somewhere else I could build a bit of a reputation. I really fancied my chances of being the Face around the Ipswich scene.

This was a good time to find myself in Ipswich, while Herman's Hermits were Into Something Good in the charts, most of the grammar school lads seemed to be heavily into Blues music. Accordingly, the three weeks of visiting Bluesmen was being eagerly anticipated, although there were exceptions like Brian, who for some strange reason owned and listened to everything that Buddy Holly had ever produced. These guys were the intellectuals of the local scene and had middle-class backgrounds, similar to my own. Once I made that clear, I was soon accepted into their circle despite being at work and a few years older than them. But the important thing about them as a group was that they tended to shape the thinking that pervaded the scene and, once you were part of that, you could start to increase your own influence. My knowledge of the Blues also stood me in good stead as I was able to talk to them about the finer details of the music and its role in the latest music releases and before long we had decided to set ourselves the task of finding the original recordings that were influencing groups like the Stones so that we could pursue our debates further.

Having gone to the grammar school Col was a natural fit into the group but Tom was a sort of honorary member who had been brought into the group by Col after they had started working together. Sometimes this led to Tom being the butt of some quite cruel comments because of his secondary school education, but he seemed to take it all in his stride. It wasn't quite the same with the local girls. While they did stick to their school groupings, it wasn't as unusual to find girls from other walks of life mixing with them. Long term friendships, often from junior school days, seemed to be more important than what they were currently doing. The one area where this was different was at local youth clubs. Youth clubs down in Romford were for kids and we had no time for them, certainly wouldn't have been seen dead going to one. But in Ipswich even the hard-core mods would regularly go to their local youth club and socialise with kids from across the whole teenage spectrum. When I was asked to go along I nearly died laughing. 'Bloody hell that's where my kid cousin goes, I'm too old for that sort of boring crap.'

'No, you've got it wrong there's plenty of guys of your age that come along, Geoff and I sometimes go to St Thomas's, some of the guys are in the bands that are based at youth clubs and others help run the places, you ought to give it a try.' Col said. Not on your life I thought, although I was to discover that the local youth clubs were the source of some half decent local bands and that the dances that they held at weekends were often better than at a lot of other more formal venues. But to go on a club night with a load of 14 and 15-year olds not on your life!

Despite being out of London the local girls managed to keep up in the fashion stakes with some of the local boutiques stocking the latest fashions. For the guys, as I had already discovered, the latest fashions were not as readily available and even where they were the guys still at school didn't have a great deal of ready cash. This led them to create their own styles using ex-army stores and the like. I at least could afford what fashions did come into the town through the one store that did stock the latest trends, but even their selection was limited and you would often see two or three guys all wearing the same outfits, not at all what I had been accustomed to in London. What really rankled was that Rick and Alex, who like me were working, would regularly go down to London with their mates and return with gear that I couldn't get my hands on. This also led to uncomfortable questions for me. Why I didn't go shopping in London as I had come up from there and had the money? All I could say was, 'I've had enough of London and those West End shops all rip you off anyway. Those prats like Rick and Alex have more money than sense.' But how I envied them. It didn't take long for me to find a solution however. Good old Mum. She always took an interest in the latest fashions and was more than happy to go shopping for me. One of the girls we knew worked in the most upmarket of the local boutiques and she would let me have the weekly fashion catalogues for guys that they received from their suppliers. From those catalogues, I would see the new styles being promoted and could ask Mum to go up West and buy them for me. She would then stick them in the post and I could have the most up to date fashions weeks before they arrived in the local menswear shops. It gave mum an excuse to go up to the West End and it also let her still be involved in my life. Despite his warning about me having to stand on my own feet my old man would also would bung me some extra cash when they came to visit; I think they both felt some sort of guilt that they couldn't protect me at home and had had to encourage me to leave.

So, I was well set up, I had cash in my pocket, style, the best set of wheels in town and two great new mates on which to build a circle of friends. Col and Tom were interesting characters and quite different in background. After going to the local college Tom had come to work at the council with just three 'O' levels. He had started on the lowest clerical grade, but in the year that he had been working he had already done some studies and had been given a couple of raises in pay. This didn't however mean that he had a lot of spare cash and after paying his keep and maintaining his old scooter, by the end of the month he was always complaining that he was short of money. It also meant that he didn't have a great deal of money to spend on clothes and would go to the cheaper menswear shops to get the nearest equivalents to the latest fashions. His mother, who was raising Tom and his brother Peter on her own, would often be asked to alter a cheap jacket so that it looked like something more stylish. He was a typical example of a seven and sixer. This, however, gave me a sure-fire way of keeping him on side. As I got sent more stuff from London I let Tom have my cast offs which enabled him to, at least, keep up with most of the other guys in town. With him I could do no wrong, I was already his hero.

Col's background on the other hand was more like mine. Although a couple of years younger, he had come to the council as a Finance Department trainee and had already passed the first set of his exams. Being a trainee meant that he had time off each week to study at the local library although, especially during the summer months, I'm not sure how much time he spent sitting in there. However, as a trainee 'professional' he was paid considerably more than Tom. Also, as Col had his own distinct idea of style, he managed to get away with spending a lot less money on cloths than most of the other guys. In addition to his old leather jacket, which he delighted in telling every-one had belonged to a biker who had been killed in a road accident, he would often be seen around in a donkey-jacket like the refuse collectors used to wear or a second-hand PVC jacket. Both of which had been bought from the local Army Surplus Stores. Under these he would wear chunky jumpers with what looked like any old shirt that he could find. All this would be topped off with an ex-US Air Force combat cap. And what really pissed me off, given what I spent on clothes, was that the girls loved him. Far from me being the bird magnet and him picking up my left overs it was me who was always getting introductions from him to the best-looking girls at any venue.

Chapter 9

During that late autumn and winter, life slipped into a regular pattern. I had settled into life with my aunt and uncle and was even getting to like my two young cousins. My uncle was still difficult, wanting to have a pop at me whenever the opportunity arose, but then I suppose it wasn't that much different to how my old man was. My aunt was a real brick, much more like my mum than I had realised and her Sunday roasts were legendary, it would take something very special to lure me away from one of those. Jean was a few years younger than Mum and my uncle was ten years older than her. In style, it was if the two sisters were aged the other way around. Mum was always dressed in the latest fashions, indeed, there were times even I thought she dressed a bit too young, but she always looked good. Jean on the other hand wore the dowdy clothes of a middle-aged woman. Calf length tweed skirts, beige jumpers and chunky shoes, I don't even think she owned a pair of high heels, and her hair was usually pulled back in a non-descript knot. It was a shame because she was an attractive woman and still only in her thirties. She had fallen for an older man who, on the face of it, could provide her with a comfortable life and the status of being the wife of a respected doctor, but I think she had begun to feel that life had left her behind. They only ever went out to church events or medical dinners, never dancing and the only musical performances they went to were classical recitals or the local operatic society. One day I came back at lunch time to find her dancing around the kitchen to music from Radio Caroline. She was so embarrassed, 'Please don't say anything, the kids would laugh at me if they knew I was listening to pop music.' I wasn't convinced that it was really the kids she was worried about and suspected that she was concerned about what my uncle would say.

'Why don't you just let them have Radio Caroline on?' I said, and that is when she confirmed my suspicions.

'Their father wouldn't be at all happy with that, so please don't suggest it to them.' I left it there but made sure that whenever I bought a new record I invited my cousins in to listen to it. I even found myself occasionally buying some pop record from the hit parade just for them to listen to. It became a bit of an act of rebellion for them to come to my room once they had done their homework and listen to music. If their father was out we would turn the volume up so that that it could be heard all over the house. I noticed that when we did that my aunt would turn the TV off and would sometimes be found sitting on the stairs listening. I really felt quite sorry for her.

At work, I had really settled in. Despite Tony, Bernard ran a very relaxed operation, and the office almost felt like a second home. Col and Tom however continued to irritate Bernard, arriving late and making Tony the butt of their practical jokes but generally that had been tolerated. They had however pushed their luck a bit too far when they discovered that, somehow, they could short out the internal telephone system and call multiple extensions at the same time. They had got away with it when they had done it to everyone in the planning and finance departments but crossed a boundary that couldn't be ignored when they had gone on to connect all the senior officers together causing all sorts of confusion as each party demanded to know who was calling whom and why. It certainly didn't help that at the time, Bill Jenkins was briefing the Chairman of the Council in his office and that the Chief Planning Officer was, allegedly, in the middle of de-briefing Mavis in his.

Together with their lax time keeping, Tom and Col's behaviour was starting to push the limits of even Bernard's tolerance and after unsuccessfully reprimanding them several times he took me aside. 'Alan, I can't seem to get through to them. Their behaviour is getting noticed by the Clerk and, even more worryingly, by Bill Jenkins and you know what an old woman he is. I really don't want him to start whispering poison in Blenkinsop's ear about them. Do you think you could have a word, they seem to listen to you? Reluctantly, I agreed despite quite enjoying the anarchic atmosphere that they engendered, I had even been party to some of their pranks. But I did as I was asked and we all agreed to step back a bit from the more extreme pranks, particularly those that were aimed at winding up Bill Jenkins. What all this made me realise was that I had established a degree of influence over the two of them, some sort of respect, and this was exactly what I had been hoping for.

The relaxed atmosphere of the office was however being spoilt for me by Wally. His continued harassment of the typists seemed to be accepted by everyone else but I found it uncomfortable.

'Hello love, what colour panties have you got on today?' Was one of his favourite greetings to the girls, along with announcing to everyone in his hearing, 'I'll tell you what love; if I had one I'd be down in SoHo making it earn money for me.' Strangely this behaviour seemed to be accepted by the senior staff who seemed to find his behaviour amusing. Then one afternoon I caught him looking up Debbie's skirt as she went up the stairs. He looked at me and said loudly, 'will you look at the arse on that, couldn't you just boy? Can you imagine that bouncing up and down on your lap, Christ I'd die happy?' Debbie looked down at him with contempt and I couldn't keep quiet.

'For god's sake Wally, don't you realise how much you upset the girls going on like you do? They really don't need all that filth you come out with. Just think about it.' As Debbie went out of sight Wally went ballistic.

'You pathetic little poof, scared of a bit of fanny are you? They love it. What they all need is a good shaggin'. You don't tell me what I can and can't say. The problem with you is that you can't find a little chum to tickle your bum up here like you could in London? I knew your sort in the army.' I glared at him,

'You're an ignorant old twat,' I said, my newly refined persona disappearing in an instant. 'If you weren't so fucking senile I'd sort you out good and proper, so back off before I do something I might regret.' I turned and walked back to the office.

Following this I was soon to learn an important lesson about the office politics at Stour.

The next morning, I was called up to see Doug Prince, Wally's boss. He gave me a real bollocking. 'Wally told me what happened yesterday and I won't have whippersnappers like you insulting and threatening my staff. I've a good mind to report you to Bill Jenkins. I managed to catch a pause and told him why I felt that Wally was out of order. 'Mind your own business, the girls know what to expect in an office like this. it's not one of your fancy London authorities. The girls are used to it and they don't mind a bit of teasing. They work for Bill and if he's not worried about it you should mind your own business. You need to remember Wally's a war hero and I won't have him upset. If it happens again, you'll find yourself in hot water.'

Later when I told the two lads what had happened I was disappointed when their response was that I had over-reacted.

'Oh, come on Ace, we all tease the girls about things like that. It's nothing to get wound up about. And anyway, you won't get Wally into trouble he's as thick as thieves with Jenkins and Prince. All bloody Masons. It's well known that Wally is useless at his job, always having to be dug out of holes but no one ever does anything about it. He's too well protected. I'm told that once Bernard tried to have him disciplined about over-claiming his expenses and even Bernard got his arse kicked.' Later Tracy caught up with me in the kitchen,

'The girls are all grateful to you for trying to sort Wally out but you shouldn't have bothered, I could have told you that you wouldn't get anywhere. Mavis even accused us of encouraging you; stupid old cow. It's Yvonne I feel sorry for, she's really scared of him, poor kid.' With that Tracy put her hand on my arm and gave me the briefest of pecks on the cheek. 'But thank you for trying.' So, the story had flown round the office, Wally even made a big song and dance over the fact he had put me in my place. It had no effect on him at all.

Bernard told me not to worry about any of the furore, 'It's just office politics every-one knows you are right but that little clique at the top have to have it their way. We just have to live with it.' None of this affected me, or the way that Bernard was placing more and more reliance on my work, although when he was away he still asked Tony to look after the office and oh how Tony liked to throw his weight around during those interludes. We all felt the effect of his prying into what we were doing but on balance we managed to ignore it. But poor old Ken the Cashier used to get the full force of his interference. Tony would criticise the way he cashed-up, when he cashed-up, how he recorded the money coming in and even the way that he stored the notes in his cash drawer. When Bernard was away for a few days you could see Ken physically weaken under his oppression, although after my run in with Wally there was no-way I was going to get involved.

There was one other member of the Finance department, Reg, the part time rent collector. Reg was an interesting character, he was in his mid-50s and worked for the council three days a week going around the villages and collecting the rents in cash from council tenants, which he would then carry around with him in a leather satchel. No one seemed to think this a security risk, it was the way it had always been done. Although he worked for the council three days a week, he would tell you that his real job was working for God. He was the Pastor of a Baptist church in one of the local villages, this however didn't provide him enough of an income to live on so he had to take a second job. Reg was a very gentle character and seemed to love nothing more than defending his faith, something that the two lads in the office seemed to relish challenging. As a non-conformist, Reg held an unshakeable view that there was no justification for iconology in Christianity and would argue fiercely in defence of his view, even to the extent of disapproving of films that depicted the person of Jesus Christ. He regularly out-debated Col and Tom and in frustration Col would fall back on a question that he obviously thought clever. 'Ok then, but you can't tell us how much God weighs can you?' Reg would smile and reply,

'You know I can't answer that, but if you have faith and belief you don't have to know.' While I couldn't agree with everything Reg believed I could respect his patience and the way that he never rose to the provocation levelled at him. His patience was however tested by Tony who whenever possible would put him under pressure about his rent collection rounds. I was beginning to see Tony as a classic bully only picking on the weakest in the office.

Socially life just kept getting better and better. I had been accepted into a good circle of friends and weekends were never dull. In those first few months I didn't look to find a steady girlfriend. There were always girls to hook up with at parties or dances although there weren't many who, like Julie, were prepared to let you go all the way with them so soon after you met them, but you could always get a bit of a fumble in a corner at a party which kept you going until something more substantial came along. Part of the problem was that there weren't many places in the winter that you could go to and be on your own with a girl to get right down to it. I certainly couldn't take a girl to my room at my aunts and the girls weren't allowed to have boys in their rooms at their homes. So, any sexual activity had to be in a semi-public place like a front room at a girl's house while their parents were in the back room or in a quiet spot at a party. This is where Len had a great advantage over the rest of us with his flat. According to him, he certainly seemed to get plenty of sex but despite all sorts of inducements the bastard just would not let anyone else use his flat.

It was the music scene that really kept me going. The charts of the time were mainly rubbish, despite Motown starting to make an impact. Groups like the Honeycombs and the Bachelors continued to be chart favourites and old fifties stars like Cliff Richard and Roy Orison were still outselling more credible bands like the Animals who with the Stones were the only real R and B bands making an impact. In the weeks leading up to the Blues Festival I saw some great bands and then as the John Lee Hooker gig got closer I started to distribute the free tickets I had been given. This made me particularly popular with those I gave them to and those of my little circle who were unlucky seemed to understand that I didn't have enough tickets for everyone. Not so the local tough guy Alex. He heard that I had some free tickets and in the pub the week before the concert he made it very clear that he expected one.

'OK new boy where's me ticket then?'

'I given them all out,' I said.

'You've got yours, haven't you? You can give that to me as you made a mistake and forgot me.' I simply walked away. He couldn't let it go however. I was in the Gents when he came in and stood next to me.

'So, about this ticket,' he said.

'I told you, I've got none left, they were for my mates.'

'Are you saying I'm not one of your mates then?' I ignored him and stared at the faded cream wall in front of me with a flaking downpipe coming down from the rusty cisterns above. He kept on his voice rising, 'You may be from London but you're a nobody here, a nothing and you don't want to cross me, do you understand? Now just give me a ticket and we'll say no more.' He was so full of himself and his reputation as a hard man that everyone feared that he made a basic mistake. I finished peeing before he did. I zipped up and walked behind him, he was standing at the urinal, feet apart, in full flow. I sized him up and kicked him hard between the legs, he squealed like a pig being castrated and doubled up in pain. As he bent forward I rammed his head down hard. His nose hit the porcelain top of the old-fashioned urinal with a satisfying crunch followed by his forehead. It was if I had coshed him, he collapsed on the floor in a pool of spreading blood and piss. For good measure, I kicked him in the ribs as I turned and walked away.

'Never leave 'em so's they can get up and come after you.' Max had once told me after he had delivered a beating to someone who had upset him; and I was a quick learner. I went back to my friends and we went on to the Manor Ballroom. I said nothing about what had happened, they would find out about Alex in the fullness of time. He was found soon after and taken to A and E where he was patched up, the only permanent damage being to the shape of his nose and his pride.

Although I hadn't said anything, the fact that he had been heard demanding a ticket from me before the incident meant that the rumour mill soon placed me in the frame; although I kept denying any knowledge. It was however fine with me if that was what people thought. I had taken out one of the two, supposed, hard mods in the town. It would however be some time before I managed to sort the other one. Alex was as good as gold after that, he had enough sense not to try and take retribution, after all he had discovered I was no-push over and he couldn't be sure how much more violence I might be prepared to use if he pushed me. As much as anything else, the benefit of the incident was the fact that he now left my friends alone instead of aiming snide little remarks at them and trying to provoke them in other ways. That however only reinforced the suspicion that I had given him the beating. Eventually, after they had kept going on about it, I told Tom and Col that it was true but at the same time extracted a promise that they wouldn't spread it about. I certainly didn't want it to get back to work, I don't think they would have been very impressed. However, amongst my friends, I did like the air of uncertainty that the mystery created but equally I didn't want to be simply known as a hard man, just as someone who wasn't prepared to be pushed about.

The series of performances that made up the Autumn Blues festival were terrific, John Lee Hooker simply wandered about the venue before going on stage talking to the kids, Ron Lesley introduced me to him and got me a signed flyer.

'This is Ace,' he said, 'he helps make sure we get no trouble here.' I wondered what the devious devil had heard now. But again, I was seen to be in the know. Outside this series of concerts, the quality of the acts appearing at Bluesville remained as high as ever, certainly as good as any venues in London. Bands including The Animals, John Mayall's Blues Breakers and Long John Baldry's Hoochie Coochie Men, who featured an unknown singer called Rod, the Mod, Stewart all came to the club. At the time, we were convinced that this Rod the Mod was as queer as a three-bob note and that he had been pulled by Long John. All these acts appeared in rotation alongside the regular visitors like The Spencer Davis Group and Georgie Fame. However, it wasn't just the music at Bluesville that was good. Local bands provided a more than acceptable soundtrack to most Saturday evenings at dances across the town usually at some youth club or other even if some of them had pretty dire names as with Murry and the Mints. It was at this time that a new band appeared on the local scene. It was said that, before being drafted into the US Airforce, Geno Washington had sung with some top American soul bands and to see him perform with the local lads in Les Blues you could easily believe it. Geno would go on to his own stardom once he left the U.S. Air Force, but for a while he was Ipswichs' own.

Chapter 10

As Christmas approached it was decided that my parents would come to Ipswich for the celebrations and would arrive on Christmas Eve. This was a real downer as I had hoped to spend that evening with my friends who had assured me that Christmas Eve was one of the best nights to be out in the town. But for me it wasn't to be and I felt the old resentment about having to be in Ipswich rise again. It wouldn't have been like this if I was still in Romford. I would have been out with my mates getting pissed like everyone else on Christmas Eve not stuck with having a family meal at my aunts. On Christmas Eve the office closed at 1pm, although we didn't get away until mid-afternoon as we were all expected to sit down for a Christmas lunch, which had been prepared during the morning by the women in the office. As soon as the doors were closed at 1pm the men all went up to the Rose and Crown where the Clerk bought the first round while the women stayed in the office finishing the preparations for the meal.

'Don't they get a drink?' I asked.

'Bill Jenkins leaves them a bottle of Sherry and they can have a glass of wine later.' Bernard replied as he bought his team a Christmas drink. By 2 o'clock all the men had all had at least four drinks and we were all exuding the Christmas spirit when we returned to the office to sit down for lunch. How the girls had achieved it I don't know but it was a first-class traditional spread, unless the alcohol just made it seem that way. A few glasses of wine later and there was a real party mood in evidence and some of the guys even offered to help the girls wash up. This was the signal for the lunch to finish and after the tables were put away people started to leave for the holiday. A small group of us adjourned back to the pub.

'Did you see what happened to Wally?' Tom asked.

'He went early didn't he?' Col replied.

Tom carried on, 'I was coming out of the bog and saw him put his hand up Yvonne's skirt. She turned round and give him one hell of a smack and then Debbie came out and told him where to go. I've never seen him look so angry.'

I looked over at Tom and said, 'Serves him bloody right maybe he'll leave them alone now.'

'Never mind that,' Tom replied, 'Yvonne had had a few drinks and I thought I would have a crack at her but after that she was in such a bad mood I didn't dare. But hell, it's Christmas Eve they'll be plenty of pissed girls out there tonight ready to give me a Christmas present, you don't know what you'll be missing Ace.' Unfortunately, I did and it didn't improve my mood in the slightest.

When my folks arrived, my uncle was still out on his rounds trying to make sure that all his home-based patients were in a satisfactory condition and unlikely to need a visit on Christmas Day. My aunt immediately offered them a cup of tea in reply to which my father said, 'After that drive I'm dying for a pint; c'mon Alan lets go over the road. We'll see you girls later. Send Michael across when he gets in.' I readily agreed and as we left the front door dad muttered under his breath. 'Miserable old sod won't join us, you just see.' While I was living at home Dad and I often went out for a couple of beers and we would just talk about life in general, I think it was his way of keeping up with some of the things I was into, although he didn't get to find out that much. This evening, after bemoaning how badly West Ham were doing, he really seemed keen to find out how my life was going and we ended up having a good chat about work, my social life and how things really were for me whilst living at my aunts. It felt good because he seemed really concerned, not just prying and we had a good laugh about my new working environment.

'Well what can you expect from a load of country boys, the 'Swedes' ain't even got a decent football team. Drink up I'll get you another beer, if you can call this willy water beer.' When he came back I started asking him about Romford. Had he seen or heard anything about my old mates. He went a bit quiet but eventually said, 'I seen Ricky on the market, at his dad's stall, he asked after you. And, from what I can recall, the lads on the site seem to think that most of your other mates are OK. He paused, but there's something I got to tell you. Your mum said I should. Something very sad and we want you to know it's not your fault.' He paused to take a pull at his pint. 'That Julie, the one that thug Max cut up, she done herself in. I didn't want to tell you but your mum thought I ought to in case you heard it elsewhere. You all right boy?' I felt the blood drain from my face. Christ Almighty, I knew it wasn't my fault like he said but it had been because Julie and I had shagged that Max had cut her. She had been caught while I had run away and I couldn't help but feel bad about that.

'How?' I asked

'Let me get you a real drink, you look as if you need it, then I'll fill you in.' It turned out Julie had taken an overdose of her mums sleeping pills saying she couldn't face life with the scar Max had left her with. 'Unfortunately, she didn't name him in the note she left so the Old Bill aren't able to do anything.' I found it all hard to take in, she had been so full of life. A great girl and so pretty before Max got at her. 'It's not your fault son,' Dad repeated. 'It's all down to that Max. I'm just glad we got you out of it. The lads on the site told me that the bastard was still harassing her after she got outta hospital. The one good thing is that I'm told that the Kray brothers have had a word with Max 'coz they didn't like what they heard he done'. I wanted to know more but, against all odds, at that point George walked in so we had to change the subject.

'I've been sent to tell you that supper will be on the table in fifteen minutes and that you have to drink up. But, with the amount of time that they spend talking, I reckon that gives me half an hour for a Scotch or two, will you join me?' I don't think I had ever seen my uncle so relaxed. It was a shame because it would have been nice to have had a laugh with him and maybe get to know him better but my mind had switched off so I simply sat there appearing surly and uncommunicative which simply reinforced his opinions about me.

Hearing of Julie's death put a real damper on the rest of Christmas for me and a couple of times I took myself off to my room feigning a headache. Which, although my parents could understand why, again didn't go down too well with my aunt and uncle. Her death hung over me even when I got back to work and was made worse by the fact that I couldn't tell anyone about it. However, it was another drama that would throw the work place into conflict and in which I got involved not because it would take my mind off Julie but because of the crass unfairness of the situation.

On the first day back in the office after the Christmas break, Bill Jenkins called Yvonne into his office and dismissed her for committing an act of violence against another member of staff.

'Wally went crying to Bill about the fact that Yvonne had slapped him and, of course, the bastard took his side.' Debbie told us later. 'He didn't even let her have someone in with her, she was terrified, she couldn't even tell her side of the story. When she came out she was in pieces.' Most of the younger staff in the office were up in arms what had happened, including myself. But the senior staff seemed to take Wally's side and that line had been reinforced by Jenkins himself when he called the departmental heads in to tell them about it. Back down in the Finance Office I challenged Bernard about it.

'Didn't anyone put her side of the story?'

'There was no side to put, she was seen striking him.'

'That's a load of bollocks,' I said, 'Wally put his hand up her skirt, legally that's bloody assault Bernard.'

'Don't be stupid Alan, it was Christmas and all just a bit of fun. I'm not saying she deserved to be sacked but she did overreact.'

'So, if Wally did that to your daughter you'd just laugh it off would you.'

'It's not the same, now you're just being silly.' Being silly; that was like a red rag to a bull and I certainly wasn't going to let it lay. I agreed to lead a delegation to see Mr Blenkinsopp and let him know the feelings in the office. A lot of good that did. He listened and then dismissed us with,

'These things happen and it's up to Bill, after all she did work for him. It's a shame though she was a pretty little thing; nice legs as well. I shall miss her about the office, she brightened up the place, but I can't condone violent behaviour towards members of staff. I'll speak to Bill and make sure he doesn't give her a bad reference.'

'But what about Wally's behaviour, he's always touching the girls?' I said.

'Wally is Wally, we all know what he's like.' He looked towards Debbie who was with me, 'you girls manage to put up with it don't you? But thank you for bringing it to my attention, I'll speak to Bill about him again. Try to make sure he doesn't overstep the mark. Now off you go, there's work to be done.' And that was it. At Stour, there was no one was in the Union so there was no help there. Subsequently I did enquire about setting up a branch but was firmly counselled by Bernard.

'If you do that it will all but destroy any chance of me being able to promote you when you qualify and it will be a black mark on your record for any future reference. You need to appreciate, Bill is a very vindictive person and has a long memory. You have already rattled his cage a little too hard. You'll have to watch yourself.' It was another lesson on the realities of power for me. I might think of myself as a bit of a player but compared to them I was nothing. Well almost.

Some weeks later I went into the gents and there was Wally up at the urinal. 'Hello poof boy, come to have a look at a real man's cock have you?' He said. I just walked up behind him in the same way as I did with Alex, but this time I grabbed him by the balls. He jumped back peeing down his trousers at the same time, but I kept a firm grip.

'You might think you're very clever taking the piss all the time you old cunt,' I whispered in his ear, 'but this time you've picked the wrong person. If you ever cross me again or if I catch you touching the girls, I will make sure you never walk again. And that's not a threat that's a promise.' I went straight back to the office and asked to speak to Bernard alone.

'Bernard I'm going to have to resign,' I said.

'What! What on earth's brought this on Alan?'

'Wally has just accosted me in the toilet, I was having a pee and he came to stand next to me. Then he swore at me, turned and tried to pee on me. I pushed him away, but no doubt he will now go to Bill and tell him I assaulted him, especially as instead of peeing on me he wet himself. You know who Bill will believe, so I might as well save him the effort and go of my own accord'

'Is this the only time recently that you've had trouble with Wally?' Bernard asked.

'Good lord no. Ever since I tried to take up Yvonne's case he has been on my back. This is the first time he's actually done anything physical. Before it has always been insults, followed by the threat that he would find a way of having you get rid of me. I reckon he's succeeded this time.' Part of this was true he had been on my back since Yvonne was sacked and people had heard him having a go at me so I should be able to get my story confirmed even if it was only by Col and Tom.

Bernard was livid, 'You will not resign. I have had enough of Wally and his running to Bill to cover his back. Leave this with me, I will sort it.' Bernard went straight upstairs to Bill and formally complained about Wally's behaviour. As I hoped, Bernard got to Bill before Wally had a chance to clean himself up and get to him. Bill, once again, tried to brush it aside but this time Bernard was having none of it and insisted that they take the matter up directly with the Clerk. This time Blenkinsopp, surprisingly, had no hesitation in taking Bernard's side and, as he told me afterwards, instructed Bill,

'There's been enough smoke generated by Wally recently for me suspect that there might be a fire. I want you to set up a formal hearing to get to the bottom of this, we can't just keep sweeping it under the carpet.' In the meantime, I had told the guys about it and they were well up for backing me as were, unsurprisingly, all the girls especially Tracy who took me aside and said,

'Alan you're a bit of a hero to us girls, no-one has ever stood up for us before, I hope you don't get into trouble, I'd hate to see you have to leave.' I was really chuffed to think that Tracy had said that to me and it fed my fantasies about her despite knowing that she wasn't available. However, I was gob smacked when Tony came forward to back my story about Wally's behaviour. I didn't think he had heard any of Wally's comments to me, but his support was an unexpected bonus as most people knew that he and I weren't the best of friends and Tony's honesty was unimpeachable.

On the day of the hearing I made an even greater effort than usual with my clothes putting on my darkest suit with a white Rael Brook tab collar shirt and a dark blue knitted tie, I even gave my Chelsea boots and extra shine. My Aunt took one look at me and said,

'I'm not sure if you look more like a lawyer from "Perry Mason" or an undertaker.'

'I'll settle for the former,' I replied. But nipped upstairs to check myself out once more to be sure.

The hearing itself was held in the Council Chamber, which was a bit over the top as it could just as easily been held in the Clerks office. As it was Mr Blenkisopp took his place on the Chairman's dais sitting on a high-backed leather chair. Bill sat to his right and Mavis to his left taking the minutes. The whole scene was more reminiscent of a courtroom rather than a venue for a disciplinary hearing. The hearing itself became a bit of a farce and Wally was completely out of his depth. I was able to run rings around him. The person I felt sorry for was Mavis who had to record all the proceedings and who turned red at the slightest use of bad language or sexual reference.

'He called me an old cunt.' Wally said.

'I hate that word! Did you say that to him?' Bill then asked me.

'I hate it as much as you do sir and, as anyone in the office will tell you, I don't use language like that.' I replied, 'surely you're aware of that Mr Jenkins?' I stressed the formality of the proceedings in my replies. Bill Jenkins nodded pompously. Others would support this statement as the hearing proceeded.

'He came into the gents grabbed me by the balls and then pushed me into the urinal.' Wally tried to look pained as he said this. Bill again asked me to respond.

'There was no one else in the gents so it is my word against his Mr Jenkins, but I can tell you quite honestly that there is nothing I would like to do less that hold Wally's balls in my hand. Was I wearing washing up gloves Wally? I wouldn't have done it otherwise.' Bill Jenkins glared at me.

'That's enough of that young man. You say that Wally tried to urinate on you why would he do that?'

'I don't know sir.' I said, sycophantically. 'Wally called me a poof and said that he had pissed better than me, then he tried to pee over my trousers. I admit I pushed him away and that's when he wet himself.' This rang a bell with those in the hearing as one of Wally's stock putdowns was "I've pissed better specimens than you." Bernard and Tony spoke backing me up and I played Wally just by regurgitating his favourite prejudices. In front of any unbiased hearing Wally would have been dead. As it was however, whilst being found in the wrong, he got away with a reprimand but, as this was delivered by Blenkinsopp himself, it was a real blow to his pride and in a small office, of course, everyone heard all the gory details. I didn't feel remotely guilty about screwing Wally, the dirty bugger deserved it and at least he kept his job which was more than poor little Yvonne had. The real surprise came a few days later when Tony and I were alone in the office.

'Shall I tell you something Alan? I wouldn't have got involved in the Wally incident if I hadn't heard you ask Bernard how he would feel if it was his daughter that Wally had been interfering with. It made me think about how I would react if it had been my Linda. So, I decided it was time that Wally was taught a lesson. Well done Alan.' Then he winked, 'However I'm not sure how much I fully believe your story.' I smiled and said,

'I'm not sure about your evidence either Tony.' As he left the office he turned,

'Remind me not to ever cross you young man; or stand next to you in the gents!' So, Tony was human after all, who would have thought it.

I didn't take my stand against Wally simply from any gallantry towards the girls, I would have enjoyed a quick fondle like the rest of the guys and if I had caught Tracy alone in a quiet spot probably would have tried my luck. No, it was because Wally was plain and simply a bully and, in that respect, no better than Max had been and I suppose there was an element of making myself feel better by taking it out on Wally. The difference with Wally was that he didn't have the balls to back up his threats against anyone except those weaker than him. The final act that proved this occurred a few days after the hearing when I caught Wally alone on the back stairs of the office. He was coming up as I was descending and I stood blocking his way,

'Get out of my way.' He demanded,

'What no poof or, better still, a please, Walter?' I asked. No one called him Walter and I suspected it un-nerved him. 'Do you know something, when I was in London the Krays ran things round where I used to live, you know who they are don't you? They used to say revenge is best served up cold. What do you think? Let a poof give you a bit of advice old man, don't try and push me around again or you might just be found in a ditch somewhere.' Of course, I was making most of it up but after I had screwed him over the last time it had enough of a ring of truth about it to make him think. While Wally never bothered me again after this he still harassed the girls, although never in my presence, but then so did a lot of the other guys in the office including Col and Tom both of whom, annoyingly, still continually voiced fantasies about Tracy and her underwear.

Chapter 11

The New Year of 1965 opened with a bit of a musical disappointment in that Georgie Fame had a big hit with a pop son, Yeh Yeh, which those of us who had followed him since his residency at the Flamingo felt was a bit of a sell-out. On the other hand, the Stones had made the charts with a Howlin' Wolf track, Little Red Rooster, we all thought that this was a sign that music was going our way, although in the end it turned out that this would be the last blues single the Stones would release before going totally pop. It was at that time that I was introduced to someone who would become a lifetime friend. Maureen had met James at a Young Farmers New Year's Eve ball. It was only Maureen, amongst the girls that I knew, who would have got invited to a ball in the first place and she made the most of it when she next saw us.

'I met this fabulous guy, his family have a huge farm and he drives a Mini Cooper, I bet you guys are jealous. He's over six-foot-tall and not bad looking either. You'll meet him when I bring him along at the weekend. He's coming to stay.' James was all she had said, six foot three tall, built like a rugby player and with that healthy ruddy complexion that you naturally associate with farmers. He was also one of the gentlest people I would ever meet, despite the looks which might have indicated otherwise, although that didn't mean that in a tight spot he wouldn't back you up; and a couple of times he did just that. James had a sense of humour together with a laugh that was so infectious that once he started it wouldn't be long before everyone around him would also be convulsed. He was very different to anyone I had ever met before and to start with I wasn't sure that I would hit it off with him. Not only was his background completely different to the rest of us but he dressed differently as well, a typical farmer-look, tailored cavalry-twill trousers and tweed sports jackets with brogue shoes. Not stylish, just very county set. Despite this he spoke with a strong Suffolk accent and he could drink beer like no-one else I knew.

Maureen was awful, she would insist in telling us all what they had been up to, in graphic detail. You could see James was embarrassed by this but it didn't stop her and anyway it made him sound like the ultimate stud. Like all of Maureen's conquests the relationship didn't last long but, unusually James continued to hang around with us and quickly became part of the gang at weekends. He never came to Bluesville however because that clashed with his Young Farmers club which in his eyes, or possibly those of his farming family, was sacrosanct. But he seemed to hit it off particularly well with Geoff, maybe because they were both a bit different to the rest of us and, in the early days of his involvement with us, he and Geoff would just turn up at whatever venue we had decided to grace with our presence on a Saturday night. As the weeks went on however my friendship with James became increasingly stronger and would eventually outlast most of the others that I manufactured during my time in Ipswich. Amongst the guys, he was the only one who, having found out my real name, called me Alan rather that Ace. At the start this pissed me off, I had carefully groomed my identity in Ipswich and didn't appreciate someone coming in and giving me a different moniker. But as we got to know each other better he started to address me as Sir Alan, why I don't really know but suspect that it started as a micky take over the way I perceived myself as the leader of our little group. However, despite this, between ourselves it stuck.

Outside work, mid-week tended to be pretty quiet as those who were still at school had homework and, anyway, I liked to spend a couple of evenings a week studying my accountancy correspondence course. However, because James also got on so well with Geoff, it wasn't long before the three of us started to meet up on a Wednesday evening to go drinking in the local village pubs. These evenings were restricted to the three of us because Tom could never afford mid-week drinking and, for some reason, Col never really fitted in with this combination of personalities. James would come and pick Geoff and I up and we would visit two or three pubs before ending up at the Westerfield Swan for a last pint and a pork pie with pickle. This became such a regular occurrence that the landlord would have the pies ready for us when we arrived. The weekly drinking event was very different from the other routines of my life at that time. Geoff and James were the same age as myself, whilst the rest of my crowd were all younger, and I found that I could be more myself with them, rather than maintaining the façade that I so relished amongst the others. I didn't seem to have so much to prove. Maybe I was growing up!

At work things had settled down after my clash with Wally which had had the added benefit of increasing my credibility in the office and especially with the women working there. One benefit of this was that, if Tom and Col were out, Tracy would sometimes come and eat her lunch with me in the kitchen. I enjoyed her company despite knowing that she was taken and we seemed to get along quite well until I suggested that she might like to go to the pub for a drink one Friday. It was, for once, an innocent suggestion but she was furious. 'I thought you at least understood my situation,' she snapped. 'You're like all the rest, can't just accept me as a friend, got to try and make something more of it.' And with that she stormed off and stopped having lunch with me at all for some time afterwards.

With the onset of the New Year, I also made myself a promise to try to become more accommodating to my aunt and uncle because I'd come to appreciate that, despite their uncertainties about me, they had gone out of their way to make me welcome. Accordingly, I went out of my way to try to engage my uncle in discussions about his Practice, Ipswich Town Football Club and any occurrences at the Council which I thought he might be amused by. But by God it was hard work. My aunt on the other hand was always ready to chat, enquiring about how I was getting on at work, what was happening socially and, more and more to my amazement, what I thought of new records in the hit parade. I became convinced that this interest reflected her repressed life with my uncle who I doubted would be able to name even one pop artist in the chart let alone discuss their merits beyond, 'Who's singing this rubbish?' Additionally, I felt that my aunt wanted to know more about popular culture so that she could interact more with the two children and particularly with Rachael who was becoming more rebellious as each week went on.

Rachael's attendance at St. Thomas's Youth Club, on a Thursday evening, was conditional on her being home by 10pm. Inevitably it would be nearer 10:30pm when she arrived home which would then cause a row with her father. My aunt tried to compromise with her, pushing back the deadline to 10:15pm and Rachael responded by getting back at 10:45pm.

'I don't know what to do Alan.' My aunt confided to me. 'I know that most of the children there are good souls but I still can't help worrying. She just doesn't seem to want to obey any of the rules we set. Your uncle has now told her she can only go if he comes and picks her up at 10 o'clock. Now she says she won't go at all and I don't want her to stop going because it is the only social life your uncle will let her have. Although, if I'm honest, I think he would be happy if she stopped going altogether so that he could regain complete control over his little girl.' This latter part was delivered with such an element of bitterness that I wondered just how many of the rules were being set by my aunt compared to those laid down by my uncle.

I'm not sure where it came from but I said, 'Do you want me to have a chat with her, I don't know if she will confide in me but I could give it a go?'

'Oh Alan, would you? My aunt said, 'I know she respects you and I am sure she would listen to you as you are more her generation.'

The opportunity to talk to Rachael arose the following weekend when she came up to my room. Peter had gone to the football with his father and Rachael wanted me to play The Pretty Things album that I had just purchased. At least I was educating her away from listening to pop songs. It was interesting that, despite any reservations my aunt and uncle may have had about me, they had no hesitation in letting Rachael come up to my bedroom to listen to music. While some parents may have seen music as being an aphrodisiac for teenagers my aunt seemed to see it as an emotional suppressant to her daughter's rebellious streak. While we listened to the raw rhythm and blues of the Pretty Things I broached the subject of her relationship with her parents.

'You and your folks always seem to be rowing, it's bloody hard work listening to you all the time. Don't you ever get fed up with it?' I said.

'It's them, they just don't understand.'

'Maybe the problem is they do understand? Just maybe they are so scared that you might get hurt that they overreact to try to protect you.'

'For god's sake, you sound just like them. I'm nearly fifteen,' she said, 'I know how to look after myself. I don't need my father to come and pick me up from youth club. Most of the boys there wouldn't know what to do even if I lay down and took my knickers off for them.'

I chuckled and thought oh yes, they would, but said, 'It's not the most who wouldn't know what to do that they are worried about. It's the few who would that worry them.' Rachael laughed.

'Sorry, you're different to them, you understand.'

'I should bloody well hope I'm different, I'm nearer your age than theirs. I'm on your side you know. Who was it that brought music into this house?'

'Sorry Alan, it's just that I'm so hacked off with them about Youth Club. I really want to go but not if he comes to pick me up. They'll all laugh at me.' I had been thinking about this and although it wasn't ideal, it would help Rachael and I thought it would give me a few Brownie Points with my aunt and uncle, so I gave it a try,

'How about I come on the scooter and pick you up on Thursday, I don't usually do anything but study so I could come and give you a ride home?' Well you would have thought I had offered her the crown jewels. She jumped up and down squealing, her long hair flying and catching the light from the late winter sun coming in through the bedroom window.

'Ooh yes please. That would be great. I could show you off to my friends. Can you come a bit early? Oh, please say you will.' I wasn't going to promise anything of the sort and I certainly only intended to do it until she had been rehabilitated. 'And can you wear your new shirt and those hipster trousers your mum brought up last week?' Oh Christ, I thought what have you got yourself into now? Then, on the other hand, I must admit that I felt a bit chuffed that she looked at me in that way. Just so long as she didn't tell all her mates that Mum had bought me my trousers.

The following Thursday night I laid it on the line with Rachael, 'I'll be there at ten, If I have to come into get you it will be the last time I do it and you'll be collected in future by your father. Is that clear?'

She smirked, 'Yes grandad and I promise I'll be a good girl and wear strong knickers.' This just reinforced my view that my aunt and uncle were going to have increasing problems with her before she got much older. I was just glad that she wouldn't be my responsibility.

The church hall stood on top of a sloping site on the Bram-ford Road and backed onto a row of terraced houses, about a five-minute ride away from where I was staying. The hall was built from cheap industrial bricks and looked for all the world like a small warehouse. I rode up the short drive to the front door and was surprised to see Rachael and a group of girls standing outside waiting for me. I rode right up to them, switched the engine off and just sat there waiting for her to get on. She looked directly at me and you could see the excitement in her eyes as she flicked her hair and said exaggerated farewells to her friends. She was really milking it. Rachael walked slowly up to the scooter trying unsuc-cessfully to sway her hips during the few steps she had to make. It was a real effort not to burst out laughing. Her friends followed behind. She then proceeded to introduce each one to me, for the life of me I couldn't take in all their names.

'This my cousin Ace from London, he's one of the top mods down there, he's got some fab clothes and that's one of the best scooters you can buy.' I could have died of embarrassment. She had obviously half heard some conversations and embellished them for her own satisfaction. The girls just stood around and gawped at me, so I raised my hand and pretending to be a lot cooler than I felt and said,

'Hi girls. Now get on Rachael, I've got to get you home before you turn into something nasty.' At that the smile left her face and she climbed onto to the pillion.

For the next couple of weeks I made Racheal come out to me, then Tom told me he was going to be there the following Thursday.

'There's this bird goes there and Geoff says she's just split up with her boyfriend. She's gorgeous and,' at which point he cupped his hands in front of his chest and went 'phoor.'

'You're a dirty little sod Tom. You get more like Wally every day. I can see you ending up just like him if you're not careful.'

'And you're just jealous coz you're not getting any Ace boy. Anyway, what I was saying was, Geoff and I will be there on Thursday, he's looking at a new band that some of the lads have formed. Geoff thinks they'll go far, the prick, and he says he's going to manage them or something.' As usual with Tom when he was excited the words tumbled out like rapid machine gun fire so you just had to try to get the gist of his train of thought. 'Come in and have a coffee with us, no need to be scared,' I thumped him hard on his shoulder and told him to piss off.

That next Thursday nothing was doing and I was at a loose end all evening so thought I might as well go and give Tom and Geoff a look at their precious Youth Club. I also knew that it would make my cousin's day as she would be able to show off in front of all her mates. I know I'm a bit of a poser and so I took a bit of trouble to make sure that I looked the part before going out. I put on the low slung blue tweed trousers, that Rachael so liked, the grey polo shirt and a striped jacket that Mum had got for me the week before from Lord John's in Carnaby Street. I stood in front of the full-length mirror that I had bought for my bedroom and thought, my god, you look good. It wasn't a cold evening so I simply put on my leather coat and one of my collection of stolen college scarves over the top to keep me warm on the scooter.

I arrived at the club just after nine, parked the Vespa so that it could be seen and admired clearly from the doorway, and casually walked in as if I had been going there all my life. Inside I paused and took in the scene. At the far end was a large stage on which the band had set up with its members standing around talking. Geoff was in the middle of the group holding court. At the side of the stage was a corridor with a hand painted sign that read 'Coffee Bar' and on the floor of the hall there was a table tennis table and a scattering of chairs. From somewhere there was music playing and all around in little knots were the members of the club. I could see straight away that there was, as Tom and Geoff had said, a wide range of ages probably from thirteen through to the older members in their early twenties. It all looked very peculiar to me.

Before I could make another move a guy approached me, he looked a bit like a 1950s beatnik and was dressed in cord trousers and a roll-neck sweater.

'Is there something you want?' He asked. I nearly gave him a mouthful because he didn't come over as particularly friendly but then saw Rachael emerge from the coffee bar and thought I had better behave myself.

'I'm Rachael's cousin, I come and pick her up each week. Tom over there said I should come in and have a coffee one evening. So here I am; is that a problem?' The last words were somewhat stressed and could have been taken as a threat but on the contrary the guy's demeanour changed in an instant.

'I am so sorry, I didn't realise, come in you are very welcome. I'm Mitch, the Youth Leader by the way. We have to be so careful because we do get occasional trouble from outsiders so I try to intercept strangers before they get in.' Trouble, I thought, Rachael has never mentioned that. I wonder what that's all about? By now Tom had spotted me and had come over as also had Rachael, so I found my attention being competed for. Simply by force of excitement Rachael won and dragged me towards the coffee bar. I turned and shrugged my shoulders at Tom who grinned as I allowed myself to be led off.

The coffee bar was down some steps in a sort of sub-basement and the music was louder down there, The Stones were giving it their all. I was put on a raised bench at a counter between two young girls while Rachael sat opposite on a stool. I looked along at the other girls who were seated around, all looked almost exactly the same, they obviously discussed what to wear before coming out. They were the same ones that Rachael had showed me off to the first night I picked her up. There was a lot of giggling and whispering and none of them were interested in any sort of conversation, that was until Rachael asked me to tell them about when I lived in London. So, I told them about the Clubs and from which shops I brought my clothes. You would have thought that I was the Messiah, they sat completely in thrall of me as I told them everything I thought they would want to hear, including celebrities that I claimed to have met. I put up with it for about ten minutes to please Rachael and then finished my coffee and said,

'Sorry girls but I have some business upstairs about the band. I might be able to get them a gig and need to have a quiet word. I'll catch you later.' It was all bullshit but sounded good and I left to find Tom and Geoff. 'Christ Tom,' I said, 'you might have saved me from that.'

'I thought you'd enjoy our little gang of Lolitas. Some of them are real goers despite their age.'

'And you think I'm into that sort of gaol bait, do you?' Geoff came down to join us.

'What did you think of the band then, they're called The Cellar Fellas, great weren't they?' He said

'I've only just arrived so didn't hear them Geoff.' I said.

Tom added, 'Well besides being out of tune, not playing well and not knowing the words they were OK I suppose'

Geoff looked hurt and said, 'Be fair Tom, they weren't that bad.' Tom winked at me.

Changing the subject, I said, 'That guy Mitch said you sometimes have trouble down here, what's that all about? Rachael's never said anything about trouble.'

'Oh, you know that twat Rick, his little gang hang around the pub down the road, every now and then they get bored and turn up here to make a bit of trouble. They beat a couple of the older lads up the last time when they tried to persuade them to leave.' At this point another guy joined us. He was tall and skinny and about my age I supposed but he looked older with his short goatee beard which gave him a world-weary look and he was dressed quite flamboyantly with a paisley cravat and a worn velvet jacket.

Geoff said, 'Ace, this is David'.

He nodded at me and ignoring him, I said, 'Surely you lot could sort out a few yobs?'

'That's not the way we do things here,' David said. 'The Rev Dick and Mitch have both made it quite clear that we are not to react violently and that they will take a stern view of anyone who goes against them.'

'What even when people are getting beaten up? That sounds like cowardice.' He walked off looking hurt but I really couldn't care. I found out later that the way they usually dealt with such incidents was to lock the doors and send someone over the back wall to call the police. It was just that the last time the gang got in before they could lock up. It still sounded alien to me, I was brought up to hit back hard in circumstances like that, not turn the other cheek, but if that was how they wanted to do it, that was up to them.

'So, who's that long streak of piss?' I asked looking at the retreating six-foot frame of Dave. Geoff explained that he had been coming to the club longer than most people, was considered to be a mainstay of the place and was the Deputy Youth Leader.

'He's also heavily into the Ipswich amateur dramatics scene and plays the trumpet in a local Trad Jazz band. He also plays the guitar and writes songs, a lot of the kids really look up to him.' Great I thought, what a wanker.

A few weeks later, for a laugh, Tom, Col and I decided to go and see Dave's jazz band. Although they weren't to my taste they played well and towards the end of the set Dave came to the front of the stage and announced, 'the next number we will be performing is one that I have written especially for the band and it will be my great honour to be leading the vocals on it.' After some introductory instrumentals Dave stepped forward and sang,

'Down and out in old Ipswich Town
I ain't got nothing more to lose,
I'm down and out in old Ipswich Town
just me and those East Coast Blues.'

Cheeky bastard, I thought. He had virtually stolen the whole song, my favourite blues, and was now claiming it as his own. A few weeks later I was having a drink at a local pub, not far from the Youth Club, with Tom and Col when David walked in and came over to join us. He then proceeded to spend the evening telling me how interesting he was and how he was going to London the next year after working for a couple of years at a local building firm.

'I wanted to see some real life before giving myself to the Arts, I shall go to London and work in the theatre.' I thought, it's a good job I've given up swearing. After a while he invited us back to his parents for a coffee where he proceeded to get out his guitar and sing us some of his songs. Most were dire, except for the one which he had claimed to have written himself for his band.

I went over to his record collection, naturally all methodically filed, and found a copy of the blues compilation album that I had. I pulled it out and making a great show of studying the play list said,

'Don't you just love this album and by the way, you're right to be proud of that song you've written', 'You'll be known as the next Bob Dylan before long.' He coloured up and said,

'I didn't think anyone around here would have got that recording it's very rare. I suppose my song is quite similar to many on there, but it's not exactly the same. They sound similar because I used the same old country blues melody as a root and then tweaked it to make it into a jazz number rather that the simpler blues riffs that you will find on there.' I winked at him and he went even redder. I thought, I'm a bit of a bull-shitter myself but this guy's a real professional! You might fool some of the kids with that but, as my mother would have said, "I've heard ducks fart before". I bet you won't try that one with me again.

Strangely, despite my initial reluctance, the Youth Club came to be yet another circle within which I moved. It was mainly because I went down there to pick up Rachael every Thursday, but they were a nice bunch of people with whom I could relax. I found myself going down earlier just to sit and have a coffee with the older members that I had come to know. It was there that I first met the Reverend Dick. He was the Vicar at the local church to which the youth club was affiliated and he would occasionally visit to make sure that the behaviour at the club kept within reasonable bounds. What he would have thought about some of the fumbling that went on in the passage behind the Club God only knows. That was not for me however, this was one environment in which I wanted to keep a clean nose. There were too many underage girls there who were so precocious it was hard to be sure if they were over sixteen or not and I certainly wanted to avoid any complications of that sort. Tom had already had a close shave after one youth club dance where he had arranged a date with the sister of one of the girls at the club.

'I met her at the local park the next day and she was sitting swinging on one of the swings, showing me her knickers every time she swung forward. She was obviously up for it and was quite happy to come over to the woods behind the park. I thought I had it made. Then just before we set off one of her mates said. You know she's not fourteen until next month, don't you? I nearly shit myself. Talk about a lucky escape. I really thought she was Daisy's older sister, honest'

'Christ Tom', I said 'you really need to be more careful. You'll get yourself locked up'. He just grinned sheepishly but that incident simply reinforced my determination not to get involved with any of the girls at the youth club.

It was David who introduced me to the Vicar, 'Reverend Dick, this is Ace,' - he managed to sneer my name- 'he's Rachael's cousin from London. He's not really a member but just comes in to pick her up.'

'Well you are very welcome here whatever your status.' Did I detect a touch of sarcasm in his response to David? He continued 'Are you Michael and Jean's nephew?' I confirmed that I was and we went on to discuss the difficulties in moving to a new town as David hovered round trying to get into the conversation.

'I was a military chaplin and they used to move us around all the time. It is so difficult for the family to adjust and it must be the same for you. You will be very welcome at the church anytime you know.' I didn't think so; the last time I had been to church was when I was at school and, even then, I would get into trouble from the priest for laughing. But possibly the Reverend's military background explained his rapport with the kid's all of whom genuinely seemed to respect him.

Chapter 12

As many of the group I was hanging around with were still in the sixth form at school there were times that there seemed to be very few people about including some weekends and if Geoff was working it would leave me at a loose end. At times like that Alf and I would sometimes go and give a local dance or pub in one of the nearby towns a look. That was exactly what happened one Saturday that Spring. I was drinking on my own in the Vaults, Geoff was working behind the bar and everyone else seemed to have other commitments which had stopped them coming out that night. Alf walked in and we sat discussing what to do.

'Well there's no parties that I know of,' he said. 'But there's a good pub over in Woodbridge we could go and have a look at if you fancy it?' It seemed as good an idea as any. 'We might even pick up a couple of girls hitching back from the airbase if we're lucky.' In response, I pulled a face.

In the same way that anyone from London was a bloody cockney, like those who were sent to Ipswich during the war from the East End slums as evacuees, so all US servicemen were still considered to be "oversexed, overpaid and over here". Memories were long and prejudices deep in Suffolk. The Americans even had their own cars brought over, big American V8 saloons that, when they left to go back to the States, were left to rot in car grave yards on the Base's perimeter. However, the Servicemen at RAF Bentwaters and RAF Woodbridge did attract the girls and, generally, you could find some of them every Saturday hitch-hiking up the A12 to Woodbridge on the way to dances at the Bases.

'They're as rough as a badger's arse.' Col opined, in one of his well-known generalisations.

And while it was true that some were undoubtedly prostitutes going out to the base to try their luck, many were just girls from the town who sought the music and glamour of the USA, some hoping that the U.S. Airmen's largess would stick to them or, if they were really lucky, that some Yank would take them back as wives when their tour of duty was over. As many of these girls didn't mix with the local lads the idea of trying to pick up a couple of them didn't fill me with much enthusiasm but, as there wasn't anything else doing, I agreed to go along.

The pub wasn't up to much but we stayed for a few anyway and as we left Alf drove out towards the Base and returning along the back road. Just before we got to Woodbridge two women stood in the road waving us down. In the headlights, you could see the short skirts, leopard skin fake fur jackets and high-heeled shoes, outfits completely unsuitable for hitching. Alf had to pull up quickly or he would have run into them

'Can you give us a lift boys, we're really stuck?'

'How come?' Alf asked.

'It's a long story but we'll make it worth your while.' This was said by the taller of the two who had obviously dyed-blond hair.

'In that case you're on, get in.' Alf said, 'Ace you get in the back with one of them the other can sit up front with me, I need somewhere to keep my hands warm.' I wasn't so sure; I know we hadn't scored that night but these two were not the sort I would normally go for at all. My uncertainty showed and Alf went on, 'For God's sake Ace they're all the same in the dark, just get in the back and have a shag.' As we drove through Woodbridge the girls filled us in. They were unashamedly on the game and had gone out to the Base to get some business. At the end of the evening a couple of the servicemen had offered them a lift back to Ipswich but after the girls had given them a freebee the guys had thrown them out of the car in the middle of nowhere.

'Give us a free shag as well girls and we'll see you safely home, that's a promise in't it Ace? Alf said to them, 'We'll see you home safely'. It seemed to satisfy them although the fact they were prostitutes didn't make them any more attractive to me but Alf was determined. Just outside Ipswich he pulled the car over onto the heath and proceeded to paw the girl at his side,

'Let me get me knickers off, bloody hell you're in a hurry, haven't you had it lately?' I knew I would have to follow suit or it would be all over the town that I didn't take up the offer, Alf would love spreading that about. There was little formality about it and the act was soon completed.

'Come on girls how do you fancy swapping over for another go, to compare and contrast?' Alf asked. They thought it was a great laugh and readily agreed, the blond in the front hauled herself over the back of the front bench seat almost sticking her arse in Alf's face. 'That's a new perspective on life,' he said as he watched her naked behind slide into the back while the girl I had just had had moved to the front. I noticed that she looked a bit uncomfortable but I thought no more about it. With the stamina of youth, we were soon at it again, I almost forgot that this was what they did for a living.

Then, 'Shit,' came the cry from the front.

'What's up Alf?' I said.

'The bitch has peed on me.' My response was to laugh which didn't go down well, no wonder she looked uncomfortable. She jumped out to finish the job and Alf got out after her, I had never seen him look the way he did at that moment. His face contorted in anger and he screamed at her, 'You fucking tart you did that on purpose', and before I could get out and stop him he hit her. 'You can both bloody walk back from here, you fucking bitches.' I got between them and I pushed Alf back against the car none too gently,

'If they walk back I walk back too, we'll have a big falling out, and Alf, I promise you, you don't want that.' I paused to let him consider the implications, he seemed to sense that it could get nasty and I just stood looking at him, almost daring him to say or do something. 'It's only a bit of piss, you can sort yourself out later but let's get these two back into the town like we promised.' He wasn't happy but I told him I'd keep quiet about what happened if we kept our side of the bargain. I put the girls in the back of the car and sat next to Alf to make sure he didn't try anything stupid.

When we got them back to Ipswich I asked the girl Alf had hit if she was OK.

She said, 'I've had worse; the bastard' and then the blond added, 'I'm not sure about your mate but, you're a gent, anytime you want a freebee you can look me up at Quick Snax.' I never did.

That incident led me to rethink my opinion of Alf, he had really gone over the top and that worried me. The next weekend however his behaviour was even more bizarre and would change my view of him forever. Unlike the Saturday before all the guys were around and we had decided to have a lads' night out at a Works social club on one of the big council estates on the edge of the town. David's Jazz band were playing there and we thought it would be a laugh to go and see them, but as this wasn't our usual stamping ground we were all a bit on edge in case there was any trouble. Alf and Geoff had driven and Geoff brought along with him a mate, Jim, who was on leave from the army. Jim had just returned from Aden and looked as if he could handle himself. Not only was he tanned but he had a physique that was toned from regularly working out and a face like a professional boxer and I don't mean rugged, I mean battered. He had obviously seen plenty of action. The hall was laid out with long tables with benches to sit on and we took over the end of one of them and had a few beers to get the evening off to a good start. It was then that a bunch of lads, from the estate sitting at the next table and who were bored with the music, decided that we were interlopers and that they would have some fun by flicking beer and peanuts at us. It was all very silly and as there were more of them than us we should have ignored it but Jim was not happy.

'You splash my suit again and I won't be amused,' he said to the lads at the next table and gave them a look that should have warned them off. But they were on their home turf and outnumbered us, so they felt secure in pushing it. After a bit, another shower of beer came over obviously aimed directly at Jim. He spun round off the bench with a speed that no-one could have predicted and poured a half-full glass of beer over the mouthy ringleader on the next table.

'OK you arseholes, outside, I'll take all of you on, one at a time or all together. If you think you're hard enough.' Only of course it didn't work that way and outside it was obvious that this local gang were intent on giving Jim and the rest of us a good hiding. We of course were there to offer Jim support but it didn't look too good and I suggested that we beat a tactical retreat, but Jim was having none of it. He hit the leader of the gang hard between the eyes and he went down. Then before his mates could pile in Alf came around the corner from the car park.

'Back off.' Alf shouted.

'Bloody hell! He's got a gun,' someone yelled. Jesus Christ, he had too! Even in London I had never seen anyone daft enough to pull a trick like that. He just stood there, arms stretched in front of him like an American policeman, holding a pistol in a very deter-mined manner. I went cold; this wasn't good, the last thing any of us needed was to be picked up by the police in the company of a nutter with a pistol. The local lads sensibly took to their heels but this didn't stop Alf who fired off a shot in their direction. Luckily, he missed.

'For Christ's sake Alf!' I shouted in panic, 'what the hell are you thinking about. Piss off. Right now. Scarper.'

He looked at me and laughed,

'I always knew you weren't as tough as you pretended to be. Couldn't even give a tart a smack. Who wants a lift out of here?' No one volunteered and he turned and walked away throwing back a sneering 'you're just a bunch of chickens'. Jim took offence at this and started after him.

'Jim, no,' Geoff grabbed his arm. 'We don't want him around here any longer than necessary, let him go. We need to get gone as well,' Geoff said. Six of us got into Geoff's car and the rest took a short cut through some walkways towards the town.

'Geoff, did you know he carried a gun?' I asked.

'I thought it was just an air pistol,' Geoff said. 'He kept it in his glove compartment with his johnnies and his tissues. Said he liked to be prepared for all options.'

'You prat! that was no air gun, that was real. Christ, he really could have dropped us in the shit!'

Geoff dropped us off in Town and then went back to look for the others. When we were finally reunited, all of us were severely subdued and when I was asked about the tart comment, I related the previous weekend's incident including how Alf had hit the girl. The consensus was that we all had too much to lose hanging about with a loose cannon like Alf and we resolved to shut him out of our circle. As it happened that proved to be unnecessary because he disappeared off the scene of his own accord. Geoff said that he had heard that he got scared that someone would shop him to the police so had decided to keep a low profile, while another rumour was that I had sorted him out. It wasn't true but I didn't do anything to dispel the idea. Why would I when it made me look good?

Chapter 13

1965 in Ipswich would stay in my memory as one of the best years of my life. I had a good job, great friends and a social life that I would have never dreamt possible when I first arrived in the town. There were times of course that I still missed the vibrancy of life in London and the edginess of the scene down there, especially the East End, and it was still frustrating that I had to rely on clothes' parcels from my Mum to ensure that I was keeping up with the fashions of the time. There was a new menswear shop that did its best to have the latest styles, the problem was that with a limited stock you always risked finding someone else in the same gear when you went out.

Best of all in 1965 was the music. One week we would see The Spencer Davis Group with a sixteen-year-old Steve Winwood on organ, singing in harmony with guitar notes played by Spencer Davis, as though his voice were an extension of the instrument itself; the next week it might be John Mayall, with Eric Clapton laying down evangelical blues riffs to accompany the soaring Hammond organ of John Mayall. Georgie Fame, who we had now forgiven for having a hit single, would take the Jazz influence a further stage and, with Speedy, his percussionist, laying down a grove on the Conger drums, they would light up Bluesville. Not everyone was as keen on Georgie Fame's musical influences as myself, Tom moaned that he didn't pay out good money to listen to modern jazz in an R and B venue. Then there was Brian Auger's Steam Packet combining the bluesy voice of Long John Baldry the raucousness of Rod Stewart and the dreamy sensuality of Julie Driscol. They were probably one of the earliest Super Groups. However, it was a wild quartet who were the most spectacular; The Graham Bond Organisation featured Jack Bruce on base, Ginger Baker on drums, the virtuoso saxophonist Dick Heckstall-Smith and Graham Bond, usually as high as a kite, on Hamond P3 and alto sax. The friction between Bruce and Baker was palpable and yet Graham Bond seemed oblivious to it as he created swirling sounds from the keyboard with one hand while playing soaring notes from the sax with the other. It was a fusion doomed to burn itself out, providing an early preview of what would become Cream, although it was somehow a purer sound because of the innovations these musical geniuses created. However, while there was this great innovative music in the clubs, the charts generally continued to churn out dross with the likes of Roger Miller's, King of the Road and other middle of the road groups like The Seekers topping the hit parade.

It was around this time that I had my first steady girlfriend. Up to then, as in Romford, my involvement with girls had been fleeting and cursory. One-night stands or brief encounters at parties were the norm. I certainly didn't want any form of commitment, girls were for fun, nothing more; accessories. But Sally was different and between April and June we were a constant item at weekends. Three months, now that was a commitment. We met at a dance in Debenham, a small country town, 12 miles from Ipswich and we just seemed to click. Sally worked for her father who had a garage and who would bring her over to Ipswich at the weekends to meet and stay overnight with her old friends from a local private girls' school. During those ever-lengthening spring and summer evenings I started to go over to pick her up and take her to Bluesville, this was one trip that her father drew a line at, especially if she had used him as a taxi service the previous weekend. Another of my mother's quips used to be that "the lure of a woman will draw you further than gunpowder would blow you", and, in this case, it was spot on. I would have gone anywhere to spend a bit of time with Sally. Whilst she always dressed in the latest fashions, she wasn't what you would have called a Mod, more a classic English rose. She had long blond hair and the most amazing blue eyes that I had ever seen. She also had a fabulous figure, I was completely blown away by her.

While she knew some of the girls in our group, she had her own circle of friends and this was where the conflict lay. It was expected that if we met a girl or boy friend that they would become one of our circle, but with Sally she expected me to become at least partially part of her circle of friends and this I found difficult. It didn't help that she clearly disliked some of my friends, especially the Grammar School girls who for some reason she seemed to consider inferior. I managed to play a balancing act between the two groups through the Spring but as Summer came along life started to get more fraught as she tried to appropriate more and more of my time. Then one Saturday she informed me that we were going to go out with two other couples that she knew to a dance at the Young Conservatives Club.

'You'll love it,' she informed me. I had other thoughts.

'Who will I know there?' I asked.

'You'll get to meet some really nice people, not like those childish mates of yours. These are some of the young people in the town who are really going to make a name for themselves'. She added, 'they are more your age group than the school kids you go around with,' This was like a red rag. I had never been told by a girl what I was going to do or who I was going to be friends with nevertheless I held my tongue and agreed to go along to see what it was like. What a disaster that turned out to be.

When we arrived, I was greeted by a guy who was with one of Sally's friends. He was dressed in a check shirt, cavalry twill trousers and a loud sports jacket, which appeared to be the uniform of the Young Conservatives who were gathered there. 'You must be Alan, aren't you from somewhere in London?' So, Ace wasn't good enough for her friends. I smiled and said nothing although I was already starting to feel pissed off. We sat around in the bar well away from the music which the others decided got in the way of conversation. And what conversation, nothing about music, the latest scene or even football, but what different friends of theirs had been up to, who was getting engaged to whom, what their parents had been discussing over dinner and, even worse, local politics. They were even excited about going out to canvas for the Conservative Party leading up to some election or other. For Sally's sake, I tried to not rock the boat but how that evening dragged. Eventually I had had enough and I tried to take Sally for a dance, 'No Alan,' and this was the first time she hadn't called me Ace, 'It's far more fun sitting and catching up with all the gossip.' Then, having none of it, went back to talking to her mates while I was lumbered with the two boring pricks.

When it got to about ten, Joseph announced. 'Let's trot off and find somewhere for some supper?'

I looked at him, 'I had me tea before I came out,' I said, this got me a Gorgon's stare from Sally, who replied,

'That would be lovely Joseph, come on Alan I feel quite peckish. We can go on your scooter.'

Joseph then pipes up, 'Aren't you a bit old for all that, shouldn't you have a car by now, or can't you pass the test or something?' I could have happily smacked him in the mouth and I made a note that if I was ever lucky enough to meet him on his own I would do just that. Sally however kept on about how she wanted to eat. I had had enough.

'Let's go,' I snapped 'I promised that we would meet the guys in the Vaults for a last drink. I'll buy you some chips if you're good. Get your coat we're off.' She reluctantly followed. As we left I said, 'What a bunch of pricks. What on earth do you see in them?'

'They are my best friends,' she replied

'Well they are not mine and you can do better than that boring lot.'

'You don't mean that, you'll get to like them you'll see. Tomorrow when we meet up at the cricket you'll get on a lot better,' she said.

'Cricket, what cricket? Tomorrow we're all going to Felixstowe.'

'No, I promised Fiona that we would be there. You can go to the coast anytime.'

'You didn't even bother to ask me. I'm not going to no cricket. I can't stand the game,' by now I was well and truly hacked off. 'You're my girl you'll do as I say.'

'I will not. I'm going for something to eat,' she stated 'I don't want to go to the vaults, it's rough and full of school kids. Just take me to where the others are going to eat and we'll talk about this

106

tomorrow.' I dropped her at the Berni Inn where her friends were going and left her to get on with it. I couldn't give a stuff what they thought, there was no way I wanted to mix with that load of prats.

I think she expected me to call the next morning but I had no intention of doing that. There was no way that I was going to be dictated to by some girl, however sexy she was. If she didn't like my mates she knew what she could do. There ended a beautiful friendship and I got on with enjoying the Summer. When I told Maureen, who had been at school with Sally, what had happened she gave me a big hug, kissed me on the mouth and said, 'Well done, I knew she wasn't right for you, you're completely out of her class. You're much better without her, believe me.' Sally tried a couple of times to reignite our relationship however I knew that she would have never been satisfied with the group I kicked around with and just wanted me to change and become one of the set that she was in. During our last telephone conversation, I told her, 'It's no use, I would go mad sitting around with your lot every week, there's no excitement. They're so staid. They've already become their parents. I think I would rather die than become like that.'

Her response was supposed to be cutting but it just reinforced my views, 'You're not a teenager any more Alan.'

'Ace,' I snapped back, 'You were happy to call me that when we first got together.'

'Whatever; but you are going to have to grow up and my friends would have opened more doors for you than those kids you hang around with. You'll just end up a looser if you're not careful.' I hung up, what was the point. I knew what I wanted from life and her model didn't appeal to me. Anyway, I had a date arranged for that night and I knew that with any luck that would end in sex without any strings and certainly no bloody psychoanalysis or lifestyle advice.

What Sally would have thought if she had been party to the conversations I was having with Geoff and James during our weekly drinking sessions while she and I were an item I dread to think. Certainly, I think it would have offended her finer sensibilities. The three of us had decided that we should go on holiday together but where?

'We could go to the Costa del Sol, it's cheap enough if we go by coach.' I suggested. I really fancied the idea of sun, sea and sex and I had read that all three were freely available in Spain.

'I don't like foreign food and anyway it's all right for you, you might think it's cheap but I can't afford that.' Geoff said.

While James liked the idea of Spain he said, 'Twenty-four hours on a coach, with my size I'd be a cripple at the end of the journey,' so that idea was kicked into touch. After we had gone around in circles over a couple of weeks, dismissing the Channel Islands, boring and too expensive, Calais -why would we want to – and a few other weird suggestions which came mainly from Geoff and tended to involve driving long distances to obscure places in Britain, we settled on Butlins. Butlins Holiday Camp at Skegness on the sunny Lincolnshire coast. The other two wanted to go South to Bognor Regis or even just down the road to Clacton, but there was no way I was going to risk going somewhere that anyone from my old life might have turned up to. So, Skegness it was, despite James bemoaning, 'We're only likely to meet Northern girls up there and I can't talk the language, will they even want to talk to us?'

If Sally had been aware that we were planning to go somewhere like that she would have been appalled, far too common for her middle-class sensibilities, plus at that point, even though we had only been going out for a couple of months, she wouldn't have been happy that I was planning to go off with my mates and leave her behind. Of course, as it happened it didn't matter because I had finished with her before we had come to a final decision. So, I didn't have to deal with any of the possessiveness that seemed to be part of most relationships at the time, with her trying to persuade me not to go on holiday with my mates. While it wasn't Spain, Butlins at least had the reputation as a fun destination for young people, it was by the sea, hopefully there would be plenty of girls - all that was missing was the guaranteed sun. Although if you saw the adverts and posters for Butlins Holiday Camps you would have thought that even that was promised.

Sharing a chalet, the cost of a week's holiday was going to be £12 which was no problem for James and me but Geoff was going to struggle as this was more than a week's wages for him. So, we decided that to give him time to save we would go in the first week of September, when the kids had gone back to school, and so we made the booking and paid deposits. As it worked out, Geoff needed to come up with the balance well before we went, so James and I lent him the money which he duly paid us back in instalments by way of him paying for our drinks during our Wednesday evening drinking trips throughout the summer. I would have liked to have gone mob-handed, with Tom and Col coming as well, but there was no way that we would have all got the time off together so the trip would be limited to the three of us.

Chapter 14

B y now I was well known in the area and had acquired a bit of a reputation as someone not to be messed with, whether this was fully deserved was a moot point but certainly Alex no longer tried to intimidate me or any of the guys I knocked about with. This was a good thing as most of the guys were lovers not fighters. They wouldn't have lasted 5 minutes down in the East End but this added to their appeal to me as life was generally aggro free when we went out. This didn't mean that they were cowards and a couple of times that we had encountered trouble the guys had backed me up fearlessly and between us we had seen off the opposition which only reinforced the view that while we didn't go out of our way to find trouble, as a group we weren't to be trifled with.

The one thorn in our side that remained was Rick and his gang of little thugs. A lot of the gang that Rick led were a new generation of mods, younger guys who dressed in Ben Sherman shirts, Levi jeans with some of them wearing dark blue Crombie coats which would later become associated with Skinheads. These fifteen and sixteen-year olds, mainly from the local secondary schools, seemed to only be out to find trouble. We had to step in one Sunday when a few of them started to beat up a guy we knew at Felixstowe just because they thought that he wasn't good enough for the girl that he was with and that it would be fun to see if they could take her away from him. Rick wasn't there, and so a few slaps soon put them in their place, however it didn't endear me to them or to Rick who, as their leader, seemed to revel in the notoriety that they gave him. As a group, they had been driven out of Clacton after they had a run-in with some London guys.

Tom, whose brother was there, gloried in telling us about what he had heard about this including how, 'One of the lads got hurt quite badly when one of them hit him with a cosh covered in beads.' I had to smile at this because I realised they must have run into some of my old mates and I thought about the fact that I had a similar weapon hidden in the bottom of my chest of drawers. The story then got darker, 'another one of the Ipswich lads ended up in hospital, apparently he just bumped into a GT 200 owned by some guy called Max who then gave him one hell of a beating and told the lot of them to stay away from Clacton if they didn't want to end up with their faces slashed.' And so the spector of Max still managed to intrude into my new life and if anything he seemed to have become even more unpredictable.

After this Rick and his gang tended to avoid both Clacton and Felixstowe, the latter which was by now our territory, instead they would go up the coast to Great Yarmouth where they established a reputation for being a nasty violent bunch who would regularly scrap with the mods from Norwich. I suppose we could have taken more robust steps against the Bramford Boys, as they liked to call themselves but there was another complication in that as Tom's younger brother Peter was one of them I couldn't expect Tom, who was normally always on my shoulder during any of our scrapes, to throw his weight behind any action which might involve him.

The other aspect of the Bramford Boys, that we made sure we avoided, was that they relished in being pretty criminals; shoplifting, theft of purses and wallets from unsuspecting kids and, their speciality, stealing fuel from garage forecourts at night. The two-stroke petrol and oil mixture that the scooters all ran on was mixed in stand-alone pumps that stood on the forecourt, the fuel being pumped out manually by a handle on the side. At night, some garages simply put a lock on the nozzle and left the pumps out on the forecourt. Rick and his gang would come along with a hack saw, cut through the pipe that delivered the fuel and pump the contents into their scooters and into cans from which they proceeded to try and sell cheap fuel. Not the sort of crime that Max would have entertained but they were in all other respects similar scum bags.

Early that summer Col and I had already had a run in with the gang. Col had dated a girl from their end of town for a while. Christine had gone to the youth club and Col had fancied his chances from the off. They had gone out together for a few weeks and for a while it was quite intense. I had even gone a double date with the two of them and Jackie, one of Christine's girlfriends, to a riverside pub. After a couple of drinks Col said, 'Come on let's take the girls for a fumble down by the river,' subtlety never being one of Cols strengths. We walked along the river bank and found a secluded spot where it was decided that we would stop for a while. It was a beautiful June evening and the hot sun had scented the grass with a warm smell which mingled with the sweet salty smell of the freshly washed seaweed. Some late bluebells caught the last of the daylight and in the distance a cuckoo called out a last goodnight. Col noticed none of this. As soon as we sat down on the grass he was at it with Christine, it was all quite embarrassing, especially as Jackie didn't seem to be as enthusiastic as Christine to get out of her jeans in front of an audience.

When Col striped off his pants I decided that that was enough for me and I said to Jackie, 'fancy a walk?'

'Yes please, anything's better than watching those two at it.'

'Anything?' I said.

'Don't push your luck,' she replied. In truth, I was disappointed. Jackie was a good-looking girl and it would have been great to get into her knickers but if she wasn't up for it I couldn't see the point of wasting the effort. We walked on chatting, on glancing back I could see Col getting comfortable on top of Christine. Bugger I shouldn't have looked, that really started to make me feel randy. We walked on and around the corner out of sight and Jackie took my hand, we paused, and I gave her a kiss to which she responded.

'Oh!' I said, 'that's better.'

She laughed, 'Now we've got some privacy you can push your luck a little if you like. Just don't say anything, I don't like being talked about, especially by Christine, I don't want people thinking I'm easy like her.' Easy or not, Jackie was a revelation, very enthusiastic and as the light finally gave up its battle against the night

I laid back on the grass feeling very satisfied with my evening. 'Come on let's get back,' she said, 'I don't want them to guess what we've been doing. Don't forget your promise.' We straightened our clothes and walked back along the foreshore.

'Christ where have you been?' Was the less that fulsome greeting we received from Col.

'We walked along the shore towards Nacton,' I said.

'Well I'm glad you've had fun; it's been a bloody disaster here.' I gave him a questioning look. 'We had been really giving it some and I was just about to come when a sodding great dog came and stuck its bloody nose up my arse. Scared me half to death. Then, after it had gone, she wouldn't let me have another go in case someone else came along. If you'd stayed you could have kept watch and at least one of us would have got some.' I looked at Jackie and we both collapsed in hysterics which didn't help Col's mood any.

It wasn't long after that that Col and Christine were history. Col had dumped her, 'All she could do was shag. She had no conversation, no interests, too bloody boring for me. You need something to talk about between shags, I got fed up with it.' Normally dumping a girlfriend would have caused no trouble, but in this case it was who Rick stepped right into Col's shoes, or in this case slipped into something else wet and warm that Col had just vacated. Rick had no trouble with a girl who had no other interests but sex, but he did have trouble dealing with the fact that Col and, maybe a dogs' wet nose, had been there before him. This came to a head a couple of weeks later when Col and I were at a dance and barbeque in a village to the west of the town. We had hoped to meet up with some of the other guys but it soon became clear that they weren't going to turn up. Rick however had, with a couple of his gang, and it wasn't long before he and Col were facing off.

'Going with you on the rebound is she, suppose you have to find someone who's easy and not too fussy?' was Cols opening gambit which didn't help much.

'She left you 'coz you couldn't handle it; she says you only got a small cock,' Rick said, trying to score some points of his own.

'After that dog had been sniffing round her, I didn't fancy it any more,' the story of the dog had been told and embroidered by Col himself as a cheap way of getting back at Christine and Rick. 'but I don't s'pose' she notices any difference shaggin' you.'

One of Rick's mates stepped forward and I moved between him and the other two. 'Don't even think about it,' I said, and he backed off.

Rick looked at Col and said, 'I'm going to fix you, you little twat, you'll wish you were never born.'

'You and whose army, prick, not so hard when your mates aren't around,' Col said.

Col's bravado didn't last long however when Rick told us that he was expecting the rest of his gang. 'The other guys are due any time, then I'm going to put you in hospital, your hard mate here won't be any help and if he tries we'll do him as well.' This was something that we hadn't factored in. If the rest of his gang were coming along then we would be in trouble. I briefly considered taking the three of them on there and then but realised that if their mates arrived while it was all kicking off we would be dead meat.

As Rick walked away I said to Col, 'Come on let's get out of here.' Col was all fired up but I calmed him down promising, 'We'll find a way to sort him out good and proper, just in our time and at our pace.' I still didn't know how, but at least that promise got us out of there. Riding back towards Ipswich we met the rest of his gang coming the other way, someone waved and I thought you wouldn't do that if you knew what had just occurred. As we rode back into town Col shouted in my ear,

'Let's get a beer.' I pulled over to the pub just past the youth club and parked out of sight, just in case Rick came looking, and we went inside to the bar. Over in a corner sat David scribbling into a notebook. Christ out of the frying pan into the fire. Col said 'we had better join him otherwise he'll get all hurt.' As we sat down he tipped at least half a pint down his throat in one and then looked longingly at his empty glass.

'Go on I'll get you a beer you tight bastard,' I said.

'That's jolly good of you and some crisps while you're at it. When you bring it back I'll tell you all about my new play that I'm writing.' Whoopee I thought. But at least it was better than getting beaten up by Rick's gang; well just. After a half-an-hour discourse on his brilliance David sat back and waited for Col to offer to get him another beer. When he came back with the round David looked at us appraisingly, 'do you two always dress in matching outfits like the girls?' It just so happened that that night we were both wearing blue striped matelot tee shirts which had just come into the Ipswich boutique and almost-white jeans. We thought we looked good.

'Why?' Col asked.

'Well if I didn't know you better I would have thought you were a couple of poofs.' At this Col blew him a kiss and said,

'Doesn't make us bad people dearie.'

David went red and I took the cue, putting my arm round his shoulder I whispered in his ear, 'Don't knock it if you 'aint tried it David. You might even like it.'

This made him splutter into his beer and drawing on all his artistic brilliance delivered what was meant to be his most devastating riposte, 'I was looking for two perverted characters to write into my next play and I think you two have just provided me with the models.'

'Ooh.' Col said, 'to think in the last Panto I was promoted from being the arse end of a cow to Dick Whittington's cat. When I write my memoirs I shall call it, From a Pussy to a Poof. There shall be a whole chapter dedicated to my muse, David, who discovered my ruminant arse and helped me find my inner pussy.'

'Now you're being puerile and offensive. I didn't come into my local to be humiliated, I'm just going to leave you to your childishness,' and with that he walked out with an exaggerated swagger, which unfortunately translated into more of a mince than a swagger.

'Oh, the poor darling,' I said laughing. 'Are you sure he's not queer?'

'Good god no, one of the reasons we think he does the plays

is that it gives him the chance to walk into the girls dressing room while they're changing and have a little fondle, "let me adjust your costume dear". And he's been through a lot of the older girls, even since I've been going to the Youth Club. I don't know what they see in him.'

'A bit like you then.' Col punched me on the arm.

'Cheeky boy.' He replied.

Although we had got away from Rick unscathed the problem was still there and when we weren't mob-handed we made a point of avoiding him and his gang. Similarly, I could never catch him on his own to sort him out and so a standoff existed between us as the summer went on.

Chapter 15

At work things ticked along as before with no further aggravation although I did try to introduce new systems and procedures. It was like trying to swim against the tide, surprisingly I did find one supporter in Bill Jenkins who obviously aspired to replace the Clerk when he retired and was keen to update the working practices at the council. Between us we persuaded Bernard to refurbish the cashier's office including having a low screen to improve security. However, my suggestions for having the rent payments paid in any way other than by a cash collection fell on stony ground as did my continuing concerns about Reg going out on his own collecting large amounts of cash and using the same route ever week.

'You could set your watch by him,' I argued. 'He is such an easy target.'

'Who'd want to rob dear old Reg?' was all the response that I got and sadly it would be me that was proved right.

It was late on a Thursday afternoon when the police came into the office and asked to see Bernard in private. We were all agog with curiosity. Tom said, 'Maybe Bernard's been a naughty boy?'

'Shut up and don't be so stupid.' Tony responded. For once I couldn't have agreed with him more. After a while Bernard came back into the office, you could see from the grey pallor that he had taken on that he had received some bad news.

Tom and Col, naturally, blurted out, 'What's happened Bernard, go on fill us in?' Tony and I could see that whatever it was, it was serious and I grabbed the two lads by the arms and led them out of the office before they could make life any more uncomfortable for Bernard.

'I don't know what's happened but can you two just make yourself scarce while Bernard gets himself together,' I said. Col started to protest but I cut him short. 'Bernard obviously needs to get himself together without the risk of any wise cracks from you two, I'll fill you in as soon as I can but for now give him some space. Go buy some ice-cream or something.'

I went back into the office and Tony said, 'It's Reg. He's been attacked and robbed. Bernard's taken it very badly.'

'What happened, what did the police say? I asked.

'I don't know much more than that,' Bernard said. 'The police say he was just leaving the East Bergholt estate when someone attacked him and stole the cash bag. They've taken Reg to the General. He was found unconscious by the side of the road. Oh God, I had better go and tell Blenkinsopp and Bill. He'll be sure to blame me. I should have listened to you Alan and done more to protect him.'

'Bernard, you're not to blame, no one can even think that, and don't forget, Bill wouldn't agree to Alan's suggestion for changing the rent payment system.' Tony said. However, none of this seemed to mollify Bernard who continued to blame himself for Reg's attack. Although Tony's support of my part again took me a bit by surprise.

As the days passed, we learnt a little more from the police, but not much. Reg had apparently been beaten quite badly about the head and shoulders with a cosh but couldn't remember much about the incident at all. No one in the area had admitted to having seen anything suspicious and other enquiries by the police had drawn a blank. It was a week later that I was allowed to visit him; Bernard and Tony had gone first and had been upset by the condition they found him in. Tom, Col and myself had gone a couple of days later and found Reg still with black eyes and with bruising and indentations all over his face. I had seen this before when a guy had been hit with a filled rubber hose which had been bound round with electrical cable. I'd also seen the results of beatings before, but this was particularly bad, more like a punishment beating than a quick thump to encourage someone to hand over a bag.

The following night in the Vaults I was talking about poor old Reg when someone piped up,

'You know who did that don't you?'

'What do you mean, how should I know?' I said.

'Well, a friend of mine says that Rick has been mouthing off about how he did a rent collector over and how he's in the big time now.' I didn't know if I believed him although it made some sense. He was certainly capable of that sort of violence. But it left me with more questions than it answered, and I didn't know to find out more.

The next week Tom and I were covering Reg's work, collecting the rents on the same round that he was on when he was attacked. The people on the estate where it happened all wanted to know how he was doing. I had not realised just how liked the old boy was, everyone wanted to talk about him and the round was taking a lot longer than it should have. I was giving the same update as I had probably given a dozen times already to a woman mowing her lawn when she said, 'Those scooter boys need a good threshing, first it were Clacton, now they're mekin' trouble here. The police need t' do sumit about it.'

'What scooter boys Mrs Roberts?' I said.

'Well there was a bunch of them racing through the village just after old Reg was attacked,' she said.

'Have you told the police about this?' I asked.

'Oh no, I 'int gonna get involved. It's the police job to do that.'

'But if the police aren't given the information how can they follow it up?' I said.

'You do it boy, but just you leave me out of it.'

I went on, 'Did anyone else see them?'

'Don't think so, no one else's said nothing to me.' I left it there but as we were heading back to the office said to Tom,

'I'm going to speak to the police about this. It backs up what Jim was saying on Friday about Rick, doesn't it? I wonder how Rick found out about Reg's round though?'

Tom didn't say much which was a bit surprising since he usually had an opinion on everything.

When I spoke to Debbie's husband Paul, down at the police station, he was sympathetic but didn't seem that enthusiastic and he told me that the story about Rick was only hearsay and the information about the lads on scooters wasn't very helpful as they could have come from Colchester, Ipswich or any points in-between. The next time I visited Reg I asked him about the scooters and it seemed to jog his memory a bit.

'You're right Alan, the lad who hit me was wearing a mask but he was wearing one of those smocks like you go around in.'

'You mean a parka Reg?' I said

'Yes, his had white fur round the collar.'

'Well done Reg,' I said, 'that could be really helpful. Now what about the copper-coloured scooter he was riding?' I knew I was leading him on but I thought if I could just get him to say he had seen a scooter like Rick's then I could maybe get the police to act. With the painkillers he was on, it was actually quite easy to get him to say he remembered what I wanted him to and then persuade him to ask to speak to the police again. 'Don't forget Reg the scooter was green with copper sides.'

'And he had really short hair,' Reg said.

'What did you say Reg?' I asked.

'Didn't I say before? The lad who hit me had really short hair, not like those long-haired youths you see.' Result, Rick had only recently had his hair cropped short for the Summer.

'Make sure you tell the police that as well,' I said.

Despite this new information, Paul told me that the police still didn't have enough to pull Rick in. Enough was enough, I was furious. I was going to have to sort something out.

I suspected that Rick had found out about Reg and his round from Tom's brother. There had been a lot of talk about security in the office and I could just imagine Tom going home and talking about it to his mother over supper in front of his brother and then that being passed on to Rick by Peter. I didn't blame Tom and in fact it gave me an idea about how to get even. To start with I let it be known that I had had enough of Rick and that I was going to sort him out once and for all. This story spread like a wildfire and before Bluesville in the Mulberry Tree the next week Rick was there with his mates. We glared at each other across the bar like two dogs baring their teeth at each other over a piece of waste ground. All it needed was for one of us to piss against the leg of one of the tables. He had got the message and I moved on to the next stage.

I told Tom and Col that I was going to take Rick out but didn't go into details, hinting that I had lined up some heavies to help me. I also showed them the cosh that I used to carry down in Romford and told them, 'I'm going to take his face off with this. No woman will ever want to look at him again.' They looked at me in disbelief, I had kept the cosh as a keep sake of the Romford days never intending to carry it again, but now, well this was different it was personal. The two of them were full of questions which I avoided, they thought maybe some guys were coming up from London to give me support and I did nothing to dissuade them from that idea. They were also worried that the police would get involved and I would get done, but I assured them that that wouldn't happen. 'They know what's going down and won't get involved,' I said, and they seemed to believe me. Col was particularly upset that I wasn't including him but I explained that with him there it would get too complicated and that I wanted Rick to be focused on myself and not be distracted by Col being there as well.

As for Tom, I told him, 'Try to persuade your brother to keep away on Saturday I don't want him involved if we can avoid it.' I didn't really care one way or the other, I was more interested in protecting Tom than his brother, but I couldn't let on.

I admit the rest of the week was quite uncomfortable. Both Tom and Col thought I was wrong to plan to do what I had intimated. They both told me that the level of violence that I was planning was unnecessary, even against Rick, they also tried the line,

'You know Reg wouldn't want you to do this,' but I wasn't prepared to be persuaded. I knew things were really working out though when Tom told me that Rick was calling in all his favours to make sure he had the numbers to counteract any threat on Saturday. I didn't have to ask how he knew; Tom had obviously been talking to his brother about it.

On the Friday night, we met as usual for a few drinks and while the others made plans for the next evening I stayed out of it. There was however a real atmosphere and as we split at the end of the evening Col tried again to get me to agree to take him along.

'OK,' I said, 'meet me in the pub near the Youth Club at eight tomorrow night. Don't bring any weapons of any sort, OK?' I could see he was uncertain, but he agreed.

Promptly at eight he arrived, I had already got him a pint in. He looked round confused,

'Where are the rest of them?' he asked.

'There's just us.' I said.

'You're a mad bastard, you can't take that lot on by yourself.'

'I'm not going to; I've got you here now so there's no problem' I said.

At that moment, Debbie's husband came into the pub and walked over to us and said, 'Well you were right Ace, we got the little bleeder bang to rights. He was carrying a cosh like you said and I bet when we examine it we will find bits of your rent collector on it. But best of all when we checked over his scooter we found a couple of rent receipts in the side panel with Stour Council printed on them. They're off to get a search warrant now to see if they can find anything more at his home. I'm not going to ask how you knew this was all going down but good work mate.'

Col looked at me dumbfounded; he still hadn't worked it out. After Paul had gone, I said, 'I set him up Col. The prat was so keen to take me on that he swallowed the whole "I'm coming down to get you" story that I spread around and he came out with his cosh for protection. I suspected he would if he thought I was going to be carrying. I also guessed that Tom would warn his brother and that that would get back to Rick and reinforce the threat. We got the little sod.'

'You were never planning a fight?' Col said.

'No, I just wanted to be sure that he believed I was.'

'But surely the police didn't just turn up on your say so?'

'True,' I said, 'but I also whispered in David's ear and of course, because he likes his Brownie points, he told the Rev. Dick that he had heard that the local gang were planning to come out with weapons and disrupt the Youth Club dance tonight. The Rev. had no option but to tell the police. I'd already told Paul that Rick was likely to be carrying and he took the hint that there could be a connection.'

'Tonight wasn't anything to do with the attack on Reg then. It was really lucky they found those receipts,' Col said.

'Oh, wasn't it just.' I said grinning.

'You didn't plant them? You really are a devious bastard Ace.'

'Who me? Let's get some more beer, we're celebrating.'

In the aftermath of Rick's arrest, along with a couple of others in his gang who had foolishly brought weapons with them that night, his gang simply folded. Tom, or more accurately Tom's mother, had succeeded in keeping Peter away from the action that night by the simple expedient of insisting that Tom and Peter went with her to visit their Grandmother and, such was the authority that their mother wielded, an instruction like that was not to be disregarded, even by rebellious teenagers. I remember her telling me, much to Tom's embarrassment, 'I keep the boys and the dog in order with a loud voice and a whippy slipper.' I am not sure how true that was but despite that both lads idolised her.

When the police searched Rick's parents' house they discovered a stash of cash and more pills than could be justified as being for his personal use. The embarrassment that this caused his father contributed to the most satisfying outcome of Rick's arrest, a few days later, when the police released him on bail. The story of what occurred was soon around the town, having been spread by people who knew the family. Apparently when Rick returned home his father took him outside and beat him black and blue with a length of hosepipe and then threw him out and he had to move into a Bail Hostel. What none of us knew was that, in addition to facing the embarrassment of having their house searched, his parents were members of a non-conformist church and their sons' attack on a Pastor from a similar church was seen by them as totally unforgivable. I was just pleased that as well as everything else, he had got the beating I would have so liked to have administered to him myself.

Chapter 16

Sadly, Reg had lost so much confidence that he would never return to work at Stour and he retreated into the work of his ministry. I went to visit him at his home one evening, it was a dark Victorian cottage, on a coffee table in the middle of the lounge sat a large open bible and anti-macassars adorned the arms of the faded maroon brocade three-piece suite. It smelt of dust and felt a lonely place, Reg confided to me that he missed the wider social contact that collecting the rents at Stour gave him. He went on, 'I even miss you lads challenging my beliefs. It kept my mind sharp.'

'I hope you realise that it was never meant seriously Reg,' I said.

'Of course I do, but I also believe that the Lord works in mysterious ways to challenge our faith and I feel that you lads were part of that. Similarly, I hold no grudge against the lad who attacked me. He has brought me back to focus on the Lord's work and for that I shall always be grateful.'

After an intensive period of work and much appreciated overtime, getting the tax bills out in the Spring and then finalising and closing the accounts, the Summer months at Stour were a quiet time. A time when most afternoons were spent doing word puzzles in the daily papers. On sunny afternoons Tom would be sent out to buy a block of ice cream, which would then be sliced up and sandwiched between wafers. Other times we would be sent out to try and identify properties that had been improved without being revalued for tax purposes. But often we would simply be told to get off home leaving the Finance Department with Bernard on his own. It was an idyllic working environment. That was as long as Wally could be kept out of the equation with his foul mouth and innuendoes. It still amazed me that he could still say and do what he did and still have the support of Bill Jenkins. But he did and we all had to be careful not to get into Jenkins' bad books if, as expected, he was going to take over from Blenkinsopp when he retired.

Socially the summer was a brilliant time. The light nights enabled us to hold beach parties, often at Felixstowe but sometimes further afield up the coast or on the foreshores of the local estuaries. This was when the guys with cars became particularly useful, transporting blankets and booze to wherever we were headed. Once at the chosen site, a fire would be built, blankets spread on the ground and the evening generally spent drinking and laughing. There was never any trouble and often two or three parties in the same location would merge into one. Little food was ever brought along, although usually, if we were on a town beach, as the evening wore on, one or two of the guys would be sent off for fish and chips. There was always music playing, with three or four transistor radios all tuned into Radio Caroline or Radio London. Both pirate stations were broadcasting three miles off shore, their lights on the horizon, twinkling against the darkening sea as the sun set behind us. By eleven however the transistors were usually tuned into Johnny Walker on Radio Caroline, firstly because he played, what we considered to be, more credible music, but also because at eleven he had a "kiss in the car" spot, when couples would park up on the cliffs and seafronts and flash their headlamps at the Pirates to acknowledge that they were enjoying the music whilst having a session with the opposite sex. We simply used it as an excuse to have a fumble with whichever of the girls we happened to be around with that evening. Usually that was as far as it went. While one or two of the girls had reputations as being easy and letting you go all the way, most would only let you go so far, the fear of pregnancy was very real to them even if the guy used a Johnny.

After Sally, I was in no rush to find a steady girlfriend, they were just too much trouble and restricted my opportunities too much. So girls, well they came and went. I was well regarded around the town and still way ahead of all the other guys on style, personality and, most importantly, cash. This meant I could have a different girl each week and if they weren't prepared to take the risk to give me what I wanted, especially given that I would always use protection, then I could look for someone else who would. I considered myself to be The Ipswich Face in all but name and there were some girls who were prepared to go all the way just to be seen out with me.

1965 was also probably the apex of the original Mod culture. New scooter models had been launched, although you didn't see many of them in Ipswich and certainly none of the customised Eddy Grimstead ones. But clothes that the previous year had only been available in London were now more widely available in the provinces. There was certainly a lot more style on the street than there had been when I first arrived, but I still managed to keep ahead of the game by getting Mum to shop for me in London. My weekly parcels from home seemed to be as keenly anticipated by my cousin Rachael and my aunt as they were by myself and they usually led to long discussions about the fabrics and cut of the clothes. One week I would get a pair of canvas sneakers the next a designer tee-shirt and another, the talking point of the summer, a pair of pale orange jeans from Lord John's in Carnaby Street.

Bluesville was still serving up its weekly treats including the regular bands who continued to be recurring visitors. We even managed to catch The Who at one of their early gigs, they had released their first single the previous December and followed it up with two further hits in the summer of 1965, The media immediately latched onto them as the Mod band. We were more dismissive and they didn't cut it with those of us who considered ourselves to be original mods; to us they were a bunch of kids who dressed as mods and released catchy pop records. When we saw them live however, we found that their set included a lot of the classic R and B numbers that we considered to be our standards and their performances, even of their pop songs, was something to behold. Even then few of my circle would admit to liking them as we felt that to admit to following a chart act like them was beneath us. Of more interest were The Yardbirds. Now they were different, their sound seemed to be moving in a completely different direction to The Who, with soaring and ethereal guitar they took you away from whatever else you were doing. Their first record, For Your Love, had aroused my interest with its bongo beat opening and almost classical undertones and I had resolved that as soon as I was able I would get to see them again live. I even considered going down to a London gig, but good sense prevailed and I decided to wait and hope that I would be able to see them somewhere in my current neck of the woods.

As the summer ended those of my circle who were returning to school started planning what, in most cases, would be their last year with the majority planning to go onto university. It was the start of what we all knew would be a major change in the dynamics of our social scene despite all the promises of not letting it get in the way of our friendships. It was also nearing the time that Geoff, James and I were going off on holiday and, given that this was for all three of us our first holiday without parents; this was causing us a serious degree of anticipation.

With the assumed rehabilitation of my cousin I was going down to the Youth Club less and less and this had become an issue with the two lads from work who liked to have me there to add credibility to their own aspirations of status. In contrast my Wednesday drinking sessions with Geoff and James were becoming increasingly important to me. The three of us were all the same age and with them I felt that I was with equals. This was despite the three of us all being very different, neither James nor Geoff ever tried to be on trend about anything whether clothes, music or attitudes to life generally. In fact, they were the only ones amongst my friends who could get away with taking the piss out of me and my pretentions. Certainly, Tom and Col wouldn't have dared to laugh at me the same way that James and Geoff did.

Inevitably during our sessions throughout the summer, the subject of the holiday arose. The three of us were sharing a chalet and naturally the issue of how we were going to manage any situation where one of us wanted to have a girl in the room arose, 'Well you and Geoff can sleep on the beach if I want the room, that's not too much to ask, is it?' I said.

'On your bike, you can take any girls you meet to the beach you can,' was the short shrift I received for that suggestion.

'Any luck they will have their own chalet that we can use,' James said.

'But what if there's two of them?' Geoff added.

And so, the discussions had gone on through the summer as we got ourselves wound up for the holiday not really knowing what to expect when we arrived at Skegness. Another discussion we had was over who was going to drive us there. Geoff would have loved to do it, 'My car is bigger and more comfortable and it'll have room for all of Ace's clothes, he'll need at least two changes a day no doubt. It'll also look really impressive when we pull up in the old girl.'

James wasn't so sure, 'It's a long way Geoff and I'm not really sure that I trust your old car to make it.'

'You're happy enough to come out drinking in her every week I can't see any difference,' Geoff said.

'There is Geoff, one hundred and forty miles' difference and your old Austin only does twenty to the gallon,' to which I added,

'And that's just the oil, it smokes like an old steam engine. James's Cooper will be a bit of a squeeze but at least we know we'll get there. You and I can take turns in the back. I'll pack light let's make a rule just one holdall each. OK Geoff?'

It was the first Saturday in September when James picked Geoff and I up for the holiday. My holdall filled the boot.

'I thought you said we were going to pack light?' James said.

'No, I said one holdall, and you wouldn't want me to be less than perfectly turned out for the girls, would you? Those Northern tarts won't know what hit them when they see me in all my splendour.'

'Get in and stop acting like the flash prat that you are, Geoff and I will have to put our bags on the back seat and you can take the first stint being squashed in with them.' James said. I had to admit that I had packed to impress. Well you couldn't go off for a week on the pull without making sure you had the right gear. I had also been to the hairdressers. The best men's hairdressers in

Ipswich at that time was in the basement of Ridley's, a traditional men's clothing store. Their barbers shop was an all-male environment. Women weren't allowed beyond the top of the stairs, even having to deposit their small boys there to be delivered back to them after having their hair cut. A lot of the guys called it the poofs parlour but they were just jealous because they couldn't afford the prices that they charged. So I'd had my hair styled just right for the trip. James and Geoff were their usual dishevelled selves and I couldn't help wonder whether with them in tow I had any real chance of scoring during our week away, despite having been told that all the girls from up North who went to Butlins' only went there to get pulled.

It took us over three hours to get to Skegness, no dual carriageway up there. Across Suffolk, through Norfolk and into the flat lands of Lincolnshire, it was a long uncomfortable and boring journey. Eventually we arrived, drove into the camp's car park and walked through the gates to the reception and checked in.

Geoff looked at the entrance of the camp and said, 'It looks like a bloody prison camp.'

I couldn't disagree with him and said, 'Look at those sodding great gates and the barbed wire on the top of the walls. Do you think the whole place is behind walls like them?' And it was: fenced, and walled, with only a couple of gates complete with uniformed guards to get in and out, it really did feel as if you were being locked in. We were allocated our chalet, given the row number and the chalet number.

James didn't help, asking the fearsome looking woman checking us in, 'Do we have to wear a uniform and our camp numbers on our sleeves?' She said nothing but gave him a look that would have frozen a kettle of boiling water. Our chalet was situated amongst those that had been allocated to single campers and there were already little knots of eighteen to twenty-something year-olds mingling on the grass between the rows of chalets. Ours was in the middle of the row and we let ourselves in. It was certainly compact, while you could just about have swung a cat around in it anyone else in there at the time would have had to duck. The three beds, which were arranged against the two sides and the back wall were covered in faded bed throws and between the beds, the bare boards had a rug with a distinctly worn patch in the middle. At the bottom of one of the beds stood a wardrobe and at the bottom of the opposite bed was the door to the bathroom. Everything about the room was tired and had seen better days,

'The Ritz it aint', Geoff said 'but hell we're here on holiday so let's just get on with it. We're only going to be sleeping in here so it will do.' James gave me a smirk. He and I had already decided that, as we had rarely seen Geoff score with a girl, the chances were that it would be us using the room for other purposes and we would have to persuade Geoff to just keep out of the way when we needed it. We unpacked some of our stuff but left most in the holdalls to be sorted through as we needed it. Geoff brought out a pack of twelve Durex and put them in the draw of his bedside table. 'Gotta be prepared lads, have you got yours?'

We exchanged another look, James raised his eyebrows. Later I took James aside and said, 'The chances of Geoff pulling are nil, you know what he's like. He embarrasses the girls as soon as he starts chatting to them. When you and I get hooked up we are going to have to spend some time with him as well otherwise the poor bugger won't have anyone to talk too.'

James said, 'Let's agree that we'll always eat together and at least have a couple of drinks with him so he's not on his own too much. That won't be too much to ask of any girls we pick up, will it?'

That evening we had our first experience of the culinary delights of the Butlin's dining room. It was more like a works canteen than a hotel restaurant and the food was nowhere near as good as that I was used to having at my aunt's. Meat pie and chips was the dish of the day although just what sort of meat none of us wanted to guess. Every now and then one of the serving staff would drop a plate and the whole room would erupt in a chorus of cheers. After we had eaten we went to find what entertainment there was to be had and watched some of that evening's show, but family variety shows weren't what we were there for so left after only a short while looking for a beer to wash the taste of the pie from our mouths. We started in the Tudor lounge for a first beer but it was like being in an old folks' home so we moved onto the Pig and Whistle. By now the show had turned out and the bar was heaving, six-deep at the bar itself and everyone talking in broad Northern accents which were completely alien to us. From the ceiling hung all varieties of strange objects and there were even some seats hanging from it. These all seemed to be taken by girls who were surrounded by little knots of guys making lewd comments while trying to see up their skirts. We eventually managed to get a drink, mainly due to Geoff's ability to sneak his way to the bar, this was a well-known talent that he had and for which we had often been grateful. But it wasn't a comfortable place to be, all the tables were taken and wherever we stood we got jostled and there was little chance of catching the eyes of any of the girls as they all seemed too busy trying to stop their pints being spilled. I have to admit that it was the first time I had seen so many girls drinking pints and I found it slightly unnerving for some reason. A lot of them were also very loud as was the whole room.

I turned to the guys and said, 'Christ almighty this lot would suck you in and blow you out in little pieces.'

'That'ud do me,' was Geoff's response.

But I had had enough and I pulled the guys towards the door, 'Come on there's got to be somewhere better than this.'

We got outside and James said, 'I saw something in the brochure about a Beachcomber bar let's give it a look.' I'd have tried anything by then, so we went to find it. The Beachcomber was decorated to look like a tropical beach bar. There were artificial trees with plastic palm fronds surrounding a pool made to look like a lagoon and projected on the wall behind it was a tropical ocean scene across which the clouds moved accompanied soft Hawaiian music, tropical bird song and insect noises. In keeping with this theme, the furniture was cane and on each table there was a cocktail list. The bar was probably meant for young married couples to have somewhere to go for a romantic drink, but it suited us fine as it wasn't crowded,

'A bit sophisticated for the usual clients I expect,' I said when we each got a bottle of beer and took over a table with a beach umbrella stuck in the middle. After about fifteen minutes the projected scene on the back wall got darker and to the sound of rainfall a storm was replicated with thunder, lightning and other requisite sound effects.

'Can we shelter under your umbrella before we get wet?' I looked up to where two girls holding cocktails that looked more like fruit salads than drinks stood grinning at us. Geoff leapt to his feet almost knocking over the table in his eagerness to make room for them.

'Of course you may my dears, let me draw you up some seats,' he said. I could have killed him. This pseudo old fashioned courtesy was exactly what turned the girls off him and if we weren't careful it would reflect on James and me. As he rushed around reorganising the seats I gave the girls a once-over. They were certainly a couple of lookers.

'I'm Gill,' said the taller of the two who had long brunette hair and a fabulous smile, 'and this is my friend Steph.' Oh my, what a stunner. She had short blond hair cut in a bob and was incredibly pretty, if a little serious, no warm welcoming smile like her mate. Both were dressed in ski pants and tight ribbed sweaters and it was all I could do to stop myself staring at the shapes that the clothes were accentuating. It was only as Gill was introducing her friend that I noticed the broad northern accent which was so different to anything I had come across before. They sat down and before long it felt as if we had all known each other forever. They both came from Leeds, which accounted for the accents, and like us had been totally turned off by the other drinking holes in the Camp. James and I managed to position ourselves next to the girls and by unspoken agreement he focused on Gill while I paid most of my attention on Steph. Geoff was sent off at regular intervals to get the drinks and was given no chance to make a play for either of them, but he seemed happy enough.

Every half an hour the storm rolled in again and towards the end of the evening, when yet another repeat performance started,

Gill moved towards James and said, 'that storm makes thee want to snuggle up with someone.' James took the opportunity, put his arm around her and she moved over to sit on his lap. I tried the same thing with Steph and while she didn't stop me, she was less than responsive to the squeeze that I gave her. Poor old Geoff took his cue and said he would see us back at the chalet.

'We could go for a walk, or I could walk you back to your Chalet.' I suggested.

Steph said, 'A walk would be nice but then I think we can find our own way back.' So, a walk it was. James was obviously getting on a lot better with Gill the I was with Steph and that night after a walk around the grounds he got a very encouraging snog, while I got a peck on the cheek and a promise that we would get together as a group the next night.

Gills parting shot was, 'and don't forget to bring Geoff, you can't leave him all on his own.'

As we walked back I agreed with James that he had seemed to make good progress with Gill and he was certainly hopeful of more, 'When we had that snog I tried to have a feel of her tits but she wouldn't have none of it, but I'll be inside her knickers by Monday night, mark my words boy. You'll be up there as well I bet.' I wasn't so sure but didn't say so. In fact, I had been hoping we would pick up a couple of girls who were a little less classy that Gill and Steph, both of whom seemed very self-confident and certainly Steph was not as easy a girl as I had been hoping for, I hadn't even got a kiss.

The next day turned out to be one of those beautiful early September days that seemed to forget that Autumn was around the corner. The sky was deep blue with the sun shining fiercely and threatening everyone who had exposed skin with sunburn. Not that that deterred many people and although we got to the pool straight after breakfast it was already crowded. We had just decided to go to the beach instead when Geoff said,

'Oh my god will you look at that? Bloody hell.' We looked in the direction he was staring.'

'What's the problem Geoff mate?' James asked.

'Oh, just look at that, isn't she just magnificent and look one of them is out again. Do you think I should offer to go and give her a hand to catch them?'

It was James who twigged what he was on about first. 'You can't mean that big bird over there surely?'

'Oh yes I do, she is magnificent.' Over by the other side of the pool sat this quite enormous blond girl straddling a sun lounger. She wore, and I use the term loosely, the smallest bikini I had ever seen from which acres of white flesh seemed to be making a determined effort to escape.

I said, 'Geoff look away now or you'll go blind.'

'Don't be silly, ooh look at that.' By then you couldn't miss it. She was applying suntan lotion to the mass of exposed flesh and as she stretched over with her right hand to do her left shoulder her right breast popped out from the fragment of material containing it, at which she would scoop it up and tuck it away again. As she reversed the procedure with the left hand, so that breast also made a dash for freedom. It was like watching someone trying to restrain two unruly puppies that were trying to escape from a basket.

'Geoff, come on, let's get down to the beach.' I said.

'No, you two go on. I'll catch you later. I'm going to go and say hello, chat her up. Look she's on her own, her mate's over there, I saw them at breakfast together but now she's chatting up that Red Coat over there. I won't get a better chance. I'll see you two later.' We looked over to where a very pretty, petite brunette was all over a good-looking young Red Coat.

I said to James as we walked off, 'Isn't it funny how often you get a very pretty girl going around with someone you wouldn't want to be seen dead with.'

'Yeah well I never do fancy yours!' 'Do you think Geoff will really manage to cop off with her.'

'I do hope not, she'd eat him alive and spit out the pips. Poor old Geoff.'

Geoff didn't catch up with us that morning and we didn't really give him much of a thought because we met Gill and Steph on the beach. Wow, they looked even better in their swimsuits than they had the previous night. While they were really pleased to see us, they made it very clear that they were not up for anything more than a bit of sunbathing and once again Steph seemed particularly standoffish to me. None of us fancied the dining room for lunch and so, after getting dry burgers and soggy chips from a stall, we did some more sun bathing with the girls but still saw nothing of Geoff. James said, 'You don't think he's pulled, do you?'

'Nah,' I said, 'he'll be in a bar drinking beer with some guys he's met. Mark my words.' How wrong could I have been? Later that afternoon, on arriving back at the chalet to get ready for the evening we walked in on him and the big bird from the pool. Geoff's scrawny white arse was pumping up and down like a good un on this mass of red sunburned flesh.

'Guys give me another ten will you, be a sport?' We turned and made a quick exit before collapsing on the grass in hysterics. Bloody hell Geoff had scored before either of us, who'd have thought it. After a while they left the chalet and Geoff gave us a wave as he walked her back to her chalet. The gent as always.

I said to James, 'I bet he even said, please and thank you.' Still killing ourselves with laughter we started to get ready and waited to hear all the gory details.

'Three nil, three nil, three nil to me,' Geoff chanted as he walked, adding 'that is unless you two've been at it all afternoon as well,'.

I said, 'Don't take the piss Geoff just because you've had it away at last.'

'No, straight up lads, we did it three times since we come in before lunch. She's bloody amazing. Her name's Polly, she's from Liverpool, says she knows the Beatles' families. Bet you wish you'd made such a good start.' James went and checked Geoff's stash of johnnies.

'Bloody hell he is three down. You jammy sod Geoff. Not that I would have wanted to go where you've been, she'd scare the life out of me, I'm surprised you could find you way back out once you were in there.' I just shook my head in disbelief. And that was the way it went for the rest of the week with Geoff. We only saw him for breakfast and dinner then, following a quick beer, he was off the rest of the time with his big bird and at it again. We'd laughed at him bringing a dozen Durex with him yet by the end of the week he was having to borrow extra ones from us.

For James and me things got more complicated that Sunday evening when we hooked up with the girls again. We had a good evening, James and Gill really seemed to have hit it off and I could see them going to bed before long, but with Steph I just didn't seem to be getting anywhere, she simply remained aloof, albeit while being good company. We walked the girls back to their chalet that night and Steph said good night and went in without even giving me a chance to give her a goodnight kiss so I left James to say a proper goodnight to Gill and walked back to our Chalet. Lucky bugger I thought, I may have to dump Steph and look for someone else if I want any action. When James eventually came back he had to admit that he hadn't got very far but went on, 'I don't know what's going on but Gill says she wants to talk to you alone tomorrow morning after breakfast.'

That conversation was certainly one of the strangest I had ever had. Gill came right out with it, 'You know how Steph's been keeping you at arm's length?'

'That's pretty obvious.' I suppose I sounded somewhat bitter, but she carried on.

'She just don't fancy you lad, but she really has got the hots for your mate James. She's really mad for him but won't do anything if it means me being on me own for the rest of the week.' I just stood there I didn't know what to say. She continued, 'so I was wondering would you swap and hang around with me and see what happens with those two, like give them a chance? Would you do that for a mate?'

This was all getting a bit surreal for me and I guess it showed. But I gave a shrug and said, 'That works for me' and it really did, Gill was a dream and I fancied my chances with her no problem.

Then she went on, 'problem is however Ace, I don't really fancy you either. Not in that way. You're just too flash to be my type, so I can't let you say yes to this if you think it's a way into my knickers, 'cause it won't happen.' Bloody hell I thought what's wrong with these Northern tarts, back home they were falling over themselves to go out with me. This felt like a real kick in the balls and I would never live it down with the guys if this got out. She must have picked up on my mood because she added, 'you don't need to tell James the last bit, you can pretend we were at it like rabbits and he'll never know different from me. I think we could still have a lot of fun as friends, don't you? Go dancing and such like.' What could I do? I couldn't just drop James in it and take away his chance of getting it together with Steph. I was already jealous about him being with Gill because she obviously had a great sense of fun and anyway, I was sure that if were together for a bit I would be able to work the old charm on her and get her to agree to a bit of how's yer father. It had always worked before. So, I agreed to speak to James about it and, as proposed, we swapped girls.

That was the making of James's week, while he wasn't at it as much as Geoff, he and Steph spent every evening alone in the girl's chalet while Gill and I gave them space. Gill was right however we did have a lot of fun together. We went dancing, did some shows but most of all we people-watched and laughed so much that it hurt. But, despite her continually flirting with me, she would still not let me near her. In fact, after a couple of days I didn't even try and I resigned myself to a celibate week. The days the three of us lads managed to keep for ourselves, by Tuesday we had managed to extract Geoff from his big bird during the day and we got involved in the usual holiday camp activities, a couple of games of football and some silly activities around the pool, I even played some tennis which I hadn't done since school. But the evenings, after dinner which didn't get any better, were reserved for the girls.

As the week drew to an end Geoff and James both started getting morose about leaving the girls behind, I didn't help, 'They're only a holiday romance you didn't come her to find wives.' They didn't see it that way and were already making plans for letters and visits. I began to feel grateful for what Gill and I had shared without any of the emotional hang-ups that the others were having. At

Friday's breakfast Geoff announced that he was going to spend the whole night with his big bird, her mate had made arrangements with her Red Coat, so that they could sleep together.

James looked at him sullenly, 'You lucky sod, I would love to spend the night with Steph. We'll never get the chance again. Last week you hadn't even had it away before, now you're spending a whole night with your woman. It's not on. Alan, can't you get Gill to spend the night with you?' I hadn't admitted that I hadn't got anywhere with Gill and with the fun that the two of us had been seen having together it must have seemed that we had developed something special between us, but I couldn't tell them that now, could I?

'Go on boy, ask her to spend the night with you, you won't have to ask her to marry you.' Geoff insisted. By god they were really putting me in a difficult position.

'You're the one with the reputation with the ladies Sir Alan, it should be easy for you.' James said adding his two pennyworths. Shit this was going to be difficult.

As it was the last day we had agreed to spend all of it with our girls rather than just the evening. Gill and I went for a long walk along the beach and I became even more aware of how much I envied James and the romance that had developed between him and Steph. Gill was undoubtedly the most interesting girl I had ever spent time with. I could have so easily fallen for her if she had given me even an ounce of encouragement. Although I had decided that I would plead James's case for him I was unsure about how to approach it. After a while we sat on the dunes watching the sea. 'Do you think James will stay in touch with Steph?' Gill asked.

'I reckon so, he seems head over heels with her and he's one of the good guys. He wouldn't do anything to hurt her.'

'Not like you then, I bet you have no problems loving and leaving them.' she quipped before carrying on, 'You know they want to spend the night together, don't you?' I should have realised the girls would have discussed this. I laughed. 'What's so funny?' She asked.

'I was trying to work out how to bring that very subject up.'

I replied. 'And how we could work something out so that they could.'

'Well there are three beds in your chalet aren't there? I could have one of those,' she said.

'If you'd do that I will give you my word that I won't try anything on, I'll even sleep in the bath if that would make you feel more comfortable,' I said. Although I don't know why being an extra three foot away from her would do so, it just felt like the right thing to say.

'Don't be a clown, if you say you'll behave then I'll trust you, you've been a gentleman all week, but it was sweet of you to offer' and she gave me a brief kiss on the lips. With that it was settled. I thought to myself that even though I hadn't scored this week, by spending the night in the chalet with Gill, James and Geoff would have no doubts when I said that we had been at it and they would raise no doubts when the stories were told to the other lads when we got home. After all, I still had my reputation to think about and it wouldn't hurt Gill as it was unlikely we would ever meet up again. We had a wonderful last day together; walked along the beach hand in hand for miles, chased each other across the sand with wet seaweed and did all manner of silly things, anyone seeing us would have thought that we were a couple of lovers and I wished that that could have been.

We didn't see the others until dinner and when I told James what had been arranged his response was, 'I knew that, Steph told me she had asked Gill to work on you and I bet you won't regret it. Imagine, you can and do it all night wake up with each other. It will make this a holiday to really remember Sir Alan.' If only he knew, the lucky bastard.

That evening the six of us all ate together for the first time, although you could sense that Geoff's big bird, as James and I cruelly kept calling her, was uncomfortable in the presence of the other two girls and as soon as we had finished eating Geoff disappeared off with her. James and I walked the girls back to their chalet and he and I waited outside while Gill got few things together and came out with them in a large handbag.

'Can I dump these at yours before we go anywhere?' she asked, and with that we walked through the chalet lines to our chalet. 'God this somehow feels really wicked,' Gill said sounding quite excited, 'it feels like we are going away for a dirty weekend.'

I said, 'I should be so lucky,' and she punched me on the arm.

'Naughty boy, don't spoil things by forgetting your promise. As if I could, it was crazy, but I had ended up with a real ice queen. Despite this we threw ourselves into enjoying the last night of the holiday. At, what we had come to see as, our table in the Beach-comber bar we had a few drinks, I even let her persuade me to have one of the extravagantly decorated cocktails and then she said,

'Come on take me dancing,' and so I did, and we danced the rest of the evening away. Eventually, when the band stopped play-ing and they closed the bar, we had to go back to the chalet. I felt uncomfortable as I was sure that this was not what she really wanted. When we got back she asked, 'Which bed shall I take?'

'Well not Geoff's, that's seen too much action this week, the one over there is James's but if you like you can have mine, it's up to you. You can have the blankets to put over you if you don't want to get between the sheets.

'You keep your bed, I'll be OK,' she said and with that she picked up her things and went to the bathroom. I took the op-portunity to quickly get in my pyjamas and into bed. I wasn't sure how you were expected to behave in a situation like this, but it seemed the right thing to do. After a few minutes the bathroom door opened and Gill walked through wearing a big smile on her face and nothing else. My god she was naked! Not only was she naked but her body was absolutely fantastic. Every image I had formed in my mind about her over the past week was exceeded. I was gobsmacked. Now, although I had had plenty of sexual expe-riences over the previous few years I had never seen a fully naked woman before, pictures of course, but in the flesh never. Sex had always been undertaken surreptitiously, always just out of sight of someone. A bedroom at a party when anyone could have walked in. More riskily, sofa in a girl's house after her parents had gone to bed, the park and many other places where discovery could have been just as imminent. In all those scenarios the ability to straighten your clothes out quickly tended to be a priority so no one ever got fully undressed. I just stared slack jawed at the sight of her standing there.

'e lad hast thou not seen a naked woman before?' she asked, putting on the broadest of Yorkshire accents. I could feel myself start to blush. On registering my confusion, she went on 'my god you haven't have you. It's not all a front is it; you're not a virgin as well are you?'

I spluttered and found my voice, 'No, I'm not, it's just that you took me completely by surprise.' I said.

'That was the whole idea and I hope it's a nice surprise,' She said, 'You have been really good to me this week and I have decided to give you a treat.' The slipping back into a broad dialect, 'Now get thy kecks off lad, it's thar birthday.' As I got out of bed she laughed, 'Ooh nice pjs. I bet they keep you nice and warm on a cold night, they're just like me dad's.'

'Well if I'd known you were going to keep me warm I wouldn't have bothered.' and with that I took them off and dropped them by the side of the bed. Again, she managed to disconcert me by standing back and giving me the once over, again no girl had ever seen me like that and I felt embarrassed at her appraisal of my old man standing to attention for her, I almost felt like covering it up with my hands.

'Mmm. I couldn't have hoped for more than that, you're certainly a big lad, you'll get no complaints from me there.' and with that she came up close and kissed me, 'let's get to bed it's very small so we're going to have to stay very very close all night. I hope you have got plenty of stamina.'

I had no idea sex could be so fantastic, all week I had thought of her as an ice maiden and that night she proved how wrong I was in that evaluation and she kept coming back for more. Eventually we went to sleep waking as a soft dawn light started to creep into the room through the thin curtains. 'I need a pee,' she announced and when she came back to bed we made love again. It was the first time I had ever thought of sex as making love but what we had done through that night could not be described in any other way. She had totally captivated me.

But then it was morning and we all had to face reality. A quick breakfast then throwing our clothes into our holdalls and out of the camp by 10am. It was a brutal end to the week for all of us. James, Geoff and their girls really didn't want to part. Steph, in particular, seemed inconsolable and Geoff's big bird looked as if she was trying to eat him alive while his hands were doing things that should never have been seen in public. Gill and I just stood holding hands, she seemed simply resigned that it was over.

'I hope you enjoyed your farewell present,' she said as I gave her a last kiss. I had written out my contact details for her and she told me that she would write to me and let me have hers. With that she got on the coach for Leeds and sat next to Steph whose tear stained face was pressed up against the window. Gill just looked straight ahead as the coach departed not even giving me a farewell wave.

I looked at James and said, 'I'm going to have to see her again.' I was in love.

Chapter 17

By the time the three of met up the next Wednesday for our regular drink, James had already arranged to visit Steph in Leeds although I hadn't yet heard from Gill. I had hoped that after the fun we'd had and our night together she would have been immediately in contact. Surely it had meant as much to her as it had to me? Geoff was also pondering what to do, but Liverpool was a heck of a journey from the east coast and his old car was unlikely to make it there and back in one piece. Equally the train journey was not only torturous but expensive which made James and I doubt whether there was any sense in Geoff pursuing the relationship. But Geoff still made plans and we didn't try to dissuade him. That first weekend back he had revelled in describing his adventures to the guys who in turn laughed behind his back as they related what they considered to be his fantasies to the girls. It was all getting pretty cruel, 'Don't mock what you don't understand,' I said to one group. 'Geoff was a revelation, at it right from day one, you shouldn't be laughing you should be jealous.'

'Don't be daft, poor old Geoff wouldn't know where to put it,' came one reply.

'Trust me he certainly does, he got more than James and I combined,' I said. The fact that it was me supporting Geoff's story gave it credibility but, despite this, there was still some sniggering behind his back. Although when the guys discussed it with the girls even they seemed suitably impressed, despite that being combined with a large degree of disapproval at a girl who would be so casual with her favours. One thing that this prejudice and double standards brought home to me was that I hoped Geoff didn't succeed in pursuing his big bird. It was obvious that if he brought her to Ipswich she would never be accepted by the local crowd, her size and background would have made her a laughing stock. Col and Tom of course wanted all the details, but I kept them guessing about my experiences, for the first time I didn't want to boast too much about my time with a girl. When James went up to Leeds a fortnight later I still hadn't heard from Gill and I convinced myself that she must have lost my address, so I gave James a letter for her. When he returned, I asked if he had seen her but he said not and that Steph had said she would deliver the letter for me and so my waiting started again, but there was still no reply. During the weeks of waiting and hoping I couldn't get interested in any of the other girls, such was my infatuation with Gill. I sent two more letters to her via James and Steph but gradually reality kicked in, although I still held on to a vague hope that she would write.

However, James and Steph's relationship seemed to get stronger and he told me, 'The next time we meet it will be down here, I'm going to introduce her to my family.'

'Is that wise?' I said. James had often laughed about his parent's hopes that he would marry a nice farmer's daughter and expand the farming dynasty, James bristled,

'Why shouldn't it be, what's wrong with her?' He asked.

'Nothing to my mind mate, but what about what you have always said about your parents; Steph's hardly farming stock is she?'

'It's got nothing to do with them, I'm in love with Steph and they are just going to have to accept it.' I wished him well and we agreed that while she was down we would get together for a drink.

It was great seeing Steph again. I met up with them in Stowmarket and you could see that they really had something special going on. It did however bring back all my longings for Gill and I kept asking about her and why she hadn't been in touch. I noticed that as I asked James and Steph exchanged glances and then he nodded his head to her. 'You have got to forget Gill.' James said 'Steph has something to tell you.

She looked at me uncomfortably, 'There's something you need to know. Gill and I have been close friends since school, junior school in fact and I was going through a difficult time so she agreed to come with me to Butlins, so that I could get away.' James sat nodding at the truth of what was being told. 'And she really got to like you, she's told me about your last night together. I was really surprised because she had said that that wouldn't happen. But then she said that she felt like just having a one-night fling to remember the holiday by. The thing is Ace, Gill's married, to a guy in the army who's stationed overseas. He's coming home soon so she can't risk him guessing anything because of the baby.' Steph paused to let that sink in. 'She has a daughter, her mum looked after her for the week so that Gill could come with me. I don't think she meant to hurt you, but it was just a night of casual sex to her, so you can understand why she can't have you writing to her let alone seeing you again.' I just sat there stunned, I felt upset and used. Upset because it seemed so wrong that she was married and had betrayed her husband, not to mention doing that when she had a child and yes it made me feel stupid for holding on to my hopes for the past weeks when she had simply wanted me for a night of sex.

'How long have you known?' I snapped at James.

'I only found out last week but Steph asked me to let her tell you herself. I 've told her she shouldn't, but she feels as if it's her fault.'

'I'm sorry I shouldn't have snapped it's nothing to do with you Steph. I'm just so sad about it.' She reached over and touched my hand.

'I don't know if I should say this, but,' she paused again, 'Gill told me that she doesn't regret what happened and will always remember the time you spent together, not just that last night, the whole time. If it wasn't for the baby I think she might have tried to see you again.'

I had to accept that I would never get together with Gill, but sometimes in quiet reflective moments that Autumn I found myself daydreaming about how Gill might still get in touch and how we would look after her daughter between us. It was all quite worrying really, but eventually I got over it and started seeing local girls again and by Christmas that holiday was no more than a distant memory to be laughed about with the guys. Geoff's big bird wrote to him once and then also disappeared into the archives of life but James and Steph seemed to go from strength to strength, despite the doubts of his parents about whether she would be able to cope with being the wife of a farmer. Sadly, their doubts were to be proved right when Steph came to stay for a week before Christmas. James had confided to me that he hoped that they would get engaged in the New Year, something that I saw as the beginning of the end of his freedom and our relationship. Engagement meant marriage and I didn't have any married mates and I knew that it would change my social life for the worse. After she had returned to Leeds James asked me to go for a drink with him. He was unusually quiet and seemed to brood over his pint as if he wanted to sink into it.

'Is there a problem mate?' I asked and when he looked at me such was the look of despair on his face that I thought he was going burst into tears.

He swallowed hard and with a cracking voice told me, 'Steph and I are over.' I stared at him but couldn't bring myself to ask why. He went on, 'You know we have to get up really early on the farm, well every morning I got the same old thing, couldn't I stay in bed, and then when I came back for breakfast she would still be in bed and want me to join her. She had no idea. She even told me that when we were married she wouldn't expect me to be out for so long and when I tried to explain that this was in fact the quiet time of the year she really went off on one. And, of course, my folks didn't help did they. The final straw was when she told me she wanted me to wear an engagement ring. I told her that I couldn't because it would be dangerous with all the equipment we use and she went off on one again saying that if I didn't it would prove that I didn't love her. Even when I told her that I could easily loose a finger if I got the ring caught her response was that I should get a normal job and that we could then move up to Leeds. It just made me realise that, just like Mum said, it would never work. So, I finished it and do you know I think she was quite relieved. I don't think she had really thought about what farming entailed until this week, she probably thought of it as glorified gardening. I know it's for the best but it really hurts'

'I'm sorry James,' was all I could think to say. But I thought, just what his parents wanted. For the three of us that was the finale to our Butlin's adventure. In one way or another that week had affected all our lives.

For me the rest of that Autumn had gone by uneventfully and I had taken my final accountancy examinations, over which I felt relatively confident. The weekend after the exams I even chanced an evening visit to Clacton with the lads to see Lulu and her Lovers. It wasn't my style of music but as there was a space in one of the two cars going I allowed myself to be talked into it in the full knowledge that none of my old mates or enemies would dream of attending a gig of that nature. The event was at the Town Hall and it was packed, mainly with teenagers and despite everything I had to admit that Lulu was amazing, burning through a whole raft of American R and B classics. However, the highlight of the night for some of the lads had to have been the ultra-violet lights that the venue had installed which, when the other house lights were dimmed, exposed all the girls wearing white underwear. Tom was in his element. You would have thought that he had never seen bras and pants before, but it least it kept the lads occupied and meant that no one was interested in creating trouble.

There was one other strange incident that Autumn. On coming in one evening my aunt asked, 'Have you seen What's New Pussy Cat, you know the new Peter Sellers film?' When I said that I hadn't she went on 'Well I would love to see it, there is no way your uncle will take me and none of my boring friends are up for it so will you come with me. That is if you wouldn't mind being seen out with an old lady?' I found this latter self-put-down rather sad as she was still only in her 30's and I thought that if it hadn't been for my uncle she could have still been out there enjoying life, so I agreed to accompany her to the cinema, hoping that it wouldn't become a regular expectation.

I thought that the film was okay but my aunt loved it, as we left the cinema she said, 'It was so surreal, wonderful. I don't get to see anything like that these days and the Tom Jones song, I love it.' She was like a teenager. 'Do you fancy a drink Alan? I haven't been out to a pub in years. Where do you drink?'

'The Vaults,' I said, 'but I couldn't take you in there it's full of underage drinkers, you wouldn't like it.'

'Long ago I used to go to the Red Lion is that still OK?' she said, I replied that it was and so we went into the lounge bar and sat down. 'I'd like a Gin and Tonic, a large one,' and getting some money out of her purse added, 'and have whatever you would like Alan, it's on your uncle.' We sat talking about the film and then we got onto music, 'You know I really loved to go dancing, but that was before I met Michael, that is your uncle.' I sat and nodded. 'He has never liked popular music especially Rock and Roll, I used to listen to it on the radio and thought it so exciting.' She paused and seemed to lose herself for a moment. 'But otherwise we have a good life and the children are such a joy, even if Rachael can be a bit of a handful.' We laughed about Rachael and were chatting some more while finishing our drinks when my aunt suddenly said, 'this has been such a nice evening and sitting here having a drink with an eligible young man makes me feel quite young again. Thank you Alan.'

'For goodness sake Aunt, you are still quite young.'

'I don't know about that, I feel that I am a real old fogey, life has passed me by without me noticing it.'

'You shouldn't put yourself down like that,' I said, 'since you have been listening to pop music on the radio you have become quite with-it. You should go out and get some trendy clothes, people will think you and Rachael are sisters.'

'You charmer,' she said, 'now I can see what the girls see in you. And by the way you can stop calling me Aunt that really makes me feel ancient when it comes from someone of your age.'

We finished our drinks and caught the bus home, by now Jean was quite giggly and obviously having a great time, 'I do hope Michael isn't home from his meeting he'd be really cross with me for getting squiffy.' Oh Christ, I thought, this could be another black mark against me if he thinks I led her astray. When we got back he hadn't returned from his Parochial Church Council meeting so that didn't arise but I still felt I had had a narrow escape. Jean made some coffee and said, 'I'm off to bed so he doesn't guess that I've had a drink. If he comes in soon keep him talking for a while to give me a chance to settle down.' With that she gave me a hug and a kiss on the cheek and went up. It was only as I sat there with my coffee that I realised just how flirtatious she had become over the evening and while I hoped that she was just taking the opportunity to let her hair down it made me feel good to think that we had connected in that way rather than me simply being a tolerated house guest.

Certainly, after that evening we had a far better rapport and would often find ourselves laughing over some silly situation that had arisen or discussing the latest trends. Whether it had anything to do with that evening I am not sure but Jean also started to wear more fashionable clothes, I don't mean miniskirts and ribbed sweaters, but certainly a world away from the tweeds and brogues that until then had been her trademark. I also sensed less tension between her and Rachael and often I would come home and find the Radio Caroline playing, at least when my uncle wasn't around, so maybe that evening we had together had led her to realise that she could still relate to younger people.

By now it was heading towards my second Christmas in Ipswich and I had a quiet word with my parents to make sure that they didn't accept an invitation to come up on Christmas Eve. Mum seemed to understand and I think the old man was quite pleased to have an excuse not to spent more time than he had to with Michael, so now I was able to make plans to be with my mates on Christmas Eve.

Chapter 18

Christmas Eve at the office started off with the usual early closing and Bill Jenkins' largesse up at the Rose and Crown for the men of the office. Bernard and I had already irritated Bill because we had brought a couple of bottles of Asti Spumante sparkling wine for the women to share whilst they were preparing the Christmas lunch, making his bottle of British Sherry look extremely mean, so to show his importance he paid for a second round of drinks in the pub. This, when added to the Departmental Managers buying their teams a drink, together with the drinks bought by and for individual colleagues, meant that by the time we got back to the office a good few of the guys were well away, very jovial and loud.

As we walked into the offices we were met by the rich spicy smell of Christmas. As usual the girls had done an amazing job preparing the meal and the aromas of Turkey with all the trimmings, Christmas pudding and homemade mince pies overcame the usual musty office smells that we lived with day by day. To accompany this the Clerk had provided his usual contribution of Yugoslavian Riesling and Bulgarian Bulls Blood red wine and after the puddings had been cleared he stood up,

'Ladies and gentlemen,' he called out, whilst tapping his evil smelling pipe on a glass and scattering ash into the wine. 'I have an announcement to make. Last week I informed the Chairman that on the 31st of next May I shall be retiring.' This was followed by a ripple of applause, although the expressions on people's faces showed just how surprised and shocked they were. Even though we all knew that he was approaching retirement age, no one expected him to actually go. But after a few draws on his pipe he carried on as if it was of no great importance, 'so to mark my last attendance as Clerk at our Christmas lunch I have provided some cheese and Port. You'll find it in my office if someone would care to fetch it.'

With the beer, wine and the port the place was really buzzing, lots of laughter; Wally in the corner telling his dirty jokes while some of the younger guys helped the girls clear the tables. After a while I went off to the gents and as I returned I could hear that the volume of laughter and raucous comments had increased and I pushed open the doors to the Council Chamber to see what all the noise was about. What greeted me was the sight of Col and Tom holding Tracy upside down, her skirt and petticoats hanging over her face and all the men standing and leering at her.

'*PUT HER DOWN.*' The rage in my voice must have been obvious because Col and Tom immediately did as I had demanded. 'How could you be so bloody mean?' And with that Tracy ran from the room.

'We only wanted to see if she was wearing suspenders,' Col said.

'And what colour knickers she was wearing; after all she wouldn't tell us.' Tom added

'Good for you lads, the sight of her pretty little arse has made my Christmas.' It was a good job that I didn't see who said that because I could have easily hit him.

'You perverted bastards.' I said, 'How could you be so cruel?'

The old Clerk just stood there grinning then Bill Jenkins interjected with a slurred, 'It was only a bit of seasonal fun, no harm done after all. I'll get her some chocolates after Christmas, that'll make her feel better. And you shouldn't be so sensitive young man.'

At this Bernard bundled me out of the office before I could get myself into some real trouble. 'For goodness sake Alan, don't make it any worse. Bill is likely to take over from Blenkinsopp. If you want that promotion you must stop alienating him,' Bernard said. But at that moment I really couldn't have given a shit about the promotion. Bernard went back into the party and I got my parka on to go home. I wasn't going to wish any of those jerks happy Christmas and I would certainly be having words with my two lads later when we met up. In fact, I was seriously considering giving them both a smack.

As I went into the hall Tracy was coming down the stairs. 'Are you OK?' I asked.

She nodded and putting her hand on my upper arm said, 'Thanks for what you did in there, it was very kind, but you shouldn't have, you'll get yourself into bother.'

'Don't worry about me I can look after myself.' I said, 'but you don't look so good.'

'Oh, it's too much fizzy wine, I'm not used to it.'

'How are you getting home?' I asked.

'On the bus like usual I expect,' she said.

'Come on,' I said, 'I'll give you a ride home on the scooter.'

She paused and then said, 'Well they'll all be at work so no one will see me I suppose.'

'I'm only offering you a lift.'

'I know, but I also know what my parents are like. I don't want it getting back to Jim. He can be so jealous about the daftest things.'

By the time we had got back to her place the beer had made its presence felt and I was dying for a pee, 'Can I pop in and use your toilet?' I asked as soon as we arrived. 'I should've gone before I left the office.'

'OK,' she said, 'as long as you're quick.' When I came back downstairs Tracy was standing in the front room. She turned and said, 'I really am grateful for what you did you know. It was awful having all those blokes leering at me like that.'

'That's OK.' I said, 'But those two lads are going to have to be taught some manners.' She must have heard something in my tone of voice.

'Please, don't take it out on them. I do like them, they'd had a lot to drink and it was the others who were egging them on. For my sake just leave it Ace.'

'If you insist,' I said. 'I'll just settle for a kiss instead.'

'Why would I give you a kiss?' she said.

'Well it is Christmas,' I replied. With that she stepped forward and kissed me, gently at first but then it got more intense and we fell back onto the sofa. I almost felt guilty as I slipped my hand up her skirt, negotiating the voluminous array of petticoats, and explored the area of smooth skin between her stockings and her knickers. Then, as she didn't complain, I carried on and she even started to join in. It was all very enjoyable, not something I had expected at all, but then she pulled away, sat back and biting her lower lip looked at me.

She grinned, 'I don't suppose you've got a Johnny on you?' She asked, I was almost struck speechless.

'Why?' I said, returning her smile.

She giggled, 'Well it is Christmas and every good boy deserves a treat.'

When it was over, I went upstairs to dispose of the evidence and when I came back down Tracy was staring out of the window. Without turning to look at me she said, 'You have got to promise me you won't go telling the others about this. If this got out we'd be in real trouble. Ace, you have to promise me.'

By now she was sounding quite tearful and I went over and put my arms around her, 'Don't worry Tracy, I wouldn't dream of telling anyone. That's a promise,' I said.

She turned around and stared at me, 'And don't think there will be a repeat, this was a one off. Do you understand that?' I nodded. She stood quietly for a moment and then added, 'If things were different, if I wasn't engaged. But you see it's, like, a family thing, his family and mine are old friends, they meet all the time at their works club. Even if I wanted to I couldn't change things, they've gone too far. You have to leave now I can't have my parents coming home and finding you here' and with that she virtually pushed me out of the front door.

Christmas Eve, after my session with Tracy, seemed a bit of an anti-climax even though we were supposed to go to a party at one of the nurses' flats. Even being on a promise from one of the nurses dimmed in comparison with what had happened in Tracy's front room and I couldn't even hint at that with the guys, much as I would have liked to. Her implication that if she hadn't been tied down by circumstances then we might have been able to see each other had left me confused and feeling powerless. It made me realise that, it didn't matter how important I considered myself, there were some things I couldn't control. The evening started out gently with a few pints in the Prick and Pudding and then on to a new pub, The Running Buck, but we only stopped for one drink. The place was heaving with underage drinkers all trying to outdo each other in noise and bad behaviour while the jukebox blasted out The Who's My Generation on what seemed like a continuous loop. By then there was, Tom, Col, James, myself, the girls and a couple of other guys from our Bluesville crowd. Geoff couldn't be with us as he was working the bar at the Vaults and so we went there to catch up with him. The usual crowd were in and we pushed our way to the bar, Geoff was there with a couple of barmaids working flat out. The landlord, as usual, was nowhere to be seen. We all thought he kept out of sight on nights like this so that he could deny any knowledge of underage drinking.

'Hello lads,' Geoff greeted us with his usual bonhomie, 'havin' a good night?' We all agreed that we were and ordered drinks. Geoff managed not to ring them up. 'The boss won't notice a few on a night like this.' He then went off to pull a few pints before coming back. 'It's been manic in here tonight, bloody landlord's been out back with a woman all evening and hasn't shown his face, had a bunch of schoolgirls drinking Babycham and brandy, making a nuisance of themselves with the guys. I had to tell them to leave, they gave me a right mouthful, you wouldn't have thought private school girls would know words like that. I haven't bloody stopped. I doubt I'll get to the party. And now I've got to sort those two guys out in the corner.' We just stood listening to him knowing he would tell us why without being asked. 'Maggie,' he nodded towards one of the barmaids, 'tells me that they've got one of them school girls that were in here between them and are busy touching her up, she saw them at it while collecting glasses. Maggie reckons they'll take her out back and give her one before they let her go. Buggered if I know what to do about it.' I pushed over to take a look and was shocked to see Rachael looking somewhat uncomfortable behind one of the tables, trapped between these two thick-set lads.

I went back to Geoff, 'That's my cousin, how long's she been here?' I said.

'She was with that group of schoolgirls I had to throw out, she stayed behind with those blokes.'

'*Shit*, she's only fifteen I'm going to have to do something,' I said. 'I can't let her get into trouble even if the stupid little cow deserves it.' I looked Geoff in the eyes. 'There's two ways I can do this Geoff. I can go outside and talk to one of the coppers on the Cornhill, but they will want to know why you're serving underage girls with booze. Or I can try sort it; although that might get messy.'

'Be my guest,' Geoff replied, 'try not to make too much mess'. Tom, James and Col had been listening,

'Want some help?' they asked.

'Thanks, just come over if there's any trouble.'

'You reckon you can take them both on?' Tom asked.

'I hope I won't have to.' I said, although I suspected that wouldn't be the outcome. In the event a couple of the other guys pushed through with us but I went up to the table on my own.

'Hi Rachael,' I said, 'you enjoying yourself?' She gave me a look of relief, she's scared, I thought.

The guy on her right snarled at me before she could answer. 'Piss off, she's with us, find your own tart'.

'Hey cool it man, she's my cousin I just came over to say Happy Christmas.' I said holding my hands out in front of me to show I didn't pose a threat. The disappointment on Rachael's face was obvious.

'I don't care who she is if you want a go at her you'll have to wait till we've finished,' the guy on the left said. 'I've got something here that wants to get a close look at her. Now bugger off.' As he was saying this he half stood with on hand on the table and the other rubbing his crotch.

I knew that I couldn't do anything with Rachael trapped between them and the table between them and myself. I gave Rachael what I hoped was a reassuring smile and went back to the guys. I told them, 'I am going to have to take them two out but I can't do it while they are sitting behind that sodding great table. That bloody girl has got herself in a real fix this time round.'

As I finished my beer James said, 'Alan, they've gone.' It took me a couple of seconds to realise what he was saying.

'Shit where'd they go?' I said.

Cathy replied, 'I think I saw them going out the back.' That was all I needed. We pushed our way through the throng, past the toilets and out into the back yard. It was barely lit and littered with piles of crates and stacks of empty beer barrels. At first I thought that Cathy had been mistaken and that they had gone somewhere else, then I heard a cry from the far corner of the yard which was screened by the barrels. I ran and found Rachael bent over double and being held down by one of the guys while the other, having pulled her pants down, was standing with his trousers around his ankles about to rape her. He was so intent on what he was about to get that he didn't hear me coming until I hit him as hard as I could in the kidneys. As he went down I kicked him in the crotch and then stamped on his head as he lay on the ground whimpering. Tom and Col had grabbed the second guy and the others were standing around him.

'Why aren't you giving him a bloody good hiding?' I demanded and went over and punched him in the face. He cried out and tried to shield his face with his hands, I knew I'd hurt him because I'd felt the pain that shot through my fingers when I hit him. But the red mist had descended and my response was to continue to punch him wherever I could.

Tom and Col eventually let him go and he fell to the ground but before I could start kicking him I felt James's big arms close round me, it was like being held in a vice. 'Enough, Alan, enough. You don't want to become the bad guy in all this,' and, reluctantly, I let him lead me away. My mates all looked stunned, although they had heard the story about Alex and been in a few scraps with me they hadn't seen me use that level of violence before.

Meanwhile Cathy and Maureen had taken Rachael into the ladies' toilet to sort her out and calm her down. Geoff gave me a very large scotch and when I had stopped shaking he said I'm going to have to call an ambulance and I don't think any of you should be around when they get here. I went into the Ladies to see how Rachael was.

The girls tried to shoo me out but I explained, 'I need to get her home as soon as possible, especially as there are two injured guys in the yard who may need attention. I don't want her or myself to be around if the police turn up.' In fact, Rachael seemed remarkably calm about things, although that might have simply been a combination of shock and alcohol.

Before we left the pub, I went over to the bar, 'Geoff,' I said, 'you'll have to mop up a bit of blood in the yard and you better call that ambulance, but I don't think they'll give you too much trouble now.'

'It'll be a pleasure; you've done me a good turn there; I owe you one Ace.'

I hustled Rachael out of the pub and the guys followed. I was furious with her, 'How could you be so bloody stupid, didn't you know what was happening?' She said nothing just stood there looking surly. I turned to the guys, 'You'll have to go on to the party without me, apologise to Shirley, tell her I'll catch up with her another time.'

'Maybe she'll let me instead,' Tom quipped.

'In your dreams Tom,' I said. Now I've got to get this one home. Have a great Christmas guys.' Cathy, Maureen and I walked Rachael up to the taxi rank, or more accurately guided her as the alcohol had really kicked in. Luckily, as it wasn't yet turning-out time, I was able to grab a cab quite quickly, 'you were supposed to be in by ten,' I said to Rachael. 'I dread to think what your dad's going to say?'

'I was only having a bit of fun, I didn't think that they would really do anything like that,' she said. Her naivety was scary.

'You were about to be raped,' I told her. 'It would have been no use you saying no, they would have shagged you anyway.'

She was quiet and then said, 'You won't tell Mum and Dad, will you? In an instant, she had become a child again.

'It's alright I wouldn't do that to you,' I said. 'If I were you I would tell them you were left behind by your mates and that you went looking for them, something like that anyway.'

She was quiet for a while and then as we went down the Norwich Road she spotted a group of girls. 'Stop!' she said, 'it's my friends I can walk back the rest of the way with them.'

'Not a chance.' I said and she went back into a sulk. When we arrived, I paid off the cab and led her up the steps to the front door. As we got there it was flung open by my uncle. Until then I had never understood the phrase, "his face was contorted by rage", but now I did.

'How dare you?' he bellowed. She was supposed to be back for Church at ten-thirty.' Taking in her state he said, 'what have you done to her? I knew you'd be trouble.' There was a pause as my aunt turned up.

'Has she been drinking? she asked. 'You know she's underage, how could you?' and with that she pulled her away and led her upstairs.

I was bloody cross myself by now, the assumption that this was all down to me pissed me off. I should have let her walk home with her mates I thought and gone back to the party. I didn't know what to say because I had promised not to drop her in it so said, 'I found her down town like that and paid for a cab to bring her home.' But my uncle was in no mood to listen.

'A likely story', he said. 'I want you out of my house after Christmas. I don't care where you go, as long as it isn't here. I shall tell your parents tomorrow. And if you have interfered with her in anyway I'll have the police on you.' With that he turned, stormed off and slammed the door of his study shut behind him. My aunt was looking down the stairs at me with an expression of sorrow on her face which could have meant you're lying, or just maybe it was an expression of sadness over the thought that I had let her down.

I didn't sleep well that night, mainly because I knew I would have to face my parents in the morning when they came for Christmas Day, but also because once again my life was being thrown into uncertainty. Where was I going to go? After those first months with my aunt and uncle, when I was desperate to get away, I had become quite settled and comfortable with them and they generally let me do as I liked, within their rules, which hadn't restricted me in any material way. I didn't go down for Christmas morning breakfast, I couldn't face the family and when I went to the bathroom I could hear Jean clattering about the kitchen preparing the Christmas lunch but otherwise the house sounded as if it was empty, a sort of soulnessness, which was strange for a Christmas morning.

Later that morning there was a knock on the door and Jean came in and sat on the bed. 'Rachael has finally emerged; she has a dreadful hangover; serves her right. But I have been able to talk to her and she has told me what happened, or at least her version of things. I knew there was something not right last night. I'm not sure how much of her story I believe, but she did tell me that you saved her from being raped by a couple of thugs. She also told me that she had asked you not to tell me what had happened. I'm not sure whether I should be cross with you for not doing so, but then we didn't really give you a chance, did we? I'm not going to ask you to confirm her story. I've already done that to a certain extent. One of her friends' mothers rang me this morning, worried about whether she got home alright. After a bit of questioning, her friend confirmed her story and more. It will be a long time before she will be allowed out in the town again. But what seems certain is that not only do we owe you an apology, Alan, but our thanks as well.' She got up put her arms around me and said. 'and Happy Christmas.' I couldn't help it but I felt the tears run down my face, I couldn't say anything, the fact that they accepted the truth was overwhelming. She carried on, 'When you're ready your uncle would like to see you in his office. Don't worry he knows most of the story. I've not told him the worst of what nearly happened so I would be grateful if you don't volunteer anything. What he doesn't know won't hurt him.'

By now I had composed myself and was able to say, 'Thank you, Jean, you don't know how much that means to me and Happy Christmas to you as well'. I smartened myself up and went down to see my uncle.

He was sitting behind his desk looking all the world like the G.P. he was. White shirt with a dark tie and jacket. As formal as ever, 'Take a seat Alan and Happy Christmas.'

'Happy Christmas, Uncle,' I replied with more jollity than I felt.

My uncle had a glass of something amber in front of it and he took a large swallow from it. 'Do you drink Scotch Alan?'

I paused looking for the trap but as I felt that I had nothing to lose said, 'I sometimes used to have a glass with Dad on a Sunday.'

'This is a particularly good one Alan. A gift from a grateful patient, the job does have some benefits you know.' And with that he poured me a very large glass and pushed it over to me. 'Cheers,' he said and then sat back in his chair. 'I'm sorry about last night, I jumped to a completely wrong conclusion, please forgive me.' I looked across at him and thought this is the time to make a point.

'Thank you for that Uncle. However, I am disappointed that you would think I would abuse your hospitality in that way. I would never do anything to hurt or compromise either of my cousins. My only thought was to protect her.' There was a moment or two of silence as we both enjoyed the Scotch.

'I realise that Alan and I can guess what I haven't been told,' he added vaguely. 'I hope that it won't get you into any trouble?' He looked at my hand which had swollen up overnight, 'I probably ought to have a look at that hand of yours. Make sure you've not broken it,' he said. I moved it out of sight and I wondered if he had been talking to someone about the previous night. He confirmed my thoughts when he went on, 'you must have hit someone pretty hard to have damaged it like that. I trust they deserved it? I assume that when you say you were protecting Rachael, it was from the two boys taken to hospital last night? They were quite badly hurt and kept in. We had better have a good story ready in case the police come knocking.' I simply nodded a confirmation. I was gobsmacked. My uncle obviously knew something of what had happened from his contacts at the hospital and now; was he really suggesting that he would support a story to explain Rachael and my involvement? He poured us both another scotch. In fact, he went further, 'I am prepared to say you were both back here at the time if necessary.'

I said, 'Thank you for that Uncle. Can I just say that if I hadn't got involved Rachael would have been badly hurt by those two blokes. I also want you to know that it wasn't her fault and that she wasn't with me. The two of them jumped on her as she went to the Ladies. It was just lucky that one of the girls I was with knew she was my cousin and saw it happen.' I hoped that there had been enough truth in what I said to satisfy him.

He said, 'Well in that case Alan, Jean and I have a great deal to thank you for. However, while we are talking here, there is something I want to put to you. Your presence in the house has changed things. Your social life, which I accept is nothing to do with me, except it does raise the children's expectations of what they should be allowed to do.' I sat enjoying the smoky taste of the scotch and he reached over and topped my glass up again. 'Particularly after last night, I want to put something to you. Now I don't want to sound hard Alan, but I just wonder whether it wouldn't be better for all concerned if you had a place of your own? What do you think? You've got a good job and should be able to afford it.' I thought about what he was saying and reflected on how when I first arrived I couldn't wait for a way to get out of their restrictive welcome. Now however it seemed like a huge step. Despite my pending promotion there would be deposits to pay and rent. Not to mention cooking for myself, it all seemed like a massive challenge, but I could see inevitability of it.

'I agree Uncle,' I replied and thought to myself, you might as well go with the flow as fight against it, 'I'll start looking for a place straight after Christmas.'

My uncle smiled, 'That might not be necessary Alan. A fellow G.P. up the road has a place he wants to let out. It's not much, just a basement flat, but it's up by the YMCA so convenient for your work and for the town. You could do a lot worse and I know that, if I vouch for you, he won't want any money up front.' Crafty old sod, I thought, he's been planning this all along, just waiting for the right excuse to raise the subject. And Rachael certainly gave him that last night.

Chapter 19

I moved into the flat the first week in January after Jean had come with me to have a look at it. It was larger than I expected with two bedrooms, a large sitting room and a kitchen. It was decorated throughout in magnolia which made it look dreary.

'It really smells musty, I hope it's not damp,' she said as we walked in from the concrete steps that led down from the side of a Victorian town house. 'I'll have to come and give it a good clean and airing before I can let you move in here.' And she did, even insisting that my uncle paid for a newer second-hand sofa and bed. 'The existing ones aren't fit for use,' she said, 'and they're what makes the flat smell.' Mum came up trumps as usual and provided new linen, rugs and some decent pots and pans so that by the time I moved in the place looked quite respectable.

Dad's contribution was a case of beer, 'To keep you going son,' he said, 'and don't you bring too many girls back now you've got a new bed,' he added with a wink.

'You'll have to make sure you keep it clean and make sure you feed yourself properly,' Mum said.

'You don't have to worry about that Yvonne,' Jean said, 'I am going to come in and do a bit of tidying once a week and Alan is coming for his tea on Thursdays and for his Sunday lunch so we'll make sure he don't starve.' While this appeased my mother, I couldn't help but feel that there was an element of competition going on between the two sisters each wanting to keep an eye on me. What Jean would do if she caught a girl staying was something I didn't want to think about, especially given that having girls to stay was one the main things that I did think about.

It certainly was a new experience living on my own and looking after myself. The independence was almost overwhelming. Having to make most of my own decisions, shopping and preparing meals for myself was completely new to me. For the first week or so, I lived almost entirely out of tins, even managing to explode a Fray Bentos tinned steak and kidney pie when I overheated it. After that I started to eat a little more healthily and found that I enjoyed cooking for myself and, most nights it seemed, for one or more of my mates for whom having a meal at my place became the latest novelty.

When Maureen heard about the flat she said, 'God, I expect that will be a right tip,' and then speaking on behalf of the other girls added, 'we won't be coming round if we have to wade through dirty clothes and underwear.' So, it became a matter of pride that I kept the place looking tidy which of course was helped by Jean coming in on a Wednesday and taking my washing away. Invariably she would still be there on a Wednesday evening when I got in from work with a pot of tea waiting and something in the oven for my tea. I was still managing to be spoilt as part of my independence. Not that it was all roses. The main heating in the flat was a couple of electric storage heaters which were not only inefficient but expensive to run and the paraffin heater that I had to supplement them made the whole place smell. However, none of that mattered because the flat was mine and no one could tell me what I should do, or when.

The flat was situated below another doctor's surgery which meant that it was empty at weekends and quickly my parties became the stuff of legend. The music was loud, the booze was plentiful and the only place out of bounds was my bedroom which was reserved for my use with whoever I had hooked up with at the time, and it certainly got plenty use. I loved it. This was the independence I had always dreamt of.

It was the middle of February when I met Sophie. She had gone to the girls' private school with Maureen.

'She was on a scholarship and a lot of the other girls looked down on her so I took her under my wing,' Maureen said. Scholarship girl or not she was stunning, long blond hair flicked up at the ends, very slim like a model and a stylish dress sense all of which stood her apart from a lot of the other girls. She had only just started to come to Bluesville because until Christmas she had been at school and her parents wouldn't let her come out during the week. However, she had left school at Christmas and was now working as a secretary.

'Some sort of falling out at home and her father, a nasty bastard apparently, refused to pay any of the extras she needed at school' Maureen said when I asked about her. I really fancied Sophie and she would also look great on the back of my scooter. 'Be careful Alan,' Maureen said, 'she can be a little strange and I don't want you to get into any trouble.'

'What do you mean?' I asked.

'I shouldn't say,' Maureen said, 'but last year she decided that she wanted to lose her virginity and she went out the following weekend and just asked some lad in the park if he wanted to do it. It was if it was some step in a plan that she had.' I just shrugged my shoulders, it would work for me; with my new independence access to easy sex was just what I was looking for.

The following Friday, on our first date, she ended up in my bed but as I was putting the johnnie on she put her hand on my chest and whispered, 'Don't bother.' At first, I thought she meant that she didn't want to go through with, but it wasn't that. She didn't want me take precautions. While I may be daft, that wasn't a risk I was prepared to take.

'Can I stay the night?' she asked later.

'Won't your parents be expecting you?' She pulled a face.

'I 'spose so, I didn't say I wouldn't be back and Mum might worry. Have you got a phone?'

'No,' I said, 'I think this time it would better if I got you home.' This was too fast for me.

The following Friday however she turned up after work with an overnight bag.

'Can I stay this time?' We had agreed to meet in the Vaults that evening and this took me completely by surprise, but as I was looking forward to having her that evening I didn't feel that I had any choice.

'OK.' I said, 'but we'll meet up with the others first as planned.' I didn't want to waste the whole Friday evening staying in with her and I certainly wasn't going to let her try to rule my life like Sally had. That night was the first of what became a regular weekend occurrence, she would turn up on Friday and I would take her home usually on Sunday morning, unless I could get rid of her on Saturday night. I had never had so much sex, it was amazing. There were two things however that I found strange, in fact disturbing. Every time we went to bed she would try to get me to do it 'bareback'.

'I don't like johnnies. Can't you do something else.' Then she began to say that I was scared and that, if I really liked her, I should be prepared to take risks as it gave a lot better sensation. I would have liked to, who wouldn't, but I didn't want to get her up the spout. That would have destroyed all the independence I had just gained. The other thing I also found strange was that whenever we had sex she just laid back and took it. She never joined in or even moved about, it was like having sex with a shop dummy. I expected more; even with the quick sessions I had been used to the girls tended to participate in some way or another, but not Sophie, she would get undressed lay down and wait for me to get on with the business. Over a weekend, we would be at it a lot, but every time it was the same.

'Do you have to use one of those things? You're just chicken, let's just give it a go without, go on just the once. Nothing will happen, I can make sure I don't get pregnant.' Sophie had also started to hint that she wanted to share the flat with me,

'Wouldn't it be nice if I didn't have to go home. It would be fun, we could play house; I could cook for you and everything,' she would say, usually after we had had sex. But I was having none of it; I was enjoying my life too much. Why would I want to curtail that? I was happy for her to come around for sex but I wasn't ready for any other sort of relationship and having to share every weekend with her was already beginning to rub thin.

We had been going out for five weeks, when it unexpectedly came to a head. We were in bed on the Saturday morning and I rolled over onto her and as I was about to slip inside her she grabbed me, ripped the johnnie off my old man and then managed to slip onto me.

'For Christs sake, what's your game?' I said pulling out. She went berserk.

'You wimp, you fucking wimp,' she said, 'I just want to do it properly. It's much nicer that way but you're not man enough to fuck me properly. If you were a real man you fucking would, then you'd like it, but you're just a fucking scared little boy.' All the time that she was saying this she was punching me and I had to leave the bed to escape. I had become used to the fact that the girls I now knew didn't swear and Sophie's tirade of bad language un-nerved me.

'Hey calm down, what's wrong with you? Stop hitting me.' She had followed me off the bed and was slapping me as hard as she could. She then grabbed a book that I had been reading and started hitting me around the head with it. I grabbed her arms to stop her. 'Calm down Sophie,' I repeated. 'It's not a big issue.' This seemed to inflame her more and she kneed me as hard as she could in the balls. I let her go and gasped for breath through the pain.

'I want to fuck a real man, someone who will do me like I want. Not you, you fucking little wimp. You won't even let me move in with you, you're just frightened of everything. I'm going to Maureen's. You can decide whether you want proper sex on tap or want to skulk around with scared little girls.' With that she got herself dressed and left. I sat on the bed in agony rubbing my balls and hoping that I wouldn't have any bruises on my face. The next thing I knew there was a banging on the door.

'Police, open up.' I limped to the door just in my underpants. A couple of coppers stood there.

'A young lady has just stopped us and said that she had been attacked.'

'She's been attacked? It was her who was doing the attacking, she kicked me in the balls.'

'Well she would if she was being assaulted and wanted to get away wouldn't she. You can't blame her for that. We'll have to ask you to come down to the station with us to answer some questions now get some clothes on.' I was by now getting concerned. How could I prove that it was her?

'What about her? I asked.

'That's not for you to worry about lad, she's being looked after.' I spent the rest of the day at the police station. They wanted to all the details of my relationship with Sophie, pushing and pushing for the most intimate details until I wasn't sure that they weren't getting off on the whole thing. Then they brought in a doctor to examine me.

'Why do I have to go through this? I said. 'Is it really necessary?' What I was worried about was that the medical profession was a very close-knit community and it was bad enough being suspected of attacking Sophie without it getting back to my uncle.

'Have you seen yourself? said one of the interviewing officers. 'It might well be to your advantage to have the doc look at you.' I hadn't seen myself in a mirror since arriving at the station and didn't understand at that time what he meant. 'Anyway lad, you don't have a choice.' I was shown into another room. 'Get undressed, down to your pants, the doc will be in as soon as.' When I had done as I was told I stood there and had a chance to look down at my body. During the hours that I had been questioned the blows that she had delivered had turned into bruises. In none of the fights I had been involved in over the years had I received such a pasting, I knew she had hit me hard but hadn't realised just how many blows she had actually managed to land. Christ Almighty, this was going to take some living down with my mates when I got out. And of course, I thought, this just proves there was a fight and the police had already made it clear who's story they believed. During the day, I had so much on my mind that I had all but overlooked the discomfort I was in, but now standing there in my underpants in that cold, stark, white painted room I could feel every bruise and my bollocks still ached from the kick she had given me.

The doctor, when he entered the room was a surprise, he was quite young and dressed fashionably, not at all like the old fuddy-duddies that I had been used to seeing. Despite that he was very professional and gave me a thorough examination,

'Right drop your pants,' he said, 'I understand you have been kicked in the vitals, let's have a look.' I did as I was told and cupping my balls in his hand he said, 'cough.' After a further examination, he said, 'well young man, the good news is that it's only bruising, both on your body and your testicles, and all that will ease with a bit of rest. However, your Technicolor face might take a day or so to fade.' This was the first I had heard any reference to my face,

'What do you mean my face doctor? I said.

'Haven't you looked in a mirror? You look as if you have just done ten rounds with Henry Cooper.' Shit there was no way then that I was going to be able to keep this quiet even if I did get out of there.

'Doctor,' I said, 'I don't know if you've seen Sophie, but can't you see that I'm the one who has been hurt, not her.'

'That's not for me to say Alan, all I can do is report my findings,' he said, then after looking over his shoulder in a mock conspiratorial manner, 'But I'd be surprised if they keep you in here much longer.'

After I had dressed, I was taken back to the interview room and they brought me a cup of tea and a cheese sandwich. My last meal had been the evening before and until then I hadn't realised how hungry I was. All the police had given me during the day had been mugs of tea. By then it was late afternoon and I was getting really pissed off. If it was going to be this serious, maybe I would have to phone my father and get him to help me, although didn't relish that for one moment. But no-one came in, so I couldn't ask what I could or couldn't do regarding contacting someone to help. Not only was I pissed off, I was becoming more and more scared. Guys who had been arrested after the Whitsun weekend at Clacton had told how the police kept them inside without telling them anything and how they then had been bullied and intimidated after they had been kept in custody overnight. God, I didn't fancy that. Maybe I should have asked for a solicitor before now, but I hadn't done anything.

Eventually the door opened and an officer I hadn't seen before came in and introduced himself as Inspector some-thing -or-other, I was too worried to take it in. 'Righty-o son,' he said, 'The Quack has given us his report and it seems that you may have been telling my lads the truth. He couldn't find any injuries on the young lady but you seem to have taken a right pasting. Not much of a man are you letting her do that to you? Anyway, you are free to go, sign for your things on the way out.' When I had retrieved my things from the front desk I said,

'What is that it then, don't I get a lift home?

The desk sergeant laughed and said, 'Think yourself lucky son we might have kept you overnight just for fun. I've got a daughter about her age and if I thought she was being messed about by some little toe-rag like you it wouldn't be her you'd have to worry about. Now shove off.' I found a cab in town but it had taken me a fair bit of time to limp to the taxi rank and by the time I got home I was feeling pretty ill. Looking in the bathroom mirror at the bruises on my face didn't make me feel any better at all. So, I simply made myself a mug of coffee took some aspirin and went to bed to try to sleep it off.

It was 10:30 the next morning before I woke up and I took a few seconds to realise that what had woken me was someone banging on the door. Oh please, not the police again I thought. I hurt all over and slowly made my way to the door, once again just wearing my underpants because if it was them I didn't want to antagonise them by making them wait. I opened the door and there stood Maureen, she turned and waved and her father's Jaguar pulled away from the curb. 'Ace what on earth has happened to you, did the police do that to you? I'll get Daddy to speak to them if they did. Oh my god, you look awful.' I still felt woozy and went into the kitchen and sat at the table. Maureen went through to the bedroom and got a dressing gown. 'Put that on for goodness sake, I'll stop fancying you if I have to look at you like that for much longer.'

I appreciated the attempt to lighten the mood and said, 'be a love and put the kettle on and then you can tell me what you know.' Maureen related how Sophie had turned up at hers in a Police car the previous afternoon, it was alright for some I thought, and told her that she had reported me to the police, out of spite, after a row that we had had and how the police had arrested me. She also told Maureen that the police had somehow found out that she was lying and had taken some persuasion not to take her home to her parents.

Maureen said, 'Sophie lied and told them that she didn't live at home and the police apparently believed her, especially when she said she lodged at mine. You know how close Daddy is to the Police. We took her home this morning and then I got Daddy to drop me here. He doesn't believe a word she said by the way and I was worried about you as well. I got Daddy to ring them last night and they said you had been released with no charges.' In the stress of the previous day I had forgotten that Maureen's father was a solicitor, otherwise I might have been tempted to contact him. 'That's all I know Ace. What really happened, how did you get those bruises? Then she paused, 'Sophie did that to you, didn't she? She has always had a short fuse. Please tell me the truth. I know she's a friend of mine but I can't help her if I don't know what happened.' And so, I related parts of the story to her and when I told her about her wanting unprotected sex Maureen put her head in her hands. 'I tried to warn you Ace, but you seemed to think that you could look after yourself. Sophie is having a terrible time at home, I think her father hits her.' Again, she paused before adding. 'If not worse. She is desperate to get away. I think she saw you as a way out.'

'I don't blame you Maureen,' I said. 'She's a friend and you have to stand by them, don't you? I,' for a while I couldn't find the words. 'I was just so scared yesterday. Please don't tell the guys that I said that, but God I was so scared. We mustn't let her near any of the other blokes.'

Maureen laughed and said, 'She won't be interested in the others. You had a good job and a flat, what could any of the others give her, most are going off to college next year and she certainly wouldn't be interested in the two you work with.'

It was then I remembered that it was Sunday and due for lunch at my aunts. 'I've got to go,' I said, 'if I don't turn up Jean will come looking to see if I am alright. God my uncle is going to have a field day over this, he'll love it.'

'Don't worry Ace' Maureen said, 'I've got some concealer and make-up here. I bet I can disguise the worst of the bruises on your face for you, if you'll let me.'

While this worked up to a point, as soon as I arrived for lunch Rachael said, 'Are you wearing make-up?' and this caught the attention of Jean who came over to inspect me.

'Now what have you been up to? She asked and when I was reluctant to reply she shooed Rachael out of the kitchen. 'Now tell me what happened? She said.

'I was beaten up by my girlfriend' I said. Jean almost collapsed with laughter, not the response I expected or even would have hoped for given the discomfort I was still in.

'Oh dear,' She said, 'Fancy that. I know I shouldn't laugh but maybe now you'll be a bit more careful about who you go out with.' I felt quite hurt that she was so unsympathetic and I went on to tell her about how Sophie had had me arrested and what had happened at the police station which again for some reason she also seemed to find amusing.

'Do you think Uncle will hear about this from the doctor? I asked. 'Because he seemed to know all about the incident at Christmas.'

'I doubt it,' Jean replied, He got that from his contacts at the hospital but doesn't have so much to do with the Police Medical Examiners. Now let me have a proper look at your face. Mmm, you're certainly going to brighten up the town with those bruises, Maureen's not done a bad job in disguising them, but you'll need a good story for work tomorrow. Now Maureen, that's the sort of girl you should be looking for.'

Chapter 20

I wouldn't have thought it possible but my encounter with Sophie managed to put me off girls for a bit. I suppose you could say that it dented my confidence, I didn't want to leave myself vulnerable like that again so, despite having my own place, I stopped inviting girls back for a while. It somehow felt safer. However, at work things were going from strength to strength and Bernard was relying more and more on my input and ideas for bringing the old processes up to date. I had passed my final exams and was now a qualified accountant, Bernard had shown me the department's budget proposal that he had submitted for the next year, which included money for appointing me as Deputy Finance Officer. I knew that he was getting anxious that I might leave Stour Council for a promotion elsewhere and what he was proposing would give me not only a substantial raise in pay but, equally important, a significant raise in status.

'All you have to do is keep your nose clean Alan. Don't go upsetting Bill. It has certainly helped that you're seen as a steadying influence on the other two lads.' I couldn't help but smile at this. How different my work persona was from that within my social life where I was perceived as anything but a good influence on anyone, let alone Tom and Col. All in all, 1966 was shaping up to be another great year.

Socially life was good, Ipswich still attracted some of the best club bands around and even my cousins and their friends were starting to listen to bands like The Spencer Davis Group who had topped the charts with Keep on Running. This was again almost seen as a betrayal by the Mods who had supported them over the years. Our music was supposed to be the cutting edge, new, a bit inaccessible. It was pop music that made the charts and we disapproved of all of that. However, our narrow view of what was acceptable was being challenged by the chart success of more and more soul artists like Otis Redding and Lee Dorsey who we had been hearing on imported discs played between acts in the clubs for some time and who were still producing the dance tracks of choice. The Pier Pavilion in Felixstowe was also attracting some big names. They had already announced that The Who would be performing in the Autumn and, although we liked to say that they were merely a pop band and nothing to do with real Mods, this was generating a fair bit of anticipation. However, what was exciting me more was the news that they had booked The Yardbirds. I had first heard them at The Crawdaddy Club in Richmond in 1963 when they were being used by Sonny Boy Williamson as his backing band. At that time, they had Eric Clapton as their guitarist and, even then, he shone out above the other guitarists on the club circuit. The live album of that gig had, however, only just been released and listening to it created in me bitter-sweet memories of the good times I had growing up down in London. How long ago that all seemed. The Yardbirds however had moved even further away from their early interpretations of American Blues and some people criticised them for selling out, not least of all Eric Clapton, who had left them because of their change of direction, and who we now saw at Bluesville playing with John Mayall. I however loved The Yardbird's new material which seemed to be taking a different direction to the other bands. Their first single of 1966 also seemed to speak to me in its title, "The Shape of Things to Come". This was the future and my future looked good.

I still had thoughts about sneaking down to London to see them in one of the clubs, although when I suggested that to my parents my father said, 'Max and his family still rule the roost down here and they've long memories, so you'd better keep on steering clear of the manor for the foreseeable.' He went on, ''cause I've also heard that he's been doing more enforcin' for them Krays, some are sayin' that he might 'ave been involved in that murder of the guy that they found around this way in a suitcase.' That murder had been a cause celebre around Ipswich in the recent months as the body in the suitcase had been found on a rubbish dump in a village just down the road and, while the police claimed to have no leads, the grapevine was sure that it was a London gang murder. The thought that Max may have been so close to hand worried me for some time and I realised that I couldn't even start to hope to go to any gigs back in London.

If that information had been a shock to me it was nothing compared to the shock that came with my parents the next time they visited. I had kept up my correspondence with my old school friend Bruce's sister even after I moved to Ipswich. Sherry was a couple of years younger than me but it was her that I had kept in touch with over the years. Not that I told my mates I had a pen pal, that would have sounded soft. Her letters were always sent to my old address; I didn't even dare tell her where I was. Sherry kept me informed about the music and youth scene in California and in turn I kept her up to date with on the same from the UK perspective. Sherry painted conflicting images of a dynamic changing society, but one that was still controlled by the establishment and how that control was being resisted by the young people of California. She told of violence, shootings and of beatings by the LAPD. Her own take on resisting the establishment though was through music and from late 1965 she had been unsuccessfully trying to turn me on to the music of the Californian counter-culture. Psychedelic she called it.

My parents brought the letter to me as they usually did, it had languished at theirs for a week because they had waited to bring it with them on one of their visits, after all how important could a letter from a pen pal be? I opened it and stared with disbelief. It was only a short letter,

Dear Alan,
I can't say this in any other way. Bruce has been killed in Vietnam. They haven't found his body. They say it was a firefight in some jungle village. Mummy and Daddy wanted me to let you know.
Love are sustaining me: try them.
Sherry.

This letter seemed to break the bounds of my childhood. My friends were old enough to die. We all knew about Vietnam and most of us opposed the US for its policy there. I had also known that Bruce had been drafted to serve out there but to have been killed that just didn't seem real. Why hadn't I written to Bruce instead of his sister? But boys don't do that, it wasn't cool.

I showed the letter to my parents and, if anything they were even more shocked than I was, they had met Bruce's parents at school functions and Marcus was the first black man that my father had had to confront as an equal. 'They're not as bad as you'd imagine,' was his enlightened comment at the time, but then in reference to his white wife, 'although I don't like the idea of black and white getting together like that. It's the children I worry about.' We had argued about this and he concluded it by stating, 'well I hope you don't have any thoughts about the sister. I don't want no picaninnies in our family thank you very much!'

After Mum had read the letter, she said, 'It's so sad; how can they let their children go off to get killed like that. But it's nice that Sherry says she has her love for him to sustain her.' It took me some time to realise that Sherry was talking about the band Love, who she had been talking about in her previous letters. I didn't have the heart to tell Mum.

After hearing of Bruce's death, I found myself more and more reflecting on how violence could change life so. First there had Julie who had been so damaged by Max's violence that she had killed herself and now Bruce who had been killed, through no fault of his own, by the violence imposed on him by his country and I began to question my own involvement with violence in the past. Had any of it, even that used to help others, really been justifiable? It was a question that throughout that spring that I kept returning to.

On the day of The Yardbirds gig I went shopping and bought myself a pair of tweed hipster trousers with cuffs that were angled back towards the heel to accommodate higher heel boots. This was necessary because I had also spent a lot of money on a pair of Cuban-heeled boots. These I had specially ordered after seeing them in a magazine and I knew that, with the dark jacket that I already owned, the overall look would ensure that my position as a style leader in the area would be reinforced. I carefully dressed to go out that evening, Old Spice aftershave and all, when I was ready I admired myself in the full-length mirror I had bought. My god, I thought, but you look good. James picked me up on the way through and we met the others in a pub in Felixstowe for a few drinks before the gig. The girls were all over me, they loved the new look and I walked over to the Pier Pavilion arm in arm with Maureen and Cathy. The car park was full of scooters and a few cars.

'Wow,' Geoff said, 'look at that. It's one of the new Ford Cortina GTs.' I had to admit, it was a good-looking, car painted in a metallic powder blue and obviously, brand new. They all stopped to admire it.

I said to James, 'Two-a-penny down in North London, any Jack the Lad working on the track at Dagenham would be able to have one at a knock off price. I prefer your Cooper, more style.'

'Better than a scooter though.' Col said. 'I wouldn't mind one.'

Maureen added, 'It's very pretty, you should get one Ace then you could take me for a ride.' This latter remark accompanied by a squeeze of the arm. Everything seemed to be going my way. I was feeling so upbeat that I bought everyone in my group a drink when we got into the Pier Pavilion. The supporting act was a local Ipswich band, The Sullivan James Band whose line up included a trombonist and with that they could put down a really solid grove. The whole place was buzzing and the floor was full of people dancing. As usual we commandeered a space in the middle of the floor. Parkas, handbags, coats and other valuables were place in the middle of the space and any interlopers quickly dissuaded from staying. This was our special evening, we were a clique and tonight we wanted to celebrate that.

At the break, more drinks were ordered and James, Geoff and Col went off to do the honours while we watched the roadies set up for The Yardbirds. By the time the guys got back from the crush at the bar the band were almost ready to go on stage and we moved forward to make sure that we had a good view. I stood behind Cathy and put my arms around her waist and she leant back so that I was supporting her. That felt good too, holding her in my arms. I had already reached the conclusion that my next conquest was going to be either Cathy or Maureen, the time was right, I just had to decide which of them it was going to be. It would be good to hook up with one of them for the summer, both looked great on the back of my scooter and both would be going to university in the autumn so there would be a natural break point if I wanted it.

'Oi, watch-it.' someone had shoved me hard in the back and I wasn't going to put up with that. I turned and froze.

'Well look who it ain't, you've made my day Ace my son. I'd given up hope of running into you.' Max stood there with three of his soldiers including the two who had grassed me up over Julie. They were dressed in, what had become the look of choice for the hard mods, tight fitting Ben Sherman shirts, shiny suits and heavy boots. A look that would later be taken over by the kids who would evolve into skinheads.

At that moment the MC announced, 'Boys and Girls, The Yardbirds.'

I panicked. I was with all my mates, I should have backed in amongst them, they would have given me some protection, but no, I ran. The band struck up, I ran; ran like a terrified animal, pushing through the audience as the opening chords were played, the beat of the bongo drums seemed to pick up the pace as I ran, crashing through the first set of doors, to the sound of "For your Love." The lyrics followed as I ran across the foyer and out of the main doors. I continued towards the car park, the music fading as it followed me, but above it all I could hear the slap of heavy rubber soles behind me creating a base backbeat as I dodged between the parked cars and scooters. I would have had a chance if I had been wearing my Desert boots but in the new Cuban heels there was no way I could out run them. They caught me in the middle of the car park and I swung round to face them. Lashing out I caught one of them with a good punch, but then they were all over me, I felt the first few punches, stumbled and went over. Then the kicking started; it seemed to keep time with the repetition of the lyrics. I recall little more until two of Max's soldiers pulled me to my feet and one said, 'Gor'n Max cut 'is fuckin' face off.' I clearly heard the metallic snap of a switch blade and a shout,

'Leave him alone you bastards.' Then, except for the distant music, silence, although I seem to remember hearing Max,

'Oh fuck.' He turned, hit me again and I fell backwards.

Chapter 21

When I regained consciousness in hospital my mum and dad were sitting at my bed side. I couldn't take anything in and all my surroundings seemed to be in the negative with the monochrome walls and the all-pervading smell of antiseptic. It felt as though I was in some strange sepia picture. I managed to ask, 'What happened?'

'Don't worry about that now, we'll tell you about it when you come round properly,' Dad replied. 'It's good enough for now to have you back with us.' Mum was crying and couldn't speak. 'For now, just rest, you've had a really bad time. Do you remember anything? I had some vague recollections, some memories would become clearer later, but at that time none would fix themselves in my mind, it was like trying to recall a dream.

I discovered later that I had lost the best part of a week and had had a series of operations. A couple of days later, whilst on his rounds, the surgeon said, 'You were very lucky young man, if you had hit your head just a little harder you may not have recovered and the internal injuries from the beating you were given took some fixing, I can tell you. It's been a long time since I saw such a mess. You had a ruptured spleen, other internal bleeding and bruising to your kidneys. By the way do you feel ready to talk to the police? I've been keeping them at bay but they are anxious to talk to you as soon as you feel you can make some sense.' I had been aware that my speech was strange but that was the first time anyone had made a direct reference to the fact.

'Why can't I always get the right words out?' I managed to ask, even then I needed to pause to find the right words

'It's all to do with the bang you had on the head, you were lucky not to need another operation to relieve the pressure on your brain, but I'm confident your speech will return to normal quite quickly. Now about the police?' We agreed that I would talk to them for a short time the next day. I certainly wasn't at all prepared for the shock of what Dad told me that evening. They came in apparently full of their usual bonhomie but I could tell that this evening it wasn't natural. After the usual enquiries about how I was doing, they sat down and Dad took a deep breath.

'They tell me you're seeing the police tomorrow,' he said. 'You don't have to if you don't want, but if you are going to talk to them there are things you need to know. There's no easy way to tell you this, but during the fight your mate Col, he got stuck with a blade, he was killed. I'm sorry Alan, I know you was close. They didn't want us to tell you until you were out of the woods but you had to know before the Old Bill came knocking.' I tried to speak but the words just choked in my throat. Mum was crying and I could feel tears running down my face. 'It were that thug Max done it.' Under the stress Dad reverted to his East London background. 'They got 'im and 'is mates down the A12, south of Colchester. Got 'im bang to rights, your mates blood was on his sleeve. The police have spoken to me and I thought it best to tell them about your history with Max. So, you'll 'ave to come clean abart it all, it'll be for the best, trust me son.' I couldn't take it in. I just lay there in shock; how could Col be dead? It wasn't possible. How could it have happened? He'd been so full of life that night. None of it made any sense they were attacking me; he wasn't even there.

It took me some time to put together what happened, the police filled in some of it and, once I was allowed visitors beyond my close relations, friends filled in the rest. The police were however generally sympathetic, especially after I had come clean about the bad blood between Max and I. James and Geoff were some of the first ones allowed to visit, 'Christ boy you look rough,' Geoff said, James was more circumspect, but their presence made me feel better nonetheless. There wasn't the air of gloom that pervaded when my parents visited.

After I had managed to get the sentences together to tell them about my injuries I said, 'What really happened, how did Col get stabbed?

It was James who told the story, 'When you ran, Cathy screamed, she seemed to sense that something was badly wrong and Col was the first to react when we saw those guys chasing you out. We chased after you with the others, but Col was way ahead of us, you know how fast he could move when he had to. We heard him shout as he got to where they were giving you a kicking. One of them turned and the next thing I saw was Col falling. He didn't make a sound, just went down. But what I do know was that it was the big guy who did it, then he just turned around and hit you again before running off to that blue Cortina.'

Chapter 22

The summer of 1966 was my lost summer. That season was taken up by recovery and convalescence. three weeks in the Ipswich General Hospital, a grim old Victorian complex, followed by two weeks at the Bartlet convalescence home on the sea front at Felixstowe. That was the last place I wanted to return to but I was given no choice in the matter. Naturally I had visitors. My mother had come up to stay with her sister straight after the attack and was a daily visitor and she tried to entertain me with stories about what was happening in Romford and of her shopping trips with my aunt. The time that she spent with me dragged by, despite her best efforts. Bernard would pop in once or twice a week and fill me in on the office news. 'You know Mr B. is retiring, well they've given his job to Bill Jenkins, so we can all expect some changes and modernisations.' I grimaced, 'Oh that will be a good thing surely?' Bernard continued. 'It will mean that as soon as you get back I will be able to formally appoint you as my deputy and we will be able to move the whole place forward. That will give you something to look forward to.'

Tom also remained a stalwart friend visiting often and, when I got to Felixstowe, smuggling in bottles of booze. Tom kept me abreast of the office gossip. It was different when the other guys I knew visited; it was uncomfortable; Col had grown up with most of them and you could tell by the way they spoke that they missed him and, it seemed obvious to me, that they held me at least partly to blame. When they came, they gave the impression that the visits were getting in the way of their usual routines and needed to be ended as soon as possible. The exception to this were James and Geoff, they were constant visitors and they at least manged to make me laugh as they recalled our previous summer's Butlins holiday. They also brought me the outstanding news of the summer. 'You'll never guess what? Len and Sophie are getting married. He's got her in the club, the silly bugger,' James said. Anyway, they get hitched at the end of the month, the Registry Office.'

'Do you reckon you'll be able to get there?' Geoff asked. I shrugged my shoulders but I knew that wouldn't happen.

The only girls from the group who visited were Maureen and Cathy. 'Don't take it personally, some of the other girls would come but their parents have told them not to, you're seen as a bad influence.' Cathy told me. 'But then you always were.' Maureen said, with a saucy smile on her lips. The two girls would flirt outrageously with me and usually they would end up giggling about some or other inappropriate comment or suggestion, during one memorable visit Maureen decided to try and put her hand down my pyjamas to give me physical stimulation and she tried to reach under the covers. 'Bloody hell have they nailed these down?' She muttered as the NHS bed making did its best to prevent the intimate contact that she was proposing. But that was as far as it went.

'What's going on here?' A particularly prickly Sister appeared from down the ward, 'I'll have to ask you to leave if we have any more of that behaviour.' The two girls blushed bright red and sat back demurely.

'I was only trying to make him more comfortable.' Maureen said.

'Oh, I'm sure you were, well I won't have that sort of behaviour in my ward.' After she had moved on both girls collapsed into fits of giggles until once again they were told to behave. After they had left I lay in bed reflecting on what had happened and how Col would have loved that story. Then the realisation came that he would never hear it; we would never have those moments again and what seemed like a dense black cloud descended and threatened to smother me. The tears flowed and I sobbed uncontrollably while that same prickly Sister came and sat quietly next to, me holding my hand until I regained some control.

Two other regular visitors became very important to me. The first was a real surprise; Tracy would pop in two or three times a week after work, usually with Debbie but sometimes on her own, bringing fruit and sweets and a kind of gentle company I wasn't used to but found comforting. The visits rarely lasted more than fifteen minutes and the conversations were very stilted but as an act of kindness they were unrivalled and I looked forward to them more and more. However, after I was moved to Felixstowe the visits had to stop as she had no means of transport and she couldn't ask her fiancé for a lift down to see me. The other regular visitor was the Reverend Dick. From the start, he would just come and sit quietly with me for a time. Then after a few visits started to gently talk to me about the incident and try to draw out of me my feelings about what had happened. Never did he preach or judge but spoke to me as if we had been lifelong friends. He had gone to Col's funeral and was the only one of my visitors who could talk to me about it. 'I said a small prayer on your behalf,' he said. 'I know Peter wasn't a believer but I'm sure he wouldn't have minded.' I thought back to Reg with his unshakeable belief and found myself envying the comfort that it seemed to give these two remarkable men. During his visits whilst he didn't refer to the bible specifically, he did stress the importance of believing in something good that wouldn't die with us and how we should all try and find ways of living our lives positively without causing pain to others. I truly believe that it was he who not only started my healing process but enabled me to start questioning who I was. If I had been going back to the flat on my own I think they would have kept me in the Bartlet even longer and that would have driven me mad. However, my aunt and uncle decided that that wasn't going to happen and that I should have my old room back.

'That way we can keep an eye on you,' my aunt explained, 'and you'll have a doctor in the house if you need one.' There were no warnings about how I was to behave or any of the lectures I might have expected just a genuine warm welcome back into the family. My uncle even got his colleague to let me give up the flat, to save me having to paying rent, until I was ready to go back. One evening shortly after returning I gave my aunt and uncle a frank account of what had gone on in Romford before I had come to live with them. I felt that I owed them the truth before it all came out in Court and I like to think that they welcomed that.

That Summer, the Summer of 1966, saw my world change: my music, the sounds of the mods, changed. I had thought that the R and B, Blues and Soul music of my era would be the soundtrack for youth forever but music was taking new routes. It was dividing and mutating like a cancer in its inexorable growth. Indeed, my memories of the Summer of 1966 perceived whilst drifting through a blue haze of recuperation from both the physical and mental traumas, would be of musical change. Sometimes the days of that summer seemed to be just a blur but at last, gradually, I started to feel my life returning and my speech was steadily returning to normal. The first sign of this was finding the interest to sit with Geoff, my uncle and my cousin Peter watching the World Cup final, although in later years I would never be able to recall any detail of that afternoon.

Musically, I did as my American friend Sherry had suggested when she wrote to tell me of Bruces' death and obtained an imported copy of Love's first album and subsequently I got Mum to find some albums by some of the other new US bands that Sherry had recommended like the Grateful Dead and Jefferson Airplane. Psychedelia interacted with the paranoia of my convalescence and awoke my interest in the new music. This music didn't hark back to my past lives, it was new and full of colour and obscure movement and unlike tracks from the past, especially if they were even vaguely associated with Col, didn't reduce me to tears My cousins hated this new music, Jean couldn't understand it but my uncle, while not enjoying the experience, seemed to recognise the good it was doing pulling me away from the past and he actually encouraged me to listen to the albums.

His motives became clearer after lunch one Sunday afternoon. 'Alan, I am worried about the medication they are giving you,' he said. 'Do you know what you are taking?' I shrugged my shoulders. 'You're taking Barbiturates for depression and your pain killers are opiate based. Does that mean anything to you?'

I simply said, 'No. So, what?'

My uncle continued. 'I know you will know of Purple Hearts; well they're a barbiturate. And the pain killers are opiate based, like

Heroine. I think you are in danger of becoming addicted to both.' This gave me a real jolt. It explained the feelings of being out of it while at the same time having feelings of euphoria and then plunges into despair. He said, 'I think, if you will agree, that we should try to wean you off both medications. Personally, I don't think you need the pain killers anymore.' He paused to judge my reaction.

'But it still hurts,' I said. I was scared.

'Does it, or have you just convinced yourself that you need the pain killers? Old doctor Williams is, I fear, a bit too fond of prescribing painkillers. He finds that easier than addressing the real issues. What I would like to suggest is that we try to get you off them. They'll still be here if you need them. Similarly, with the anti-depressants I would like to start reducing what he has pre-scribed. Do you want to think about it?' This sounded terrifying to me. My uncle wasn't my doctor, he had said that he couldn't minister to me as that wouldn't be ethical, and now he was sug-gesting that I should disregard my own doctor's advice and follow his. Luckily at that moment I was in a reasonably good place and, whilst scared, I could understand what he was saying. I was also appalled at the suggestion that I was becoming addicted to drugs, after having managed to avoid that throughout my adolescence. So, albeit reluctantly, I agreed to let him try to help me.

'For God's sake though, don't let on to Doctor Williams what we are doing,' he said, 'he would have my guts if he were to sus-pect'. The process wasn't easy but with the support of both my uncle and aunt, together with the ubiquitous Reverend Dick, we managed it. This was the best advice I had ever received; my un-cle made sure that, while I was kept stable and pain free, I slowly came off the medication and this, I am sure, led to an accelerated recovery as the summer came to an end. From thinking he was the most boring person on earth he became a bit of a hero of mine. Jean was always there with tea, sympathy and the occasional scotch stolen from my uncle's study, while the vicar continued to be, in effect, my personal counsellor.

My peer support during the summer had continued to drift

away. Not only was I yesterday's news but in the early summer a great many of the people I hung around with were engaged in preparing to go to University. They were moving on and I was being left behind like never before. Tom still came to see me but the reports from work tended to be same and his visits became weekly at best. He was always apologetic about this but I could see his point and I wasn't sure how often I could put up with his speculation about Tracy's underwear and fantasies about the tits of the new typist who had replaced Yvonne.

'Why don't you just take her out and give her one?' I asked tetchily during one particularly lurid fantasy about what he would like to do to her.

'Don't be daft,' he responded, 'can you imagine what it would be like coming into the office the next morning and having to face her after having a shag?' My mind strayed to thoughts of Tracy the previous Christmas, was it really nearly nine months before. So much had happened in that time.

James, Geoff and Maureen remained as constant as ever, popping in unannounced and attempting to cheer me up. Luckily Jean liked all three, welcoming them into the house and always having coffee and slices of cake available on demand. Cathy however now rarely visited and I missed her a lot. When I asked why, Maureen said, 'Her parents don't feel that she has been concentrating on her studies enough and that she had to decide whether she wanted to spend time visiting you or use her spare time to go out with the girls. I'm afraid the girls won.'

'You mean they thought I was a bad influence, gave her an ultimatum and she gave in.'

Maureen smiled, 'That's a bit harsh, but yes it was sort of like that.'

It was during the times that she visited me on her own and spoke of her future University life that I realised how much I would miss her and the seemingly unreserved friendship that Maureen provided. I resolved to myself that, as soon as I was fit again, I would ask her out on a date. I had started to see that she was the sort person that I would like to try to build a proper relationship with. At the same time as this was happening the Reverend Dick suggested that maybe I should go up to the Suffolk Punch pub on a Sunday after the morning service. 'You'll be going back to work soon and I am sure I that having a few beers with the lads will help you get ready for that. Get Geoff to bring you along.' It did help and I started to feel that this, combined with my growing feelings for Maureen, were the last bricks in the building of my recovery.

The Reverend Dick was of course right; I would soon have to return to work with all the attendant interest that would entail. Col's death still weighed heavy on my conscience. I still had nightmares where I saw his killing in graphic detail and would wake up in a cold sweat; periods where I just sat staring out at the garden re-enacting all the mistakes I had made and times where I simply sat and cried over my part in his death. I was particularly tortured by the fact that I had never told Col why I had moved to Ipswich and that he died without ever knowing the reason for the attack. I wanted to explain but would never be able to. It was as though my life had splintered and was being refracted back at me through the broken shards. It was then the words of that old Blues song would keep coming back to me:

Down and out in New York City
ain't got nothing else to lose,
down and out in New York City
just me and the East Coast Blues.

Finally, Doctor Williams gave me the all clear and said, 'I'll sign you off to start back at work in a fortnight, you should be up to it by then, but do take it easy. No heavy drinking or late nights young man, your body and mind still need to fully heal.' I was over the moon; now I could start to get my life back. I rang Bernard to tell him, which seemed to make his day as well given the effusiveness with which he received the news. I also rang Geoff, James and Maureen and arranged for them to come for a celebratory drink in the Emperor that night. Maureen seemed to be on a particular high and eventually said, 'Guys I have news; I have met this fabulous boy. He's gorgeous, twenty-six and in the army. I've never felt like this about anyone before. I think I'm in love this time.' We told her how pleased we were for her, slyly smiling at each other as we had heard it all before. It certainly didn't alter my plans to ask her out when I got back to work. That would be my return present to myself. Given her track record she would be long over him by then.

However, as those two weeks went by, her infatuation with John grew stronger and two days before I was due to go back to work she sat over a cup of coffee with Jean and I and announced, 'John and I are getting engaged.' My aunt raised her eyebrow. 'I know it's not been long but we are so right for each other and he's due to be posted to Germany soon so we want to make it official before he goes,' she said. 'I have given up my place at Manchester. I am so happy.' I was devastated. All my hopes that I had built up regarding Maureen crumbled. Somehow, I knew she was serious, this was different, she was so intense and determined. I suppose in the same way that she would dismiss a boyfriend out of hand as soon as she knew that he wasn't right made her equally determined to keep the one who she really wanted.

I hugged her and gave her a kiss, 'I am so pleased Maureen; no-one deserves it more that you. You've been a fabulous friend over these months and I know you'll be happy.' As I said this I felt a lump in my throat and there was a knot in my stomach, but such was the intensity of her happiness I truly couldn't have been happier for her.

After she had left, Jean put her arm round my shoulder and asked, 'Are you all right dear? I know you have become very close to Maureen over the past few months and I would hate this to knock you back.' How the hell she had picked up on that I don't know? I'd neither said or done anything. 'Please try not to let it get you down too much,' she added.

I choked on my words as I acknowledged all she had said but managed to add, 'But I am really pleased she is so happy,' and I truly was, although it meant I only had returning to work, and the normality that that would bring, to look forward to.

Chapter 23

On that first day back to work I parked the Vespa in my usual spot and walked in.

'Hello Alan,' Bernard was waiting just inside the front door, 'Can you come with me, Bill wants to see you.' I thought, that's good of him, maybe this is where they get to tell me about the promotion.

'Oh, it's really good to be back,' I said as we walked up the stairs. Bernard didn't reply, 'Tom says that the new junior finance guy is settling in well, it must be good to know we'll be back to full strength.' A grunt was all that I got back by way of reply. By then we had reached the end of the corridor which led to the Clerk's office. Bernard knocked and walked in and I followed. Bill was sitting behind the desk and next to him sat David James, the Chairman of the Council. There were two chairs in front of the desk and I moved to sit in on one of them.

'You won't need a seat young man, this won't take long.' Bill Jenkins said. 'You know David James don't you.' I nodded a greeting to him but before I could add anything Bill went on. 'You look well recovered anyway.' He went on. 'However, I have to inform you that because you have brought the Council into such disrepute we are not going to keep you on.' I couldn't believe what I was hearing and stood there dumbly. I looked over at Bernard but he was just standing there looking at his shoes. Christ what a set up. 'Now there are two ways of dealing with this, either you can sign this letter of resignation, in which case you will receive three months' money and Bernard will give you a good reference. Given the disruption you have caused during your time here I think that is very generous. Should you not agree to resign you will be instantly dismissed without any reference.

My mind was in turmoil and I found that I could hardly breath let alone think. I must have looked shocked because Bernard found his voice and said. 'Bill give Alan a moment, on top of everything he's been through this will have been a real shock to him. At least we can show a little humanity surely.' I could see that Bill and David didn't like this rebuke but Bill seemed to take the point and said, 'I suppose so, you better pull up that chair and sit down.'

Bernard said, 'Sit down Alan, I know this must be a terrible blow after all you've been through, but The Clerk didn't feel that he had any alternative.

'Well I thought that would be obvious,' Bill snapped.

'Not at all, when we are sacking a member of staff who has given us valuable service the least we can do is give him all the facts.'

Bill looked blacker still, 'I think he has been told all that he needs to know,' he said.

Then the Chairman spoke for the first time, 'I don't think there is anything to be gained by raking over all the details again, the options that this young man has have been made perfectly clear to him and our position is that we don't want people of his disposition working here, damaging our reputation and the morale of the other staff. Especially as the trial is coming up. And you'd do well to keep out of it Howcroft.' With that he leaned over and pushed a paper towards me, 'Now just sign the thing and so that we can get on, I don't have all day.' I could feel my anger rising but I also knew that there would be no point in losing my temper. I reached forward and picked the letter up, it was quite simple,

"For personal reasons I wish to tender my resignation with immediate effect."

There were a few more words to dress it up, together with a space for my signature. I read it through a few times, just to make a point, then signed it.

'Bernard will show you off the premises, Bill said, 'Straight-way if you please Bernard, I don't want him conferring with any of the staff before he goes. If I had my way I would prevent you from having any contact with anyone who works here ever again but sadly that is not possible. We'll send your personal effects on later when Bernard has gone through your desk.' Bernard put his hand on my shoulder in a demonstration of support and we got up to leave the office.

Bernard accompanied me down the stairs and to the side door, 'Best you go out here,' he said, 'Bill is really worried you'll instigate a mutiny if you talk to members of staff at this point. I want you to know that I had no idea that this was to happen until Friday afternoon and Bill made it very clear that if he even suspected that I had warned you I would be out too. I am really, really sorry Alan.'

'That's all right Bernard,' I said, 'I know this isn't down to you, but it's a real shock, I was looking forward so much to returning to normality and moving on.'

'I'll come around this evening with your things and a breakdown of your payoff, if that's alright? Maybe we can chat more then.' I nodded and Bernard shut the door behind me. I stood for a few moments in the back alley, the damp, green covered walls seemed to close in on me and as I looked at my hands I could see that I was shaking. Had this really happened? It seemed unreal, yet there I was standing alone having been shown off the premises by the back door like some undesirable. But then that was exactly what Jenkins had intended. My humiliation, my punishment for Col's death. I felt tears come to my eyes and I stood leaning against the door and cried like a child.

Telling my aunt was easier that I feared, I think that she was relieved that that was the reason I had come back rather that an indication that I had relapsed into my earlier mental state. She was however furious, I think she would have gone to the office and hit Jenkins if I hadn't calmed her down. 'The ungrateful sod,' she said. This was the closest I had ever heard her come to using bad language. 'The insensitive ungrateful sod. I would like to get my hands on him, he'd know all about it. We'll get your uncle to speak to his solicitor about this, that we will.' Strangely, it was the act of calming Jean down that enabled me to start to come to terms with what had happened.

By late afternoon Tom had called me and we had arranged to

meet as usual before going on to Bluesville that evening, although he couldn't say much as he was calling from the office. Bernard came around after work with the stuff from my desk. My uncle was there and in a belligerent mood and I didn't want him to start taking it out on Bernard. 'Uncle,' I said, 'could I use your study to talk to Bernard please?'

He agreed but added, 'But first I wouldn't mind a word myself. You know this is no way to treat a person who is returning to work after injuries and traumas like those Alan has had to recover from. I'm inclined to go to the local press and see what that does to your precious council's reputation.' Bernard just stood there looking embarrassed so I ushered him into the study.

'Is he serious about going to the press?' Bernard asked.

'Oh, he's just angry, but he has his own very clear sense of justice and he does know the Editor of the local paper,' I said. I think that he sees this more of a medical issue than an employment one. He's worried that I might have a relapse,' I could see that this worried Bernard, which I suppose was my intention. I didn't blame Bernard at all, but he was the only one from the Council who was there.

'I am so sorry this has happened Alan, until Friday I genuinely thought that I would have you back as my deputy. I still can't believe that Bill would do this.'

'Don't you Bernard? The more I have thought about it today the more I have come to the conclusion that it was inevitable, he dislikes me and I have been a bit of a thorn in his side, haven't I? No, the timing could have been better but don't worry about me I'll be alright. Soon find another job. I'm qualified now that won't be a problem. I could probably walk straight into a role at the Borough.'

Bernard put his head in his hands. Then looking at me said, 'Since this morning, Bill has added a further condition to me giving you a reference. I am not to do so if you apply for any jobs in Suffolk. He says he wants you well away from here.'

'Fuck him the miserable old cunt,' I could see that this outburst shocked Bernard. I had always avoided using bad language in the office and it took him completely by surprise. 'I think my uncle is right I should go to see a solicitor and talk to the Evening Star. There wasn't anything in the paper I signed this morning about restricting where I worked. It is you who have broken the agreement, not me'

'Look Alan you have got some money out of this and I have squeezed every penny I can for you from the holiday pay that you are due.' Bernard handed me the breakdown of the cheque that he held in his hand. I could see that he had certainly stretched the point regarding what I was due but I wasn't going to let Jenkins get away that easily.

I waved the settlement breakdown in front of him and said, 'Bernard, if I am going to have to move away it's going to take me longer to get sorted out and cost me more than this to relocate, even if I can get a job quickly. I don't mind being shit on, but I won't have it rubbed in.'

Bernard smiled, 'I told Bill as much, not quite in as many words, but my meaning was clear. He won't want the local press involved. Don't quote me but, that threat will worry him more than anything, mark my words. Do you think that your uncle would mind me making a telephone call? I sat across the desk as Bernard rang Bill Jenkins at home, he put his finger to his lips warning me to keep quiet and then proceeded to fill Bill with horror as he embellished my situation to the point where I thought Bill would start to disbelieve him. According to Bernard, my physical and mental stability were at risk, my doctor had already been involved and there was talk about signing me off sick again. Also, he said that I was talking about getting a solicitor to challenge the dismissal and my ability to have signed the resignation letter in my mental state. Bernard was playing a blinder. Having softened him up, finally he told Bill about my uncle going to the local press. There was a pause and Bernard said, 'I told you that taking away his ability to apply for jobs locally would push him over the edge and now you have to deal with it. You do appreciate that, with the court case coming up, the press will see him as the innocent victim of that attack and be on his side. I think they would love this story, don't you? It might not look so good so early in your tenure as the new Clerk. I think you had better speak to the Chairman and fill him in.'

I couldn't hear what was said on the on the other end, but Bernard replied. 'I am not taking his side at all, I am just thinking about our reputation Bill. I could get caught up in the fallout from this as well you know. I am back home at present but I can return to Alan's if you need me to.' You lying old tyke, I thought. Jenkins, however, obviously thought that that was a good idea because Bernard said, 'Give me twenty minutes Bill and I'll be with him. Do you have his number?' After giving him the telephone number Bernard hung up. 'I've had enough, I think we should really screw him for everything we can. This is no way to treat someone in your position and I'll not have it. Bugger him.'

We told my uncle what was happening and he got out his best scotch and poured us all a large one while we waited. 'You mustn't ever tell anyone what has happened here.' Bernard said. I think he was beginning to feel the enormity of the things that he had just said. 'It would cost me my position if Bill were to suspect that I was in cahoots with you over this.' We seemed to wait an age and Bernard began to look even more nervous and gladly accepted a second Scotch.

When the phone eventually rang he almost jumped out of his chair and he reached out for the phone but my uncle got there first, '40567. Who? Oh' yes I'll put him on. But first let me tell you sir, you are a disgrace. You should be ashamed of yourself for treating a young man who has been through so much in this way,' Without awaiting any response, he handed the phone to Bernard.

After a few minutes listening, all I could hear was a raised voice on the other end, Bernard said, 'I'll put that to him for you Bill. Alan, Mr Jenkins says that he will give you another month's money if you go quietly and don't involve the press.'

My uncle jumped in, 'That's not enough Alan. He's taking the micky.

'Tell him I want another three months money to do as he wants, especially if I have to move away and start over again.' I said. Bernard relayed it on. There was a pause and Bernard put his hand over the receiver. 'I think he must have the Chairman there, he only lives down the road from him, shush. Yes Sir, I'll make that very clear.' He looked across at me and grinned, 'It's the Chairman, he agrees to your request provided this is the last he hears of you and that this must be the end of the matter, do you understand? This last sentence was said in as sever a tone as Bernard could muster, which I thought was as much for the Chairman's consumption as mine. I looked across at my uncle and he nodded. I took the phone from Bernard,

'I'll settle for that and you'll hear no more from me provided you keep your word and don't make any disparaging comments about me to anyone. And I will want that in writing.' There was a spluttering from the other end of the phone but before I could respond my uncle shook his head and mouthed,

'Enough.' I handed the phone back to Bernard. He spoke a few more words into the phone and hung up.

'I really enjoyed that,' Bernard said, his grin even wider, 'it's no more than they deserve and I feel that it makes up a bit for the way that I've let them treat you. I better get home now, Cynthia will be wondering where I have got to.' With that he handed me the latest copy of the Local Government Chronicle with its central yellow appointments section. 'If you keep an open mind about where you are prepared to work you could do very nicely out of this, there is no way I could have paid you as much as some of the jobs are offering in there.'

Later that evening I met up with Tom and of course he wanted to know all the gory details. 'What have you heard?' I asked, I had no intension of risking my pay-out by giving anything away.

'Bernard told us about it just after you left. Jenkins is a real bastard, you're well out of it. By coffee time it was all round the office. Everyone was totally shocked, Tracy was actually in tears' he said, 'more importantly when are you going to have a leaving do. They all want to see you off properly. The place won't be the same without you.'

'I wasn't planning to make a fuss about leaving.' I said.

'Oh, but you must, you can't let them get away with sacking you and not letting everyone say goodbye,' Tom said.

'I tell you what,' I replied, 'when I have a new job to go to, you can get together those who want to see me off and we'll have a couple of beers. Now let's go and listen to some music.'

It was the first time I had been to Bluesville since my crowd had disappeared to university and it came as a shock to realise what a gap that had left. Geoff was still there and a couple of the girls who had gone to work rather than carry on with their studies, but the majority of the Grammar School bunch had gone. Their place seemed to have been taken by a whole new population of youths all of whom seemed to be vying to make more noise than their mates. The dance floor seemed to be full of these young guys getting in everyone's way, spilling beer and generally making a nuisance of themselves. One stumbled into me, I grabbed him by his jacket but then I just let him go, I should have given him a smack and tried to re-establish myself but really couldn't find the inclination or the energy. Life had moved on during the months of my recovery and I felt left behind. I had not been there to prepare for it. Tom and Geoff seemed to pick up the same vibe.

'C'mon let's get out of here and find somewhere to get a beer.' Geoff said. 'Celebrate your freedom from working for a bit longer.'

'Piss off Geoff,' I said, 'you have no idea what you are talking about. There is nothing I would rather do than get back to work.' With that I walked away to where I had left the scooter. At that moment, I felt like I did that first night in Ipswich, completely alone, unsure and being sent into exile again. Riding back down the Norwich Road the rockers outside the Two Ages shouted their usual insults, which now just sounded inane. Everyone seemed younger than me, I even felt uncomfortable on the scooter. I was too old for all this, the experiences of the past few months had changed me and it was only now that I was beginning to realise how much. The next day I advertised the scooter for sale, it had gone by the end of the week.

Chapter 24

My job search started the next day and, to my astonishment, I had a call from Tracy, after asking how I was, she then surprised me by quietly saying that she missed me before going on, 'Debbie and I will do any typing you need while you're job hunting. We've both got typewriters at home so no one needs to know.' So, the girls were still on my side, that gave me a bit of a lift. I soon found out that there were plenty of vacancies for accountants all over the country. I immediately discounted those in London; Max's family had long memories and anything north of Birmingham seemed too alien to really take seriously. In the end, I accepted a post in Norwich as it was easy to get to and flats there were cheaper to rent, but it all took time and meant that by the time I was due to start the new job almost two months had passed making me very grateful that Bernard had helped me get a better deal. Once I had put a deposit on a flat in Norwich to rent and bought James's Mini Cooper from him, the initial payment I received from the Stour Council was starting to run down.

I didn't feel I needed to do anything special around my leaving Ipswich except for the promise that I had made to say goodbye to my old work colleagues. I was beginning to look forward to this as it would undoubtedly annoy Bill Jenkins. We met up in the Rose and Crown and I was surprised at how many people turned up. Bernard put some money behind the bar, 'From petty cash, the tea fund,' he said. Everyone seemed to want to know how I was getting on and then I remembered that only a few of them had seen me since Col's death. The whole evening was proving to be a success and I realised how much I was going to miss most of the people at the office. Bill, Robert, Wally and Doug Prince didn't attend and I was glad of that. They would have put a damper on the atmosphere and there was always the danger that I would have said or done something I would regret. After Bernard had presented me with a smart new brief case, the event wound down and I was left with a hard-drinking core of well-wishers. As I came back from a trip to the toilets Tracy was waiting for me in the corridor,

'So, you're really going away.' She said.

'Yes, a new start, again. I mustn't mess it up this time.'

'You won't. I envy you being able to get away.' She started crying.

'I'm not that much of a loss, you'll soon get over me love.' I said, trying to make it sound like a joke.

'Oh, I will miss you but it's not just that Alan, since last Christmas you have come to mean a lot to me and I hated not being able to be with you and help you when you were recovering. No, I finally found the courage to break off my engagement and cancel the wedding. Now I'm getting grief from people I thought of as friends and from my parents who seem to think I've let them down. Only Debbie has stood by me. They've made my life hell at home and I can't even go out in case I run into him or get lectured by my friends.' She paused to wipe the tears away. 'I know this sounds mad but, I would love to come with you. Even if you didn't want me as a girlfriend, I could share your flat and I would help out with the rent and everything. I have to get away but I don't think I could make it in a new town on my own like you did here.' I looked at her, despite the mist of tears her blue eyes still penetrated, as they had done every time she had looked at me since that first day when I met her in the office.

I remembered Cols words at the time, 'I should keep away if I were you. She's engaged to a tough Rocker, seriously Alan we can do a little flirting, we're thought too young to be a threat, but you; as I said, I would keep away boy.' But I hadn't and now she was not only available but asking to come with me. After one quick shag was that really sensible? She stood in that beige corridor and seemed to light it up. I had been infatuated with her since that first day at Stour but was that the same as wanting her to come and live with me, and it was only a couple of weeks previously that I had been cut up when Maureen had told me of her plans. This was all so sudden that I couldn't really take it in. But over the past couple of years if I could have chosen one girl to go out with, it would have been her. And now I was confused and hesitating. She must have sensed that because she turned away and went into the Ladies toilet. I shook myself and went through the door after her, catching her before she could disappear into a cubicle.

'Do you mean it?' I said.

She nodded and said, 'You don't seem too keen though.'

'Well it's all very sudden and you did take me a bit by surprise. But, but, yes it makes sense.' Her head dropped. 'No; I don't mean that. What I really want to say is yes. Yes, please come with me. I can't think of anyone I would rather start again with than you.' Then with a broad grin I added, 'However, there is only one bed, so it better be as my girlfriend unless you want to sleep on the floor.'

She laughed and said, 'That's amazing, I'm not doing it just to get away, I really want to be with you. Can we keep it quiet for now? I will hand my notice in tomorrow and I can join you in a couple of weeks, they owe me some holiday. Oh, Alan I love you.'

No girl had ever said that to me before and hearing it standing in the Ladies toilet seemed surreal. Is that how it happened when you fell for someone? We held each other for what I realised was only the second time, but it felt right and I found myself saying, 'You know I've wanted you since the first day I met you.'

'What even while you were with all those other girls?' She said. I decided that it would be best to leave it there because I knew that Tom and Col had always rejoiced in telling the typists what we had been up to. Tracy then said, 'Debbie will be so pleased.'

'Why? I asked.

'Well it was her idea that I should tell you how I felt and she also thought it would be good for me to move away and make a new start. She said if I didn't tell you now I would lose you.'

'How long have you been plotting this between you?' I asked.

'Oh, Debbie has known how I felt about you for ages but it was only last week that she made me realise that I was going to lose my chance if I waited until after you had left. I owe her a lot.'

The final act of my time in Ipswich occurred just before my

move to Norwich it was the trial. I had been dreading it, having my past all raked over in Court. The Barristers warned me to expect to be put under a lot of pressure about my relationship with Max and his fellow defendants and that Julie's death would undoubtedly come under the microscope. Just be open and honest about it all was their advice.

As it happened it all turned out to be an anti-climax. Max was allowed to plead guilty to the Manslaughter of Col, and with his mates, to Grievous Bodily Harm to myself. It was all over in a flash. I didn't know whether to be pleased or disappointed. I wanted him to go down for Murder, but as the legal team told me later, 'It was always going to be difficult to make that stick, some of the witnesses said that Peter might have run onto the knife. Max's briefs would have made the most of that and he might have got completely away with it.' As it happened the Judge took a firm line and Max went down for long stretch. But at least one day he would return home; something that Col would never be able to do.

My move to Norwich was uneventful, the flat was furnished so I only had my personal stuff to take. I was just happy that I had found a flat within walking distance of the offices and that Tracy had been pleased with what she had seen the previous week when I had taken her to see it.

'It's lovely,' she said, 'this will be my first home away from my parents and I know we can make it really nice with a little effort.'

That afternoon we had made love, it was the first opportunity that we had had since my leaving do. We couldn't do it at hers, her parents had refused to even meet me and although my aunt and uncle made her immediately welcome I wouldn't have taken her to bed at theirs, that wouldn't have seemed right. As we lay in bed afterwards staring at the magnolia walls and uneven surface of the whitewashed ceiling we had been aware of the musty smell and had assured ourselves that with a good clean it would disappear. But this was going to be our home and that didn't matter.

On the first morning of the new job, I walked up through the market with its colourful awnings and through huge brass doors of the Art Deco City Hall into the impressive foyer and gazed up the twin staircases. This was more like it. The offices themselves, however, were less magnificent with the accountancy staff crammed together in one large room. For the first time in my career I had a small team to manage; two trainees and a clerk. Although the job was fine and I got on with my team professionally, I found it difficult to relate to them socially. I had no enthusiasm for going out drinking with them and most of the horseplay in the office, which the year before I would have probably been leading, irritated me.

As the novelty of the new job began to wear off I found that more and more I was having doubts about my own value. Some days the light would still seem to leave my world and be replaced by a darkness that threatened to overwhelm me. It was during those times that I would wake up wet with perspiration and shaking following a nightmare. During my lunch breaks, especially during these low times, I had taken to simply roaming the Norwich streets and would look in at the many churches in the town centre, sometimes just sitting quietly for most of my break. I found that in the solitude and the almost deafening quietness I could reflect on what had gone before and the mistakes I had made. It was during one of these quiet moments that I met Robert, a young curate at one of the churches. I had been in this church a few times, when it was sunny its stained-glass windows seemed to tint everything in pixelated multicolours and I would reflect on the almost psychedelic patterns that they produced as a form of meditation. On this day, I had been sitting there for about twenty minutes when he wandered up and sat next to me. My initial reaction was one of annoyance at being disturbed, but he sat quietly next to me for a while before saying, 'The light in here's sure beautiful, don't you think?' He had a soft Irish lilt to his voice which was strangely calming. 'I've seen you in here before and was wondering if I could help in anyway. Just tell me to push off if I'm intruding.'

I smiled at him and said, 'I suppose you're trained to spot the oddballs?' He didn't respond so I carried on. 'I just like to come in here for the solitude and get away from all the work things that pile up.' He nodded. 'Sometimes I just like to get away from everything,' I added.

'I know just what you mean,' he said and then proceeded to tell me his life story which was full of anecdotes and humour. Eventually I had to tell him that I needed to get back to work. 'Well you've done me a power of good,' he said, 'I don't get many people in here to talk to during the week.' This was the start of what became a regular occurrence which would develop into a friendship.

Tracy couldn't believe it, 'A priest. What on earth do you find to talk about, she said, 'You can't have much in common?' But we seemed to have no trouble filling the time we spent together, initially in the church and later walking around the Cathedral grounds. After a few weeks of this, he and I would sometimes wander into a pub where he would have a half pint of lager.

I became fascinated about Robert's job and how someone who seemed so full of life and fun had come to go into the church. Bit by bit I found myself envying his life and the contribution that he seemed to be able to make in the community. Eventually I told him my own history. 'There, I knew there was a story to be had from you from the first time I saw you in the church. You were a troubled soul, sure, I could see that from the start.' If anyone else had said that to me I would have probably told them where to go. But Robert had a way about him that gave me confidence in what I could only describe as his goodness and he certainly helped me to feel better about myself. During my time in Norwich I would also still occasionally meet up with the Reverend Dick for a couple of pints at Scole, halfway between Ipswich and Norwich, he seemed to enjoy the chance to get away from his own patch and, crucially, the two of them also got me thinking about my life and what I was achieving.

Tracy had noticed the improvement in my mood and welcomed Robert's influence in that. However, I was also getting increasingly disillusioned about my job and although I tried to keep it from Tracy she was aware that all wasn't well. I wanted more. I began to feel that I had missed out on something and that I needed a wider perspective on life and I began to appreciate why people went off to university. However, there was something more. I had also started to believe that there must be something special that made Robert and the Reverend Dick so different to most of the people I had come across. I wanted to understand how the faith they had seemed to energise them and enable them to interact with people at a different level, I envied them that. I tried to explain this to Tracy but she just put it down to yet another symptom of my depression, but I was starting to move in a completely different direction.

One day during our second spring in Norwich, I arrived back from work to find Tracy in a high state of excitement, 'They've asked me to be the PA to one of the Directors, it will mean a big pay rise - we could start looking for that house to buy.' I told her how pleased I was for her, but the idea of buying a house caused me to pause. I had been researching university courses and had been about to tell her that I wanted to give up my job and go to university the next September. In fact, I had already found a course in Cambridge studying Philosophy and Theology, which I thought would be ideal as it would mean we wouldn't have to move too far. I had already discussed it with Robert and the Reverend Dick, the latter who was especially supportive. Now I was in a quandary when to tell her. I couldn't really let her accept the job and then leave after a few months and I certainly couldn't think about buying a house 'You're so clever, they must think a lot of you, you could get a job anywhere,' I said.

I think she must have sensed what was coming because she replied, 'I don't want a job anywhere, I want one here among my new friends. What are you getting at?' I then told her what I had been thinking. 'You've done all this without telling me?' She said, 'but you've discussed it all with your vicar friends. That puts me in my place doesn't it. Well I don't mind supporting you through university in Norwich but I'm not moving and if your long-term plans are to become a vicar, you can forget it. I'm not cut out to be a vicar's wife.' Over the next few weeks we returned time and again to the subject as I explained why I wanted to do this. In the meantime, Tracy had accepted the new job and that had put me on the spot.

'I could go to Cambridge and come home at weekends.' I suggested.

'Don't be so stupid. It would never work,' was her response and so it went on, creating more and more of a wedge between us.

Eventually she said, 'Look I can understand where you are coming from Alan and why you would want to do this. We both have our own ambitions and now I can afford to keep the flat going. I owe you so much for letting me come with you from Ipswich, I don't want to get in your way. You must do what you want to before it leads to us hating each other and that's something I couldn't bear. We can still keep in touch and be friends surely?' So that's how it happened, I went to Cambridge and Tracy made her life in Norwich.

Chapter 25

Over the years, I kept in touch with Bernard. He never progressed any further with his career, with the change of regime at the Council his face didn't really fit and eventually he took early retirement. I kept in touch with him throughout the years and even after he was struck down with dementia he would greet me like a long-lost friend and ask after my news although, towards the end, two minutes after I had left it would all have been forgotten. I lost touch with Tom for many years then out of the blue I got an invitation to his retirement. He had risen up the ranks and done well for himself, even to the extent of having had three wives. However, it did hit me hard to think that the office junior had retired, surely, he was still only a lad?

The others of my circle; well they all had gone their own ways, I heard that Geoff, almost inevitably, became landlord of his own pub although our paths never crossed again. Sadly, a couple of the group had died, Maureen taken by breast cancer and my farmer friend James, with whom I met up with in Stowmarket once a year, to Kidney disease at the age of fifty, 'Got that knighthood yet Sir Alan?' He would ask as we shook hands before sitting down to reminisce about the old days over a couple of pints of Adnams. At his funeral, I learnt that he had become a pillar of his village Church, although strangely he never mentioned that side of his life to me during our sessions. I still miss him. Tracy and I never got back together but I have shared her life with her through correspondence over the years, more a dear friend than an ex-lover. I even became Godfather to her son, Alan.

The one other guy from the Ipswich days that I did meet up with was David. He found me on Facebook and I didn't have the heart to refuse his friend request. He seemed to have actually become a successful theatrical producer and, with some trepidation, I agreed to meet him for a drink when I was next in London. We met up in his South London local pub and caught up with our news, especially all the things he had done and how successful he'd been. After about an hour we were joined by a tall grey-haired guy, 'This is my partner Lesley.' David announced and then with a wry smile added, 'I tried it and found that indeed I did rather like it and that it doesn't make me a bad person. Do you remember that evening Alan?' With this the barriers seemed to fall away and the three of us ended up having a great evening, we parted promising to meet up again some time and I'm sure we will, but not too often.

There was one other person from Ipswich that I caught up with. It was early February 1969 during my first year at Cambridge, a beautiful day pretending to be early Spring, I had gone for walk into the centre of Cambridge. As I walked up King St. I heard a shout from across the road and looking over I saw Cathy. She ran across the road dodging a bus and multiple cycles and flung her arms around me. 'Ace, is it really you? What a coincidence,' she said. 'It's wonderful to see you. What are you doing here?' When I told her that I was in my first year at college she said, 'Why didn't you look me up then?' I had to admit to her that in truth, during the confusion of my last year in Ipswich, I had completely forgotten that she had got into Cambridge. We went for tea in a little café and talked and talked. She was now in her third year of a Law degree and during that final year of her studies we started seeing each other. There were many times during that year that I had flashbacks of that walk to the Pier Pavilion, three years before, when I had promised myself that it would either be her or Maureen that I would date next. At the end of her course she went off to a job in London and my weekends were then filled with journeys backwards and forwards to see her.

The wonderful thing was that she understood precisely what was driving me and how I was starting to reshape my life. She gave me her total support. We have often said, during the forty years of our marriage, that we each seemed to know from that first meeting in the street that fate intended us to become a couple and we seem to be as happy now as we were in those early days.

Despite three children she managed to retain her career as a Barrister, which certainly helped with the family finances given the paucity of the salary I received through most of my career and she provides me with a link back to my time in Ipswich reminding me of my weaknesses and keeping me on the straight and narrow.

And me? I'm not a Face, but I am well up the ranks of the soldiers and a lot of them, and certainly the Seven and Sixes are envious and look up to me. That still makes me feel good, even if that is a sin. My clothes still mark me out and, even though I don't ride an Eddy Grimstead scooter any more, my position as Dean of the Cathedral marks me out for respect and even if I don't have the looks of my youth I can still hold a congregation in thrall when I try.

Lightning Source UK Ltd.
Milton Keynes UK
UKHW042100050219
336800UK00001B/104/P